I0733568

STEALING THE DUKE

Marrying a Mabry, Book 1

Lexi Post

© Copyright 2023 by Lexi Post
Text by Lexi Post
Cover by Kim Killion Designs

Dragonblade Publishing, Inc. is an imprint of Kathryn Le Veque Novels, Inc.
P.O. Box 23
Moreno Valley, CA 92556
ceo@dragonbladepublishing.com

Produced in the United States of America

First Edition March 2023
Trade Paperback Edition

Reproduction of any kind except where it pertains to short quotes in relation to advertising or promotion is strictly prohibited.

All Rights Reserved.

The characters and events portrayed in this book are fictitious. Any similarity to real persons, living or dead, is purely coincidental and not intended by the author.

ARE YOU SIGNED UP FOR DRAGONBLADE'S BLOG?

You'll get the latest news and information on exclusive giveaways, exclusive excerpts, coming releases, sales, free books, cover reveals and more.

Check out our complete list of authors, too!

No spam, no junk. That's a promise!

Sign Up Here

www.dragonbladepublishing.com

Dearest Reader;

Thank you for your support of a small press. At Dragonblade Publishing, we strive to bring you the highest quality Historical Romance from some of the best authors in the business. Without your support, there is no 'us', so we sincerely hope you adore these stories and find some new favorite authors along the way.

Happy Reading!

CEO, Dragonblade Publishing

Additional Dragonblade books by Author Lexi Post

Marrying a Mabry Series
Stealing the Duke (Book 1)
Painting the Earl (Book 2)

Acknowledgments

For my overachieving husband, Bob Fabich, Sr., who earned straight As in high school and became the youngest fire chief ever in the state of New Hampshire. Our conversations are always lively and engaging.

For my wonderful sister Paige Wood, who absolutely loves historical romance and helped me brainstorm the bones of this story. Your insight is priceless.

I have to thank my critique partner, Marie Patrick, for keeping my toes to the fire and reading every 5,000 words as I got them finished, no matter how rough they were.

A special thank you to Lexi's Legends, who helped with so many of the names that I needed for this story. Specifically, thank you to Lisa Staebell-Fishback, Teresa Fordice, Rochelle Ireland, Rhonda Nygaard-Beck, Bette Read, Bonne Davis, Lynda Meschino Tang, Belinda Jackson Hercule, Kim Mangels, Rita Cassidy-Kern Clements, Amy Allen Hallmark, Ashley Myers Clark, Beth Waters Cotter, Laurie Cogburn, Valerie Hills. You ladies are why I write.

I also want to thank my very knowledgeable editor, Amelia Hester, who kept my world on point, and Kathryn Le Veque for giving me the opportunity to share James and Joanna's story.

Author's Note

The Marrying a Mabry series was inspired by one of my favorite books, Louisa May Alcott's novel, *Little Women*, published in two volumes in 1868 and 1869. This was an American coming of age story about four young women in New England. They were Margaret, Josephine, Elizabeth, and Amy March, or Meg, Jo, Beth, and Amy respectively. Each tries to live up to their mother's expectations of them, which were to become good people and respectable women.

Stealing the Duke is specifically inspired by Jo March and her journey to womanhood. For Joanna Mabry, it is a journey from spinsterhood and debate to love and action. Basically, what if Jo March lived in Regency England and was the daughter of a marquess? How would a young woman of significant inquisitiveness and impulsiveness comply with societal norms? And if her intellectual equal was not a mild-mannered professor, but an arrogant and very well-read duke, how could she possibly persuade him to see her point about education for her female peers? More importantly, how could she possibly be of interest to him and he to her?

On a weather note, it should be explained that 1816 was denoted as the "Year without a Summer." This was due to exceedingly cold temperatures and torrents of rain, hail, and snow in the northern hemisphere causing catastrophic loss of life. The reason for this was unknown at the time. However, our current science is quite confident this event was caused by one of the largest volcanic eruptions on Earth during mankind's existence. The volcano was Mount Tambora in the Dutch East Indies, or present-day Indonesia, which erupted in April 1815. Its ash cloud was so extensive that it changed the weather. The fallout, no pun intended, would cause famine, riots, looting, soaring prices, cholera outbreaks, and believe it or not, due to the cost of feeding horses, possibly even the invention of what became the bicycle. On a literary note, it also spawned Mary Shelley's *Frankenstein*, another book that has inspired a romance from me.

CHAPTER ONE

London
March 1816

L ADY JOANNA MABRY looked down the corridor to the left and the right before slipping into the Duke of Northwick's library. He had to be the most antiquated, arrogant, conceited, insufferable, condescending—no, that was wrong. She quietly closed the door and stared at it, her burgundy-colored dress swishing with her quick turn. She needed to think alphabetically. Belinda said the best way to calm her temper was to distract her mind by using the alphabet. That meant the Duke of Northwick was the most antiquated, arrogant, conceited, condescending, insufferable man she had met since her debut four years ago. Though there was that vicar when she was barely past ten, but that was before she'd been fully enlightened into the great breadth of knowledge that was so easily accessed by the male gender.

Turning around to see what books, if any, the duke might have to her liking, her breath caught. She widened her eyes in awe. The large room was lined with books. Not even a bust of Caesar interrupted the pattern of leatherbound volumes. She inhaled slowly, letting her eyes close for a moment as the strong scent of leather, wood polish, and a faint whiff of something else filled her nostrils. Was that bergamot? Citrus? Opening her eyes again, she let her gaze feast upon shelf after shelf, wall after wall, covered with tomes of knowledge. As her gaze rose, her throat closed.

How could this be? How could the Duke of Northwick, a man with such outdated opinions, possess a two-story personal library, a proverbial oasis of wisdom, a sanctuary for the human mind? She stepped away from the door, trying to comprehend the wonder before her. How was she to choose? Turning to the closest book case, she scanned the titles as she walked along it, her fingertips gliding lightly over the leather bindings as if they were delicate objects likely to break.

She halted. And *this* he would keep to himself? Did he keep his young cousin, Elsbeth, from stepping foot into such a study for fear she would learn something beyond what he pronounced all women need concern themselves with: embroidery, dancing, painting, and social graces? She pulled her fingers away from the prized books and fisted her hands in the folds of her dark gown, her breathing accelerating with her growing fury. It would be a pleasure to pilfer one of the duke's books, and this one she wouldn't return. It wasn't as if he'd miss it. There may be no dust on the shelves, but that spoke to the efficiency of his housekeeper, not his time spent absorbed in the pages of so many volumes of delight. No doubt he was nothing more than a collector because it was clear his education had been accomplished in a past century. How odd, he didn't appear that old. She snickered at the thought.

Forcibly pulling her gaze from the bookshelf before her, she scanned the room quickly to find a large desk on the other side and started toward it, her footsteps not making a sound on the soft Persian carpet beneath her feet. What books would such a cynical, mocking, narrow-minded, ...hmm, ogre want near at hand? She grinned at having succeeded in her alphabetical tirade. Belinda would be proud of her. A quiet pang of loss split the irritation around her heart for a brief moment. "Oh, Bea, if only I had access to this two years ago." Her voice sounded muted, the room absorbing the sound as if only silence was welcome in such a hallowed space. It was as if it reprimanded her for speaking aloud. Her younger sister, Belinda, would also not approve of her foray into the duke's library for the sole purpose of absconding with one of his volumes. But Bea's soft voice no longer graced mere mortals' ears with its kind thoughts.

Joanna shrugged off the momentary melancholy that never failed to fill her when thinking of Bea. Instead, she scanned the bookcase directly behind the eight-foot, walnut desk. Unlike the first wall of books she reviewed, which had only subjects about plants and animals, subjects she thought herself fairly well acquainted with, this set of books had no particular focus. Her curiosity was piqued. Why would he have Radcliff's *The Mysteries of Udolpho* and Homer's *Iliad*, yet also have Goldsmith's *Vicar of Wakefield* on the very same shelf? Could it be that these were the duke's favorites, which he read over and over? She had one such area in the Mabry library. Shaking her head, she dismissed the idea. Someone like Northwick could not possibly appreciate Voltaire's *Candide* or Paine's *Right of Man*. More likely, this is where he set new acquisitions waiting to be added to other shelves by his staff. Whichever book she decided upon would not be coming back to Haven House. In fact, she planned to avoid Haven House and its owner all together.

Everything about the too-tall, dark-haired man with blue eyes the shade of the sky on a rare clear day in London irritated her like a bug in her bed at a traveling inn. Keeping her tongue silent at dinner had been a herculean effort only made possible by the constant pinches on her thigh by her older sister, Mariel, and the occasional kick to her leg by her cousin Teddy, who sat across from her. No, this book she would not return. Not only did the duke not deserve it, but he wouldn't notice it missing. With other people, she always returned the book, making an effort to get it back to the correct house or nearby at least.

As she perused the various titles before her, an iron stairway to her right caught her attention. She allowed her gaze to rise to the top where a narrow walkway encircled the entire room, bookcases rising from the balcony to the ceiling. Why must the most beautiful and endowed personal library have to belong to her newest odious acquaintance? She had no doubt that the very man at dinner, who joked that women needed no more than a shopping excursion and a ride to Hyde Park to entertain them, kept this nirvana from his lovely cousin or any other woman who wished to partake of its riches. Just the thought of young Elsbeth, with whom Teddy was so enamored, not being allowed into such a room, had Joanna's humors boiling. Licking her lips, she took a step toward the stairs when voices just outside penetrated the wooden doors. She froze. She didn't worry about being caught in the library of a peer, it had happened twice before, but since she didn't plan on returning her pilfered book, she'd rather not be a possible suspect.

The voices moved on, most likely the butler and another staff. Still, it behooved her not to tarry. Turning back to the books awaiting final placement, she scanned more of the titles. *Antigone* by Sophocles was a play she'd longed to read since seeing it performed last season. She reached up to remove it from its resting place when the title next to it caught her attention. *Educating the Female Species* by Lord Ancil Rutherford. She had read and reread Mary Wollstonecraft's *Vindication of the Rights of Woman,* finding it a forward-thinking treatise on the education of women. What could the old-fashioned duke, who thought a properly educated woman was one who could dance and embroider, possibly want with a book on female education? Pulling the large tome from the shelf, she ran her hand over the raised title. *Species.* Why would some use the word species? It was horribly incorrect, which didn't hold much promise for the book. She pondered the word, trying to fit the subject to her host.

Of course! It had to be a book on training women like brood mares. What idiocy. What ignorance. What—

The door started to swing inward, and she ducked behind the

large desk.

Footsteps tracked to the left side of the room and halted. "Place the duke's smoking materials here. This should have been done before the guests arrived."

"Yes, sir." The contrite voice of a manservant proved him duly chastised.

Soft sounds floated in the silence before a swish and a click told Joanna the two servants had exited the room, leaving her alone once again.

She quickly rose, thankful the servant had forgotten to set up for the men who would obviously soon come into the library to smoke after the meal. If not for him, she might have lost all concept of time. Pausing, she sniffed at the air. Was smoke the scent she couldn't place? No, it was something else.

She hugged the book close to her chest and padded across the room. If the tome was what she expected it to be, she wouldn't be reading it for long. It could make excellent kindling on a cold winter night though. At least it would be out of the hands of Northwick, who needed no more reinforcement. And on the happenstance that he did allow Elsbeth to come into his palatial library, at least her young mind would not be damaged by reading Rutherford's view on the education of the feminine species.

She set her ear against the door and listened. Hearing no more footsteps, she slipped into the corridor and headed for the back entrance. Occasionally, while "borrowing" a book, she ran into a busy servant at other homes, but she had no such encounter this time. That was probably because the dinner party was relatively small. There had been merely twenty at the table, though the meal, she admitted, was of the finest delicacies.

Once outside, she hurried, the cool day giving way to a colder night. She strode toward the stables where their coachman was no doubt enjoying a whisky with the head groom. There were four coaches lined in a row, but finding the distinctive crest of a silver knight's helmet with red feathers that designated the Mabry coach was fairly easy even in the dark. Opening the door on the side facing the house, she set the book on the seat and grasped her shawl. She was always careful to have an excuse in case she was caught. Pleased that she had succeeded, she exited the conveyance and quietly closed the door.

"Are you so anxious to leave my home then, Lady Joanna?"

She started at the deep voice behind her, her heart suddenly racing. Had he seen her with the book? Her hand, still on the handle of the coach door, tightened. Merciful Heavens, just her luck the bloody duke himself would come upon her. Forcing a smile, she let go of the handle and turned around. "Your Grace, I only sought my shawl, so I could be more comfortable while continuing the evening."

His brows rose. "I was unaware my home was not a temperature to your liking. If you prefer, I can have more coal placed on the fire in the parlor for after our repast."

And what if she preferred to join the men in the most beautiful library she'd ever entered? She swallowed her question, but only because of her cousin Teddy, and raised her head to meet his gaze. He was entirely too tall. "That won't be necessary." She forced herself to spread the black lace shawl before settling it across her chest. "This will do fine, but thank you."

He cocked his head slightly as he studied her, his dark wavy hair falling lower on one side of his forehead with the gesture.

It wasn't lost on her that they were clearly alone, standing in the dark, quite away from anyone but the stable hands, thereby in a highly improper setting. "Why are you out and about, Your Grace?" She raised her eyebrows in question, but wasn't sure he could see her clearly in the dim light since the coach blocked the stable lanterns.

He, on the other hand, was clearly illuminated as he stood between two coaches. His dark pantaloons blended with the darkness behind him, as did his black coat, but his white shirt and perfectly tied cravat were a strong contrast to his tanned skin. His head straightened, and he lifted his chin, the arrogant planes of his face clearly defined. "If it is of importance to you, Lady Joanna, I was called out to look in on Venus, one of my horses who is soon to foal."

He cared about his horse enough to break from his own dinner party and check on her? That did not fall into the perception she'd had of him at dinner. Then again, it may simply be a concern for his property. He probably looked at his cousin in the same way. "I had no idea you had such concern for your horses." She clamped her mouth shut on her next thought, which would have solidly baited him into an argument. She'd given her word to Teddy to keep her opinions to herself, but he would be in her debt for months, now that she understood why he exacted such a promise when she, instead of her younger sister Amelia, had joined him and Mariel.

The duke, to his credit, didn't take umbrage to her insinuated insult. In fact, his broad shoulders appeared to relax. "I did not consider the birth of a new horse appropriate dinner conversation. But if you are interested, I'd be happy to bring you into the stable to see Venus."

Her heart jumped, and she tightened her hold on her shawl. To see firsthand a foal's birth would be mesmerizing, but even as excitement at the prospect filled her, she could hear her mother's voice cautioning her to think before she acted. Why would this duke, who thought women belonged in a parlor, allow her such an opportunity, an opportunity her father had refused her when he usually granted her almost every wish? She studied the duke's face. Though he was serious, there was a sparkle in his eyes that was not there before. Was he daring her? Oh, she never could resist a dare. She parted her lips to accept the invitation.

But you promised Teddy. She snapped her mouth closed, her conscience forcing her to reconsider. "As much as I would enjoy that, I must decline as I'm sure my sister and cousin are already wondering about my whereabouts." She grasped her skirts, ready to escape his challenging presence.

"Allow me to escort you. I can't have you traipsing about in the dark while under my hospitality." He stepped closer and offered his arm.

She gritted her teeth. She wasn't a child. If she found her way out to the coach, she could find her way back inside. "I'm sure I can make my way back alone. After all, I can see the house from here. I don't wish to put you out." Pleased that none of her scorn came through in her voice, she smiled politely.

The duke didn't remove his arm. "But I insist. As your host, I am duty bound to see you safely back to the dining room, or as may be the case, the parlor, since the ladies may have already retired to that pleasant room."

Again, she had to tamp down her retort. She wouldn't ruin Teddy's chances with Elsbeth, no matter how much she wished to express her opinion. Instead, she placed her hand on the duke's arm and nodded, avoiding his gaze.

He started forward, keeping his stride short for her. He needn't have. She enjoyed a brisk walk, but since everything about him irritated her, she simply started counting. She was barely at eight when he spoke.

"I would have been happy to send a footman out to fetch your shawl, Lady Joanna. I admit, I'm not used to my guests wandering about in my courtyard in the dark of night."

Meaning, he was not used to women walking about alone in his courtyard. "Yes, I suppose you could have. I will be sure to make use of your footman if I find myself in a similar situation." Which would never happen since she planned to avoid the man's presence for the rest of the season. Amelia would just have to attend with Mariel and Teddy. She had been curious about him since he did not visit London often, and had not been in residence during her seasons. In fact, it wasn't until she'd heard Teddy mention the Duke of Northwick that she remembered he existed. Now she wished she'd never satisfied her curiosity about the reclusive man who it was said preferred the country to Town.

As they neared the house, the duke halted. They had been moving slowly, so his lack of motion was barely noticeable, but when he pulled his arm from beneath her hand and faced her, concern that he'd seen her with the book resurfaced. She boldly met his gaze, ready to brazen out the situation.

"Lady Joanna. I have the distinct feeling that you do not find my company to your liking."

Heat rose in her cheeks. She had to admit, the man was observant. Rather than tell the truth and have Teddy upset with her until the day she was laid to rest, she lowered her brows. "I'm not sure why you would think that, Your Grace. Have I not behaved appropriately?" She bit down on her smile. What would a gentleman say to such a question from a guest? She expected he'd make a hasty retreat.

She was wrong.

"Your behavior has been impeccable, as has your sister's, and I have to admit your cousin's as well. It is not that which has me questioning your sentiment. Let us say it is just a feeling."

"A feeling? That is not a very logical reason. Did you not say at dinner that logic is the only way for a man to progress in society? Or did you mean that only for those in the mercantile and trading businesses?"

His lips quirked upward on one side. "I did not realize you had been listening to that particular discourse. I stand corrected." He gave a brief nod and opened his arm toward the waiting stairs to the door. "Shall we?"

Confused by whether he meant his reasoning for thinking she didn't care for his presence was faulty, or if he now believed that she did enjoy his presence, she preceded him up the stairs. He stepped forward to open the door, but paused. "Then am I to assume you agree with me regarding the use of logic for finding the truth?"

Surprised by the question, she answered honestly. "Of course, as long as one has the education needed to follow the logic to its correct conclusion, something most women of the peerage are denied."

His whole body stiffened.

Blast, she'd revealed too much. She smiled, hoping he could see her face in the light flowing through the house windows. "Therefore, I suggest that we should join the others so we can continue this lovely evening."

He studied her for a moment, then opened the door and allowed her to pass. This time there were servants about and from the look of one of them, it appeared they thought she'd been on some kind of moonlit assignation with the duke. How far from the truth that was.

The butler stood before the dining room. "Your Grace. Your aunt declared the end of dinner and the ladies are now in the parlor."

"Very good, Harrison. Please show Lady Joanna the way, and I will repair to the library."

"Of course, Your Grace. My lady?"

She gave the duke a brief nod then followed the butler, hoping she'd saved herself from ruining the night for Teddy. As soon as she stepped inside the parlor, her sister approached her. "Where did you go off to?"

Mariel was the oldest of the four of them and already a widow three years at twenty-six. Her ability to adapt to any situation gracefully was an art Joanna often envied. Dressed in a dark forest green with her thick chestnut hair pulled tightly back with just a few whisps escaping to frame her face, Mariel exuded calm. But her emerald eyes shone with worry.

"I just went to fetch my shawl." She quickly stepped around her sister and the disapproving look she knew would come. Mariel was the only one who knew about her penchant for borrowing books from their peers and the true reason for the shawl.

She strode to where Lady Astor and her daughter, Elsbeth, sat and took the chair opposite them. Of all the ladies in attendance, Joanna found she enjoyed this lady's company the most. Though at least two score, she had a youthful appearance and her mind was quick.

Lady Astor didn't hesitate to include her in the conversation she was having with her daughter. "Lady Joanna, we were just discussing the attributes of the eligible men currently with my nephew. It appears they are all quite interested in Elsbeth, yet she doesn't come out until next month. Do you have an opinion on how she should choose her husband?"

The older woman, looking splendid in a deep gold evening dress that set off her blonde locks beautifully and complemented her brown eyes, smiled, clearly teasing her daughter, who blushed.

Joanna leaned forward as if she would impart great wisdom. "Lord Mabry. From where I sit, he is clearly a cut above the rest."

"I fear you are hopelessly biased." Lady Astor turned to her daughter. "Pay her no mind. It is clear we cannot depend upon her opinion on this matter."

Chuckling, she nodded as she addressed Elsbeth. "I must acknowledge the truth of the matter. Teddy has so many wonderful qualities, I cannot imagine I can remember a single fault. Unless of course, you consider stealing my favorite book and throwing it in with the cows at his estate as not particularly nice. We were but eight, and when I ran in despite the bull heading for me, he did come to my rescue by distracting the mean bovine."

Both ladies smiled, but it was Elsbeth that spoke. "Were you able to retrieve your book without either of you being injured?"

She widened her eyes. "It was a close thing that. The bull did indeed turn toward Teddy and rush him." She paused, watching the concern pass over Elsbeth's face. "Luckily, he is an excellent sprinter. He even took awards later at Cambridge for his skill."

"I see he has much to recommend him." Lady Astor nodded approvingly.

Feeling more comfortable, Joanna continued. "Now, if I were being objective about a husband hunt and in your circumstances, I would make my judgement based upon who was willing to wait until you are presented at your first ball."

Elsbeth's smile faltered, but her mother cast Johanna a grateful smile.

"I wouldn't listen to Lady Joanna." Lady Caroline's voice coming from behind her had Joanna looking over her shoulder. "Since she hasn't found a husband yet, her advice is suspect."

"On the contrary, my advice is sound because it comes from much experience in winnowing out those not suitable." She turned back toward the ladies and winked.

Unfortunately, the lovely blonde, who had obviously set her hopes on their host, found the need to join their conversation. She floated to the chair next to Joanna and gracefully settled into it, her very pale blue dress falling into perfect folds. It matched her eyes exactly. "Take my advice. As you study the prospects for marriage, you want to look for wealth, impeccable manners, and someone you feel comfortable conversing with over dinner."

Elsbeth's brow furrowed. "What about his carriage. Should he not be pleasant to look upon?"

Lady Astor opened her mouth to respond, but Lady Caroline waved her hand dismissively. "While that is always nice, it should not be the first characteristic you look for."

Joanna's gaze swept to Lady Astor, whose eyes had widened. "Then am I to assume you do not find my nephew to be handsome?"

Joanna sensed more than witnessed Lady Caroline stiffen. The lady had made a mess of it now. Unable to resist, she prodded further. "What is it that you find unappealing? Is it the length of his wavy dark hair, the hardness of his aristocratic chin, or perhaps it is his interminable height?" She quirked up her lips to Lady Astor, so the lady would know she was not serious.

Lady Caroline produced a lace fan as if from the air, it appeared so quickly, and began to fan herself. "I'm sure I am completely unaware of any such faults with His Grace."

"Oh, then it must be his nose." She nodded to Lady Elsbeth. "I have heard it on good authority that a man's nose is very important to ladies."

Elsbeth, for all her youth and naiveté, understood the fun they were having and directed her comments to Lady Caroline. "Pray, do tell me what is wrong with my cousin's nose. I think that I may have missed it, having grown up with him towering over me all the time. I do believe I've only seen the underside where his nostrils—"

"That is quite enough about his grace's physical attributes." Lady Astor set her hand on her daughter's lap. "Don't you think, Lady Caroline?"

The woman nodded, then abruptly stood. "Please excuse me. I just remembered I wished to ask Lady Barret what she thought of the play we both happened to attend the other evening."

Joanna held her grin back until Lady Caroline had floated off toward three ladies conversing near a bay window. Returning her gaze to the women across from her, she couldn't help the light laugh that escaped her. "That was not well done of me." She shook her head, but didn't stop smiling.

Lady Astor tried to look stern, but her lips twitched. "We should not have teased her. She did not realize we weren't serious." Finally, her own smile appeared. "But it was a bit of fun."

"Mother!" Elsbeth hissed, then let out an adorable laugh.

Joanna sincerely liked them. If Teddy did succeed in obtaining Elsbeth as a wife, she would be pleased. The woman, though only eighteen, had a sharp mind and a gentle disposition.

"And here is the esteemed personage we were just speaking of." Lady Astor's smile widened as she focused beyond Joanna.

Even without looking, she felt the approach of the duke. She turned her head slightly, in time to see his long-tapered fingers wrap over the top of the chair back that Lady Caroline had so recently vacated. She dearly hoped he wouldn't sit.

"Do sit, James. I don't believe you've had a chance to get to know Lady Joanna. She is such a delight."

A delight? She'd never had that particular word used to describe her. *Interesting* or *opinionated* or even *lively* were the usual, somewhat complimentary words aimed her way.

"Actually, Aunt, Lady Joanna and I had an intriguing conversation out in the courtyard this evening."

Intriguing. She rather liked that term. She addressed Lady Astor, whose eyebrows had risen considerably. "It was not quite as fascinating as the duke infers. I believe it had to do with footmen, my shawl, and logic. Rather boring topics compared to what we were discussing here."

The duke took a step forward and turned his gaze upon her. "And what were you three discussing?"

Before she could reply, Elsbeth answered. "Very important topics like what characteristics make for a good husband."

His brows descended slightly as he turned his attention to his cousin. "That is a meaningless topic and one only fathers and older cousins need ruminate on for those in their charge."

As Elsbeth's shoulders slumped, Joanna's irritation with the duke returned. "Then it a very good thing that our conversational path led to discussing your nose."

If she hadn't been watching, she would have missed his head jerking back in the slightest of movements. He was a master of subtle movements. "My nose?"

"Oh, yes." Elsbeth waved her hands about. "You do know how dragonflies enjoy landing on a good-sized proboscis."

The duke's brows lowered considerably as he barely shook his head.

Lady Astor covered her mouth with her gloved hand to hide what Joanna was sure was an escaped chuckle.

Elsbeth indicated the others in the room. "You will probably find much more enjoyable conversation with your friends. We will be happy to keep Lady Joanna entertained."

He nodded, obviously not sure how to respond, but did finally attend to his other guests.

Joanna looked at Lady Elsbeth. "Dragonflies?"

She shrugged, and all three of them broke into laughter. Joanna quickly looked over her shoulder to find the duke otherwise occupied, then turned back to face her new friends. "I do believe we have stumped the duke."

"Not an easy accomplishment." Lady Astor straightened her already impeccable posture. "That man has the knowledge of the world in his head."

"And he's far too proud of it." Elsbeth slipped her tongue out toward her cousin.

Joanna's food from dinner suddenly felt like a lead musket ball in her stomach. That couldn't mean what she thought it meant, surely. "Did he attend university, then?"

"University? That was just the beginning. You should see our library. I'm sure he's read every book in there, and he keeps purchasing more." Lady Astor shook her head. "He's always loved books, even as a small child. I think they kept him company."

The last was said with such melancholy, that Joanna decided it best not to comment. It was just as well because her heart had picked up its beat and a chill raced up her spine. She sincerely hoped the duke had already read the book she'd taken. Or if he noticed it missing, wouldn't associate it with her. After all, there were over a dozen people visiting his house this evening, and he may have very well entertained the night before and the night before that.

"Lady Joanna?"

She blinked at Elsbeth's question. "Yes?"

"I was wondering if you could tell me about Lord Mabry's parents. As cousins, you seem very close."

Now Teddy was a subject she could focus on with enthusiasm. He was the brother the Mabry girls had needed to balance out their antics. "Oh, I can tell you many stories about Lord Mabry." As she launched into the first day Teddy came to visit, she couldn't help being aware of where the duke was in the room. As much as she was enjoying his aunt and cousin, she hoped they could leave soon. Unfortunately, avoiding this entire family was now her main mission for the season.

CHAPTER TWO

James Huntington, Duke of Northwick looked up from the *Morning Chronicle* as his aunt walked into the dining room. "Good morning. Mrs. Eddings made seed cake for you." Which reminded him, he wanted to look up the answer to a mild debate regarding food from last night before his meeting with his solicitor.

"That woman spoils me." Her eyes lit with pleasure.

As his aunt moved to the sideboard, he returned to his paper. It appeared the author of *Guy Mannering* was soon to have another novel called *The Antiquary* printed in three volumes, and there was a new home being built on Tottenham Court Road. London was growing and almost on their doorstep, something he wasn't particularly pleased with. They'd only been in Town a month and already he missed Burhleigh Park, his country estate, but Aunt Louisa had been right, it was time Elsbeth was exposed to London's social functions before she came out officially later in the season. On that score they had agreed. Because of his own dislike for Town, a purely emotional one, he had inadvertently put his cousin at a disadvantage in navigating London society which could make or break a young woman's chances for a good marriage. Easing into the season, as he liked to think of it, put her at a slight disadvantage, but made her more suitable. Her experience would lead her to a better match, not simply the first man she set eyes on, as seemed to be the case at the moment.

"James, I must thank you."

He set down his paper and politely gave his aunt his undivided attention. "To what do I owe your gratefulness?"

"For allowing us to host last evening's dinner party. I know it is not your favorite activity. But it was an excellent introduction for Elsbeth on navigating such a setting. Shopping and coffee shops and rides in Hyde Park are all very well, and important, but social interaction is fleeting there. Having a few guests here in her very home allowed her to feel comfortable, and gave her a chance to observe and learn."

A flash of guilt swept through his chest at his aunt's gratefulness. He owed her much. It was she, his father's younger sister, who had taken it upon herself to make him part of the family. She should never feel as if she must beggar herself for a boon. "You know that I consider both Haven House and Burhleigh Park your home. I want you to feel comfortable in doing whatever you think is best for Elsbeth. I have kept you from London far too long as it is."

His aunt's brown eyes glowed with warmth. "No, you haven't. I, of anyone, understand your reticence in coming to Town, but the past is past. And the future will soon have a new mistress here and at Burhleigh Park. I appreciated the opportunity to converse with Lady Caroline at dinner. She is a very accomplished young woman."

One of the qualities he admired in his aunt was her ability to touch upon their shared past without reliving it. If he could find a wife as skilled as she, he'd be content. "I'm pleased you thought so. I would like your full opinion of her."

His aunt took a sip of tea then set the cup down gently. "In a way, she reminds me very much of myself at her age."

He agreed. Though he was young when she had taken over his upbringing, he still remembered her appearance. Had he perhaps unknowingly made that assessment and so felt more familiar with Lady Caroline? It was something to ponder. "In anything beyond appearance?"

Aunt Louisa laid her hand on her chest. "Oh, I was never so graceful as she. She has a poise well beyond her years. She listens attentively, has a lovely smile, and her manners are impeccable. I understand that she also plays the pianoforte, speaks French, and is an avid letter writer. She also has excellent skill with a needle."

He raised his eyebrows at that.

"Oh, she showed me the work she had done on her dress. It was very detailed and perfectly done. I have no doubt she will make a man an exceptional wife one day."

His aunt told him everything he wanted to hear, but he had the sense she held something back. Then again, as Lady Joanna had reminded him the night before, feelings were not logical. "Then you agree she is a possible candidate to be the mistress of Burhleigh Park?"

"I agree. But I do hope you will remain open to other possibilities."

"Of course." Since his marriage prospects were just that, *his* prospects, he would make his own decisions just as he had since he was seven years old. Self-reflection, knowledge, and observation had stood him in good stead over the years. That he had found a woman of uncommon beauty and refinement so quickly in the season made him anxious to progress the relationship. It would take someone with superior qualities to catch his attention now.

His aunt dabbed at the corner of her mouth with a napkin before carefully setting it aside. "Speaking of possibilities, Elsbeth requested to go to the Pleasure Gardens this evening."

He set his own teacup down with more force than necessary. "The Pleasure Gardens? How did she hear of those?"

His aunt waved her hand dismissively. "Really, James. You can't expect the girl to be in London a month and *not* know about them. This is a city, and in addition to your paper, there are plenty of other news sheets and conversations to be had."

"You mean gossip. I hope you informed her I would not

allow it."

His aunt's chin rose, a common habit among all Huntingtons. "No, I told her *I* would not allow it. In my estimation, I don't believe she knows what they are. She only wished to go because she overheard Lord Mabry setting a time to escort his cousins to Vauxhall."

How unfortunate that the Mabry family was interested in the Pleasure Gardens. "I'm surprised that the Mabrys would go to Vauxhall. That was not the impression I'd received."

"Elsbeth mentioned their primary purpose was a particular treat one of the confectioners produce. If it is anything like this seed cake, I'd attend as well." She took another bite of the caraway seeded, buttery cake.

"Be that as it may, we shall have to find another form of entertainment that Elsbeth can attend this week, so that she may practice her social skills. I don't want her focused on only one person when she hasn't come out yet."

Aunt Louisa held up her index finger. "I'm so glad you mention that. We received an invitation to a small recital being given by the Worthington ladies. You remember them, the pretty daughters you met at the ball last week?"

He vaguely remembered two young ladies who held conversations as if they shared a brain, one adding a comment onto the other's for a complete thought. "If you think she is ready for that, by all means, send our acceptance and I won't plan to be at something else."

"Wonderful. This will also give us an excuse to have a new dress made for her. I want her to enjoy the anticipation of the event."

"Whatever you think best." He rose. "Now, I must meet with my solicitor before paying a call on Lady Caroline."

His aunt gave him a telling look, but politely refrained from commenting.

As he strode toward the library, he counted the weeks before they could repair back to the family estate. London to him would always be the city that took his mother. It made no logical sense, but he'd long ago accepted that fact and avoided it like a wasp's nest. If not for his cousin's need to find a husband of advantage, he would have contented himself with an appropriate lady among his neighbors near Burhleigh Park and never set foot in Haven House except when in Town for business.

James opened the door to the library and quickly shut it behind him. This room was the only room he felt at peace in. It was the one change he'd made to the house upon coming into his majority. He knew, even back then, that if he were forced to come to London, he would need a sanctuary.

Striding across the carpet, he quickly came to the narrow stairs leading to the second floor. He took them two at a time then followed the balcony along the eastern wall. There had been a minor debate last evening about the favorite food consumed by the Monk in Chaucer's *Canterbury Tales*. Though he was absolutely sure that he'd been correct, he wanted to confirm his knowledge.

Passing a small nook where there was no shelving, just two armchairs facing toward the room, he continued to the second bookcase from the end and squatted. On the third shelf from the bottom, he carefully extracted a plain brown volume and opened it. Delicately turning the pages, he skimmed the words until finding what he sought. "It *is* swan." Pleased that he'd been right and could now tell Lord Landon next time he was in his company that it was indeed swan, he reshelved the book. Now, he could focus on his day.

Returning to the stairs, he descended far slower than he'd ascended, then strode to his desk. Taking a key from his waistcoat, he unlocked his top drawer and pulled out a ledger. Though his uncle had left a sizable dowry for Elsbeth, he wished to add to it as a way to make up for keeping her in the country so long. He hoped to entice as many appropriate gentlemen as possible for her to choose from.

Pulling the chair back to take a seat, he halted, his gaze pivoting to the open space on the shelf behind it. Pushing the chair back to the desk, he stared at the missing book. Had his aunt borrowed a book from his library without requesting his assistance? He shook his head. She would not. Elsbeth might, but this he also doubted, as she would inform him. Either a staff member borrowed it, which was not allowed or one of the guests had taken it.

He would not consider any of his guests close friends. He didn't have anyone whom he felt any connection with or loyalty to beyond his aunt and cousin, so it could very well be one of the men from last night. Opening his second drawer, he pulled out a large sheet of parchment with a chart reflecting the titles on this particular bookcase. This was an ever-changing place for books he was accessing regularly, those he had purchased and not yet read, and his favorite rereads, so he kept a written account of them. Looking over his shoulder, he read the titles of the two books on either side of the space and quickly consulted his chart.

"What the devil?" He stared, dumbfounded. Who would take *Educating the Feminine Species*? Had they actually opened the book, or did they really think there was such a treatise? His mind immediately flew to the three other men who had joined him last night for drinks and smoking. None had remarked on his library, something he would have been insulted by if any of them were of any import to him. The discussion had remained on politics, the clergy, alcohol, and horses.

Stymied, he sat, contemplating the possibilities. If the thief had opened the book, he could imagine any of the three men borrowing it. The fake leather cover hid the real title of the book, *The Illustrated Pleasures of Seduction*. If he remembered correctly, it was on the frontispiece in bold lettering. He'd purchased the book as an example of the common practice of fake covers, or rather common among gentlemen. The men last night were all in their prime, each a number of years younger than himself. He could easily see them wishing to review the many illustrations. He firmly believed there was knowledge to be had in every book, and despite his experience, he'd found a few scenarios in the volume that he'd not tried and planned to. But why not simply ask to borrow it?

He tapped his fingers on his knee as he pondered the mystery. Envisioning the scene in the library from last night, he didn't remember any of the men walking close to his desk. All four of them had lounged about near the fireplace, the main order of business smoking and drinking. The women had all repaired to the parlor by that time.

His fingers stilled. No. One woman had found the need to fetch her shawl before their dinner ended. "Lady Joanna?" He rose, placing his three fingers in the empty space on his shelf. Could she have taken his book? But why? To what end? Even as he tried to reconcile the idea, her words during their outside conversation floated through his mind. *Of course, as long as one has the education needed to follow the logic to its correct conclusion, something most women of the peerage are denied.*

He shook his head, unwilling to believe a lady of breeding would steal a book from his library. But even as he reviewed the lady's frowns at dinner, her body language when he found her at her family coach, and her secret smile while conversing with his aunt, he knew.

Lady Joanna Mabry had absconded with his book on seduction!

He stared at the empty space on the shelf as he imagined her opening the book to read it...and laughed.

The absurd humor of the entire circumstance was too funny to ignore. His laughter grew until he fell back in his chair, holding his stomach. When his laughter finally quieted, he wiped his eyes, but couldn't stop smiling. Lady Joanna reading *The Illustrated Pleasures of Seduction*. He shook his head. Had she opened it yet? Did she know what she had? Somehow it seemed the appropriate punishment for her crime, a shock to her senses. His smile faltered. Or would she enjoy every drawing, anxious to know the feelings produced by the dog position and how they might be different from the reverse rider?

A snicker escaped him. She did say women were denied the education of men. Maybe now, she'd realize she didn't want to learn what men knew, any more than he wished to know what ladies knew.

He sobered completely as his gaze moved to the empty space on the shelf. Still, there was the issue of her theft. Involving the authorities was out of the question. She seemed a forthright woman. He would make a call on the Mabry household on his visitations today. Maybe if he gave her the chance to confess, he could retrieve his book with no one else's knowledge. He did not wish to be the one to have revealed the secret of false book covers to the female gender.

Turning back to his desk, he opened the ledger, but didn't see the neat numbers running down the columns. Instead, his mind was filled with the image of Lady Joanna opening the book and fainting dead away.

CHAPTER THREE

JOANNA WAITED UNTIL the maid had added the final pin to her hair and left the room before she pulled out *Educating the Feminine Species* from its hiding spot at the bottom of the armoire. Ever since hearing that the Duke of Huntington had called on her while she was at the milliner's shop, a sense of foreboding had dodged her heels. Unfortunately, there had been no time to see if the book contained some secret letter or memory, perhaps a pressed flower from the duke's mother. That had occurred once before, only it had been a flower from a sweetheart, and she'd quickly returned the book with no one the wiser.

Setting the large tome on her bed, she clicked the clasp open and quickly thumbed the pages. It was easy to see there were many illustrations, but her most pressing concern was something of value between the pages. She wasn't halfway through before the sketches caught her attention. "What was that?"

Stopping, she opened the page fully and stared. A flush filled her cheeks as she gazed upon a naked woman whose own hands were in the most inappropriate places on her body. Squeezing her eyes shut, she took a deep breath. She must have misconstrued the illustration. Why, she had no idea, but her mind must have seen something that wasn't there. Convinced that was all it was, she opened her eyes prepared to view the illustration objectively.

It remained the same. It was exactly what she'd thought she'd seen. Slamming the book closed, she stared at it as if it were a wild animal. What was such a book doing in the duke's library? What kind of feminine education did he think was important? Stepping away from her bed, she grabbed up her fan and proceeded to cool her face. Maybe it was an illustration of how to take a bath, as if a woman didn't know how to keep herself clean.

A tap on her door before the knob turned had her jumping to stand in front of her bed to hide the book.

"Joanna, are you ready? Teddy is anxious to leave." Mariel's gaze swept over her as if to make sure her dress was in proper order.

"Yes. Yes, I'll be down in a moment."

"Very well." Mariel smiled. "I do believe that Teddy hopes to come across Lady Elsbeth in the gardens. I told him that would most likely not occur. I don't believe the duke is that open-minded."

At the mention of the duke, she felt her cheeks heat again. "No, I'm very sure he is not. Tell Teddy I'll be down straight away."

Mariel gave her a knowing smile. "I'm sure you will since you and your favorite confection are the reason we're going." With that, Mariel exited the room, her very dark plum skirts sweeping through the door.

Joanna spun back toward the bed. Had the maid seen the book when she'd brought out her sapphire-colored dress? She couldn't leave it in the armoire. Frantically, she looked about the room, dismissing one hiding place after another. Where would no one look?

With little time, she opened the chest at the end of her bed where additional linens were kept and buried the book beneath them. Tomorrow, she would be sure to move the book to her locked cupboard in the family library…or burn it. Even at the thought of having knowledge of any sort go up in flames, she reconsidered. Besides, she would be a hypocrite. The reason she'd been granted the locked cabinet was because Amelia, as a child, had been upset with her and threw one of her favorite books in the fire.

As she opened the door to leave, she swept the room with her gaze. It looked like it had when she'd entered. All appeared to be in its place. Satisfied the book was safe at least for the evening, she left. As she reached the bottom of the stairs, Teddy strode through the parlor doors.

"There you are. I was about to send a maid up to find you. I know how you can get lost in a book."

She swallowed as guilt over what she'd seen surfaced. "It's a good thing you know me so well, but as it happened, I tore myself away to meet your rush to leave."

Teddy, who sported thick light brown hair and a pale complexion couldn't hide his own blush. "I only thought to speed you along to your tasty tidbit. You are the one who insists on going to Vauxhall only on the evening Monsieur Armand makes your favorite dessert."

"Yes, but last month you weren't nearly so eager."

He had the grace to nod. "You are correct. There is a young lady who might be in attendance." He straightened his paisley waistcoat as if a single wrinkle would make a difference in whether the young Elsbeth would find him acceptable.

That he couldn't accept he made a dashing figure as it was with his tan breeches and light brown greatcoat was of concern to her. His reed thin frame was kept from being effeminate by his broad shoulders, but he was still young, younger than she, and she felt sure he'd fill out more in the coming years. "If the duke is a proper guardian, I doubt that you will see Lady Elsbeth this evening." Sudden doubt about the duke's true character made her pause. "What makes you think she'll be attending?"

Teddy gave her a charming smile. "Just a feeling."

She batted him on the arm with her fan. "Now you are teasing. You cannot possibly have such passionate feelings towards this young lady so soon."

Mariel walked into the entryway to join them. "Oh good,

you're ready. Let us leave."

Joanna looked about as she dawned her spencer. "Is Mother not coming?" She knew her father was at what he called his Deliberation Club, but it was no more and no less than he and his close friends discussing the latest discovery over a meal.

"No, she's tired. She asked that I let her know if I chanced upon Lady Barrage. It seems the woman complained that she could not possibly support The Asylum for Female Orphans because it did not instill a proper virtue into the girls there."

Joanna grinned. "And if Lady Barrage happens to be at the Pleasure Gardens and by chance decides to waltz with a gentleman of no relation, then Mother can argue the orphanage's worthiness."

Mariel nodded as she led them to the door, her cloak punctuating her answer as it swished when she turned. "Precisely."

In little time, the three of them were settled into the Mabry coach. As soon as the coach started forward down the dark street, Teddy was quick to continue their conversation. "Mariel, for argument's sake, do you think a young man can feel passionately for a young woman after a month of knowing her?"

Joanna frowned. He should not have enlisted Mariel's aid in this particular dispute. She was the only one of them who had loved passionately and lost her love. It had been why she married Lord Beaumont, the elderly gentleman who was their father's age, burying her grief in the running of her own household.

As the silence lengthened, Joanna elbowed Teddy. "Don't be asking Mariel about passion. She is not a young man who must marry the right woman so that he can continue the Mabry line. There is much more importance placed on your choice than on hers."

"I was just looking for another opinion." He shrugged. "Didn't you say that you would never marry unless you felt an incredible passion for the man?"

She leaned her head back against the seat and shook it. "Teddy, that is me. I do not have your coming responsibilities." She lifted her head away and looked at him. "I don't even have the same constraints as Amelia does. Since Aunt Mabry left me her fortune and Silver Meadows, I can live happily for the rest of my life as a spinster."

"Oh, Joanna, don't call yourself that." Mariel's hand reached out and tapped her knee. "You are barely twenty-four. You still have time to make a comfortable marriage."

In consideration of her sister's sad past, she reined in her first response. "But I don't want a comfortable marriage. I am perfectly happy as I am. It is not so different from you. Would you remarry? You are yet still a young widow."

Mariel shook her head. "No."

When she didn't elaborate, Joanna let her be. Her older sister knew what it was like to be married, and if she was not anxious to repeat the experience, then it could not be all that it was touted to be.

Teddy was quick to fill the brief silence. "Well, I am not only going to marry because it's my responsibility. I'm going to marry a woman I can love. And I may very well have found her."

Her cousin could be such a romantic. "Or you may not have. Remember, you need Uncle's blessing."

He lifted his hands out palms up. "What possible reason could he have to withhold his blessing. She's a duke's cousin and a marquess' daughter?"

That was true. "But what a shame it would be if you were to marry her and then fall in love with someone else."

He shrugged his shoulders. "That's what a mistress is for."

This time she punched him in the arm.

"Ow."

"Theodore Bartholomew Augustus Mabry. You will not demean a woman in such a way as to force her, who you once claimed to love, to have to endure the gossip about you and a mistress. Do you see your father or ours bedding down with some fallen woman? Do you?"

"No." Teddy's voice took on a sullen quality. "But many

gents have one."

She folded her arms over her chest. "That may be, but a Mabry would not do that to the mother of his children. I predict that soon there will be very few women who will allow for such an arrangement."

Teddy slumped down on the seat. "Please. Spare me your women should have the same rights as men argument."

"Why because you know it or because you don't want to listen to it?"

He grinned. "Because I know it?"

She harrumphed, but relented. Her family and friends were well aware of her opinions on the matter. She was in a unique position in regard to the subject of women's intellectual equality. She hadn't realized until recently how much being a wealthy unmarried woman undermined her arguments that women of the peerage be able to own property without having to hire a sly and well-versed solicitor or that women of all levels of society should be allowed to attend schools and be taught the same subjects that men were taught. When she spoke about these issues, she was dismissed because she didn't understand the difficulties of her beliefs.

She only blamed part of her frustration on society. The other part of the blame lay at her father's feet, who allowed all his daughters to pursue their own interests with his full support. Once Teddy had been born to her father's younger brother, she had no doubt her father gave a sigh of relief not to have to be the one to groom an heir for the Mabry estates.

"I hope you do find a passionate love one day." Mariel's quiet voice spoke of experience and to neither of them specifically, effectively silencing them all.

As soon as they arrived at Vauxhall's Pleasure Gardens, they paid the fee, strode through the front building, and entered onto the grand walkway. Though Vauxhall included twelve acres of sculpted gardens and outdoor buildings laid out in a grid pattern, she'd never gone beyond the supper boxes that were built in a crescent on either side of the center square. She had no interest in walking among planted trees beyond the main buildings that were a poor substitute for a true forest.

The orchestra, on the second level balcony in the tall rotunda, played a waltz, though they could not see it from the entrance. The music gave the lantern lit area a dreamlike quality.

"This is the perfect setting for falling in love."

Teddy's exclamation had Joanna taking his arm. "More like a perfect setting for wayward actions."

Mariel took his other arm. "Remember our primary purpose, cousin."

He looked at them both. "But I was."

Joanna opened her mouth to lecture, but Teddy laughed. "Yes, I know. To the supper boxes, so my ladies can indulge their palettes."

She smiled, unable to help herself. Though Teddy was often irreverent and humorous, he was rarely hurtful in his comedy. She tried to imagine him as a husband, but just couldn't do it. "If I could just convince Monsieur Armand to offer his mascarpone ice cream in his establishment on Bond Street, I'd forgo the Pleasure Gardens altogether."

"And miss all this?" Teddy splayed his hands despite having each of them on his arm. "You won't see that fire swallower on Bond Street or those dancing dogs in Monsieur Armand's shop." He brought them to a halt to watch the ladies and gentlemen dancing outside the rotunda. "It appears Lady Emily has found a new protector. Is that not Lord Reddington holding her tighter than a chimney sweep holds his broom?"

"Teddy." Mariel's warning tone floated across them. "It is not appropriate to point out someone's mistress to ladies."

He started them forward again. "I apologize, Lady Beaumont. I'm so used to escorting Joanna, that I forget myself."

"And you don't have to watch what subject you discuss with me?" Joanna frowned at him, though he kept his gaze ahead.

"You are the one who told me women and men are equal, so

that means whatever I discuss with men I can discuss with you." He finally met her gaze, "correct?"

Reluctantly, she nodded. He'd never treated her like a lady because she'd refused to allow him to do so, but he'd never before brought up such a brazen subject. Elsbeth's interest in him must have him feeling overly confident.

"Come Joanna." He gave her his most charming smile. "Is it really so onerous to see people enjoying themselves? Isn't that why you're here, to enjoy your favorite ice cream?"

"I suppose you have a point."

Even as he chuckled, Mariel spoke. "I prefer the parmesan cheese over the mascarpone myself."

Joanna's heart tightened. "Belinda's favorite was strawberry."

Teddy squeezed her arm in his. "She loved it all, even your favorite, as long as it was ice cream."

That was true. Belinda was the reason why they had an ice house on their grounds, and when she became ill, Cook had experimented with flavors not even Monsieur Armand had thought of. She missed her sister sometimes more than she could bear.

As they strolled toward the supper boxes, Joanna scanned the crowd for people she knew. Many of her friends enjoyed coming to the Pleasure Gardens with their husbands or families. She preferred her entertainments be separated. She didn't mind the mixing of classes that some objected to. Nor did she find objection to those couples who took advantage of the many hidden avenues between the greenery to steal a kiss. For her, it was the chaotic feel of so many activities happening at once, that one could not reasonably enjoy any single one.

As they approached, Monsieur Armand turned from the couple he spoke to and extended his hands toward them. "My favorite family. So good to have you here tonight." He pulled them each forward by the hands and kissed them on both cheeks. Then he winked, waving a finger at her. "I know why you are here tonight. You see my advertisement in *The Times*, non?"

She played ignorant and set her hand upon her chest. "You placed an ad in *The Times* just for me?"

Monsieur Armand laughed. "You jest, mademoiselle, but if you did not grace us with your presence tonight, I would most assuredly create one only for you."

She was truly touched. "No need for that, Monsieur. My father reads that paper from beginning to end and is always on the lookout for items that may interest me."

"Bon, then let us get you seated." He clapped his hands, and a waiter strode across the grass to receive his instructions. "Please seat my very special guests."

As they followed their waiter, Monsieur hurried off to greet more visitors.

Teddy leaned toward her as they walked. "He was only flattering you so you would come back next month."

She rolled her eyes. "We all know I need no flattery to return here anymore than I would need to flatter you to inspire you to attend an event where Lady Elsbeth would be present."

He laughed. "You know me too well, cousin."

In truth, she did. She was also absolutely certain that Lady Elsbeth, Lady Astor, and the Duke of Northwick would not be arriving at the Pleasure Gardens this evening, no matter how much Teddy hoped it was otherwise.

CHAPTER FOUR

JAMES SLOWED HIS gait once through the entrance of Vauxhall. It was his first, and hopefully, last visit to the infamous Pleasure Gardens. He was quite interested to learn firsthand what truly occurred within their environs. Passing judgement on hearsay was faulty, something he had indeed done, never expecting to set foot on the grounds.

The sound of an orchestra beckoned him forward, but he kept his gaze moving, cataloging the images as he catalogued the books in his library. There were couples, and families, groups of young men and dandies milling about. The single women he noticed were obviously not of his class nor were the varied performers that flitted about the crowd. As he strolled closer to the music, he acknowledged the orchestra was adequate.

Stepping between the trees, he found the musicians on the second level of what was a three-storied rotunda. He appreciated that having the sound come from a higher level allowed it to infiltrate further into what he would consider a park. Many of his own class, as well as what he assumed to be gentry, danced across the ground below the musicians, but all appeared to be civil in their movements. His assumptions about the place were quickly being undermined, but it was yet early in the night.

He stopped to study the dancers. Though he recognized a number of men, he did not see the woman he'd come to interrogate – his thief. After his humor had spent itself over the book Lady Joanna had taken, his insult had risen. She had been a guest in his home, a new acquaintance, and yet she thought it fit to stealthily enter his library and abscond with his property? That it wasn't one of the books he'd spent years tracking down was beside the point. What if she had taken his first edition of Dante Alighieri's Divine Comedy or worse yet, his gold gilded copy of *Plato's Republic*? It had simply been to his advantage that she'd taken a book of no merit.

Determining she was not among those dancing, he continued his search, his affront deepening with every stride. He doubted that she pilfered property from other peers, so it had to be something about himself that had motivated her. Though she had made all the proper responses, his instinct told him that Lady Joanna didn't like him.

While he'd had a few older gentlemen and an occasional scholar decide not to further his acquaintance, and which he in return agreed, he'd never encountered someone with whom he'd had so little interaction take such a quick dislike of his personage. He hadn't met any of the Mabry family until yesterday eve, but she had definitely found fault with him. He didn't like it. It made him want to defend himself when he had no reason to do so. In his frustration, he found himself striding toward a grove of trees. He stopped and looked about.

Somehow, he'd walked beyond the buildings. Quickly, he retraced his steps until he came upon a long, curved structure, much like a portico that was sectioned off to provide seating at a table for a few people each. The tables sat about a foot above the lawn on concrete with diners on two ends and the rest facing outward toward a lawn where others strolled, and where, at the moment, a man juggled flaming torches. The music filtered through the trees, but was not so loud as to make conversation difficult. Scanning those at the tables, some of whom appeared to be eating, he found the person he sought. "Lady Joanna."

Without preamble, he strode to her section where she sat

with family. "Lady Joanna, Lord Mabry, Lady Beaumont." He took in their reactions at his presence in a thrice. The lady he sought appeared stunned, while Lord Mabry instantly rose and smiled, and Lady Beaumont nodded politely, her smile kind.

Mabry held out his hand. "Your Grace, it is a pleasure to find you here." The young man scanned the area, no doubt expecting to see Elsbeth. "Are you alone?"

He shook hands. "I am." Though he spoke to Mabry, he covertly watched as Lady Joanna lifted her glass and swallowed a large portion of wine.

"Then you must join us, please." Mabry opened his arm to indicate the empty chair next to Lady Joanna.

James smiled, barely keeping a grin from forming. "Thank you."

Stepping up into the close area, he sat down, noting that Lady Joanna did not meet his gaze.

Mabry resumed his seat. "We are about to have Lady Joanna's favorite confection. Or rather, the ladies are about to. I'm having a few Shrewsbury cakes myself."

He turned his attention to his thief. "And what is your favorite confection?"

She finally met his gaze. "It is mascarpone ice cream. If you have not tried it, I highly recommend it. Monsieur Armand only serves it but once a month here at Vauxhall."

He'd expected her to reveal her guilt, but she met his gaze fully and even gave a short nod as if she were the authority on the subject.

"Then I will definitely taste it so I may pass my own judgment on this delicacy."

"Excellent." Mabry waved a gentleman over and proceeded to give him their request.

He took advantage of Mabry's distraction. "Lady Joanna, are you an expert on confections?"

"Not at all. I simply know what I enjoy."

"And do you enjoy reading?"

She looked away and reached for her wine, taking a small sip. After setting it down, she met his gaze once again. "I adore reading. Why do you mention it? Is there something you've read that you would like my opinion on?"

Her opinion? He stiffened. "Not at all. I simply thought to have a conversation."

"Then I will ask you this. What do you think of the waltz?"

He blinked, the turn in subject catching him unawares. "What is there to think of it? It is a dance that is currently enjoyed by many. Do you waltz?"

Before she could answer, Mabry interjected. "I hope she can. I had plenty of bruises from practicing it with her."

Instead of being ashamed, she appeared to gloat. "I told you it wouldn't be painless. If you hadn't told father about our foray over to the London Docks, you could have been spared. It was your fault entirely."

Mabry turned to Lady Beaumont. "Did she, or did she not, beg me to go with her?"

The lady shook her head. "I'm sure his grace doesn't want to hear about your less than appropriate adventures." She met his gaze. "I do not waltz. It was not considered acceptable when I came out, but I do enjoy watching the dancers glide about the floor. It seems so effortless."

Mabry opened his mouth then suddenly winced.

This was not what he had expected. There was an unusual familiarity between the cousins that he found foreign. For a moment he tried to envision them at Burhleigh Park as part of his family. It was impossible. He would have to steer Elsbeth toward someone with a more staid family dynamic.

Joanna abruptly set her hand down on the table, and leaned forward to view her sister. "It may look that way, but it is very difficult. Of course, it might be easier with a better partner."

Her movement caused a warm soothing scent to waft by him. It fought the crispness of the cool in the air. He tried to pinpoint it, but she quickly sat back and faced him. "Are you a good lead,

Your Grace?"

He stiffened. "I do not waltz."

Her dark eyebrows lifted. "You don't? But it is considered one of the few social graces that all men must aspire to. Surely, you haven't let studying philosophy take precedence over dance lessons? Maybe Elsbeth could teach you."

Though her tone sounded as if she thought it a pity he didn't know how to waltz, her words and gaze had his back stiffening with the sense again that she didn't like him. "Do not mistake me, Lady Joanna, I am quite proficient at dancing. It is simply that in Peterborough, I had no need and no time to learn the latest dance. I doubt very much that Elsbeth has either."

As if he'd been waiting for the mention of Elsbeth's name, Mabry immediately turned toward him. "I'd be pleased to teach her. If I can survive learning with Lady Joanna, I'm sure I could handle the gentle Elsbeth."

Feeling put upon by both cousins, he allowed his rancor to slip through. "Is Lady Joanna then clumsy?"

Her sudden intake of breath gave him satisfaction.

"I am not clumsy. It was simply something new. Whenever I learn something new, I expect to make mistakes and then I become much more proficient. Take Latin for example. When I started conjugating verbs, I made a complete mess of it. But now, I've mastered it because I learned from those errors. Would you like me to conjugate a few verbs for you?"

She knew Latin? Maybe it was time to build a locked room for his most precious books. His *Plato's Republic* could very well be in peril. "No. I didn't like conjugating verbs in my school room. I certainly don't want to think about them now."

"Mores the pity. I so rarely get to discuss Latin since all the ladies of my acquaintance cannot read it."

Before he could respond, Mabry threw his hands up. "Here she goes again. Please excuse her, Your Grace. The lady cannot seem to refrain for more than an hour without mentioning her theory that women's minds are equal to men's."

"But they are." At the wide-eyed stares he received from all three of his companions, he felt he should elaborate. "I firmly believe that both genders have the same capacity for knowledge. It is simply the type of knowledge that can be processed that is different. In fact, I've read that this is why we have two genders. One can process what is important for mankind while another can process was makes life comfortable. It firmly aligns with the theory of divide and conquer."

From the corner of his eye, he noticed Lady Joanna reach for her wine. In an instant, Mabry had clamped his hand down around her forearm. "Joanna."

Surprised by such a serious warning tone coming from the young man he thought to be far too happy and immature, he studied Lady Joanna. He'd never seen a woman in a fury, but he was fairly certain this is what he found in her gaze. Not sure if it was the lighting or her eyes themselves, but they appeared to be a mixture of colors, what he would consider hazel, only in the lantern light the green was dominant. That they were narrowed at him told him he was indeed the object of her ire. It was an odd feeling, that. He didn't remember engendering any particularly strong emotional reaction, be it for good or ill, from anyone.

After pondering that a moment, he came to the logical conclusion that it must have something to do with Lady Joanna, not himself. "It appears you don't agree. I am certainly open to other opinions."

Her eyes returned to their normal openness. Now that he paid attention, she really did have rather round eyes, not the more common shape he was used to seeing on ladies of breeding.

"Teddy, you can release my arm."

Teddy? These Mabrys were entirely too familiar with each other.

She turned her head toward her cousin who lifted his hand slowly from hers. "Thank you." Calmly, she took another sip of her wine.

He frowned. Had he imagined her fury? Women were definitely emotional creatures. It may be that now she would finally tell him what she disliked so much about him.

She set down the glass and gave him her full attention. "I'm truly sorry that your education was so sorely lacking. If you like, I'd be happy to lend you a book of mine that explains the complexities of the human mind and the lack of differences between the genders."

The calmness of her voice soothed as well as any lullaby, and he found himself nodding before her words registered. Lend him a book? "No." Affronted, he struggled for the words he needed. "I do not need a book on the subject. I am quite well read. Perhaps I can offer to lend *you* one of my many scientific examinations of the brain."

A tiny smile just barely lifted the corners of her lips. "You'd allow me, a woman, to read one of your books?"

He stiffened. How had he gone from confronting her about stealing a book from his library to offering to let her borrow one? He was saved from answering her question by the waiter bringing their desserts followed by the proprietor himself.

"Lady Joanna, a sweet for a sweet. I do hope you enjoy."

Her face lit up like a child upon receiving a new pony. "Oh, Monsieur Armand, of course I will. Unless, you made it differently." She pouted. "Please tell me you didn't experiment with your recipe."

"Non, non. I would not for you. There are so few who appreciate my love of this cheese. I could not disappoint you."

She smiled kindly. "You are such a dear."

"I do wish to please. Bon appétit." The monsieur gave a short bow and strode off.

James watched as Joanna took a small amount of the white ice cream onto her spoon and placed it in her mouth. Her eyes closed. "Hmmmm."

At her actions, his body grew alert, specifically an inconvenient piece of his anatomy. This was unacceptable behavior. Did she not know that she mimicked a woman being pleasured in bed? Of course, she didn't. He shifted in his seat, uncomfortable. If she did indeed have his book, she soon would know a lot more about the matter. When had it become *if* she had it?

Joanna opened her eyes and smiled, her gaze meeting his. "You need to try this, Your Grace. No matter how your life is progressing, it will make it better."

For the first time that evening, he was positive that her words were sincere. Could ice cream truly gentle a prickly woman like music tamed a wild beast? He looked down at the confection before him and lifted his spoon. If it did, it had powers that needed to be studied thoroughly.

Taking a spoonful, he closed his mouth around it and let it glide around his tongue. The flavor was much more subtle than the parmesan cheese ice cream he'd had, but that made sense since mascarpone had far less saltiness. In fact, the dessert tasted of sweetened cream. As it melted to liquid and he swallowed, the aftertaste, instead of satisfying, was such a shadow of the flavor that it caused a need in him for more.

A quiet chuckle had him opening his eyes. When had he closed them?

Joanna's knowing smile was conspiratorial, as if they shared a special secret about this ice cream.

He gave a short nod. "You are correct. This is a flavor like no other."

Her smile widened before she turned to Mabry. "Some gentlemen can appreciate the finer nuances of Monsieur's delight."

Mabry waved his hand. "Nuance, bah. It's downright tasteless. If I'm going to freeze my tongue, I'd much rather do it with anise seed ice cream. Now that's a flavor that will top off an evening. Better yet, a strong French cognac is more to my liking."

Lady Joanna sighed before pushing her spoon into her small bowl. "There are just some things we will never agree upon." She filled her spoon again and held it aloft as she lifted her gaze to look at him. "Do you find that is the case with you and your cousin?"

The answer to that was so obvious, it didn't warrant an answer, but for the sake of politeness he indulged her. "Of course. She is much younger, less experienced, and a different gender. I feel we have far less in common than that which we hold in agreement. It's stunning, actually. I believe it has to do with the fact she was born of my father's sister. Perhaps if he had a brother, her thought process would be aligned with mine, but I have my doubts."

Her smile appeared to have frozen, but she had not yet taken the spoonful of ice cream into her mouth. She gestured with her spoon toward him. "Eat your ice cream."

Taken aback, he wasn't sure how to respond, but since her mouth was full and her eyes closed once again, he took another bite. The conversation lapsed as they all enjoyed the confections they'd ordered. As he scraped the bowl, tempted to lift it to his mouth, but refraining in such a public place, he had to admit, his mood had improved. He needed to do further research on the properties of ice cream and their effect on the mind.

"Your Grace." Lady Mariel's soothing voice was far different from her sister's. "Were you meeting someone here in the Pleasure Gardens?"

"No. I simply came to observe them."

Mabry leaned forward to stare at him. "Have you never visited before?" The incredulity in his voice made it quite clear that he thought that fact to be unheard of.

"No, I haven't. I don't come to Town often and when I do, it is for business, not for the Pleasure Gardens."

Lady Mariel gave Mabry a stern look before speaking. "Then is this your first season in London?"

"It is." And hopefully his last. "We are here only for Elsbeth to have her time in society. She hopes to be engaged by the end of the season. She is learning quickly and will be out in a few weeks, I believe. It is Lady Astor's decision."

Though Mabry lifted his glass in salute, it was Joanna who responded. "And what of you?"

"Me?"

"Are you not looking for a wife? I'm afraid that is the impression that Lady Caroline is under. If you plan to marry someone near your country estate, you should let her know. She is on the hunt for a husband, and it would be a pity if she wasted time with you if you have no interest in her."

He blinked unbelievingly. Had the woman just advised him on how to handle his search for a bride? "You needn't concern yourself with Lady Caroline."

"That's a relief. I think you two would suit very well."

Mabry, who had obviously been drinking more than his cousins leaned forward again. "Do you think Lady Elsbeth and I would suit?"

"Lord Mabry, mind your manners." Lady Mariel's stern rebuke had the fellow slumping back in his chair.

James felt Lady Joanna's stare, but did not meet it. "I have no doubt that Lady Elsbeth will have her choice of suitors once she is presented. Friday evening, we are going to a recital by the Worthington sisters, and I understand a number of unattached gentlemen will be there."

Mabry straightened. "I'd be happy to number myself among them."

Lady Joanna shook her head. "You are to escort us to the lecture on coal lamps at the Royal Institution that evening. Sir Davy is unveiling a new design that he believes will save lives. You cannot possibly go."

Mabry frowned at her. "Your father would be happy to escort you. You don't require my presence. Last time I went with you, I fell asleep and you kicked me awake."

He raised his brows at that. To her credit, Lady Joanna appeared embarrassed for once.

"I had to. You were snoring so loud. I'm surprised I was allowed entrance to the next lecture."

She attended lectures? The more he learned about Lady Joanna, the more confused he became. He found it distracting. He needed to focus on discovering if she took his book. But how to know for certain. Nothing in the evening had given him any clues.

Lady Joanna abruptly rose from her seat, and he quickly stood. "We won't keep you any longer from your exploration of the Pleasure Gardens. I do hope you enjoy your evening." With the slightest of curtsies, she stepped behind him and off the dais.

Mabry bowed. "It was a pleasure to have your company, Your Grace. I'm usually outnumbered by my female cousins. I look forward to seeing you at the recital."

Cursing himself for revealing where Elsbeth and he would be, he simply gave a short nod.

Lady Mariel gave a proper curtsy. "I hope we didn't shock your sensibilities this evening. I'm afraid we are far too close for most families to understand, but with the death of our sister, all formality was lost. I won't ask your forgiveness, but I do ask that you reserve your judgment. Have a lovely evening, Your Grace."

Stunned into silence, he simply watched as the quiet Mariel joined her family members, and they strode back toward the entrance of Vauxhall.

He resumed his seat. He hadn't learned what he'd hoped to this evening, but he had learned much he hadn't expected. Unfortunately, it was much like the mascarpone ice cream. In the aftermath, he was left wanting to know more. On quick review of his observations, he concluded that Lady Mariel tried to serve as a chaperone and role model to her younger sister and cousin. Lord Mabry, though, had obviously been far too indulged in his youth with few responsibilities and had not yet matured to where he would make a good husband for anyone, though he did show a few signs of promise.

And then there was Lady Joanna.

James steepled his hands. She was a conundrum. Her intelligence was there to see in her eyes, but her lack of poise and fluctuating emotions were unpredictable. It was, in his estimation, a combination that portended ill. Despite his reservations, he needed to find out if she had indeed stolen his book. It appeared that guilt was not one of the many emotions she felt, which meant he must engage her in further conversation to determine if she was the culprit.

A part of him did not relish the task. However, his mind was excited by the challenge. No matter the outcome, he was absolutely certain he would learn a lot more than he knew now about Lady Joanna Mabry.

CHAPTER FIVE

J OANNA WAITED UNTIL the maid closed the door behind her then
jumped from her chair at the small table in her room, her robe
parting as she rushed to the door. She had requested she be
woken at such an ungodly hour in the morning to ensure a few
hours of privacy. Setting her ear to the wood panel, she listened
as the maid's footsteps faded. Stepping back to her table, she took
a quick sip of tea and bite of toast with marmalade before she
dropped it back to the plate and turned to the chest at the end of
her bed.

When Northwick happened upon them the night before,
she'd cursed her luck. He was the last person she wanted to see.
Once he asked about reading, she became suspicious that he
might know she'd taken his book, but as the evening continued,
she wasn't as sure. Her brief instructions in acting, when she was
young and had written a play for her siblings to perform, allowed
her to draw on those long-ago lessons to throw him off her scent.

She grinned as she knelt before the chest. If their paths
crossed again, she would take him up on his offer to let her
borrow a book. Opening the chest, she dug her hand beneath the
linens but didn't feel anything except soft material. Her heart
raced, and she quickly pulled items out, tossing them onto the
floor. Surely the maid had no need to take out linens last eve. As
her hand touched something hard, she calmed. Lifting a quilt, she

pulled the large tome from its hiding place and grasped it to her chest. She still hoped to garner some small piece of wisdom from its pages. Stuffing the various bed linens back into the chest, she closed the lid, and stepped onto the chest. She flounced across her bed before dropping down to tuck her legs beneath her, pushing her robe aside. Finally, she set the book in front of her.

The cover was well used. She couldn't resist gliding her fingertips across it, especially over the border that had been worked into the leather. Golden curls and swirls accentuated bold lettering. The title, *Educating the Feminine Species,* was gilded in gold, and bold black lettering beneath it proclaimed the book created by "Lord Ancil Rutherford." The golden clasp that locked it closed had a slide mechanism to allow the reader easy access to the knowledge inside.

The bold title was at complete odds with the delicacy of the rest of the decoration. She wrinkled her nose.

It was a horrid title, and she imagined it would be a horrid book, based on the single illustration she'd seen. Despite that, she reverently opened it, turning past the two blank pages to read the title page.

The Illustrated Pleasures of Seduction.

She frowned. Quickly, she closed the book and read the title again. Opening it, she shook her head. It didn't make sense. Was it an error? She turned another page to find the same title with a copyright date of 1815. There was no author listed. Turning that page, she read the dedication.

To all young men. Ignorance is not bliss. Only the knowledge contained herein can provide you with the skills to enjoy the true beauty and wonder of the female form. In the body of a woman, true bliss can be achieved. There is no greater pleasure on earth than when both of you reach fulfillment. Read carefully, study well, and practice often. This is your birthright as a man and your obligation to your woman. – The Author

Not comprehending, she re-read the dedication. This could not mean…surely it didn't…. Was the duke's book, this book, an educational treatise on how to seduce a woman? If so, that meant it went farther than the medical texts she'd read that explained how mankind perpetuated itself. Shocked, she kept her hand on the dedication page, fearful of seeing anymore.

Had the duke studied this text, and practiced? She swallowed. While he appeared polite, he barely smiled and even at his home she didn't see any flirting on his part, though much was done by a number of the ladies present. Or maybe he had just purchased it. After having met Lady Caroline, had he thought to learn about the marriage bed? Surely, he had copulated with a servant or while at university. Did the rather thick tome contain information even a man of his age didn't know? He had to be at least a score and ten. She'd expect by now he would already know what was between the pages, or rather, bed sheets.

At that thought, she lifted her hand from the page as if it had heated exponentially. She should close the book and find a way to return it. That was the right thing to do. She wanted to do the right thing, but the point of borrowing a book was to *read* it. Then again, she'd had no intention of returning it, of going to Haven House ever again or of looking upon the duke. Torn, she scrambled off the bed and sat at the table. Taking a sip of tea, she weighed the pros and cons, a common practice for her since learning Roman judges based their decisions on this method.

She bit her toast and chewed. The pros to reading the book would be that she would gain more knowledge. That knowledge could even be useful in case a gentleman ever thought to seduce her. She swallowed. That was doubtful, but still it was better to be prepared should such an occasion arise. Another pro could be she would learn more about the duke and whether she wanted to continue to support Teddy in his pursuit of Elsbeth. She glanced over at the bed. Right now, in her ignorance and based on her assumptions, she did not. The fact was, despite the subject, her curiosity was running wild with guesses. That would be another pro. By reading it, she would know and not imagine what the book contained.

Picking up her piece of toast, she popped the rest of it into her mouth. What cons could there be to learning something new? Maybe not knowing what a duke read was best in this case? She shook her head. Ignorance was never bliss, as the dedication stated. What if once reading the book, she couldn't bear to be in the duke's company? That had to be considered, especially if Teddy succeeded in winning Elsbeth's hand. She'd gone to too much trouble to abscond with the book, so not to read it would be a waste of effort.

No, that was another pro. She lifted her teacup with both hands. What if she learned something that would change her view of the marriage bed, or rather give her a view of it. Since she was well on the way to happy spinsterhood, that argument didn't hold a lot of weight. She tipped her cup and took a good swallow. That settled it. Setting the cup down, she stood. She would read the book. She'd always believed that what a man learned a woman could learn and this was no exception. She needed to abide by her own convictions.

Crawling back onto the bed, she settled herself in front of the dedication page and turned it over. She let out a breath as her gaze fell upon two figures, one on each facing page. A sketch of a naked man filled the left side, and a naked woman filled the right. Above each were simply the words *man* and *woman*. There was nothing new to be learned here since she was familiar with the female form, and based on the statues her younger sister Amelia insisted she view, she was somewhat cognizant of what a male body looked like. It was a fair place to start a book of this kind.

Turning the page, she let out a breath. "Oh." Now the left side contained a sketch of the male's nether area with lines pointing to specific parts. She quickly moved her gaze to the facing page. It contained the same area on a woman, but it had far more lines. Curious, she studied it. There was more there than she had realized. It didn't seem necessary to point it all out.

Lifting the page, she stilled as a sound whispered through her door. A maid?

A light tap on her door was her only warning. Without preamble, she slammed the book closed and stuffed it under her quilt just as the door opened and Amelia poked her head inside.

"Oh good, you're awake. I just couldn't sleep any more. I'm fairly bursting with my news."

Her pretty younger sister stepped inside wearing her pale blue robe, her blonde hair loosely braided from her night's sleep. Amelia never went about without everything about her in perfect order. Even when she painted in her studio, her clothing there might be a tad eccentric, but it was always impeccable. Whatever the news was, it had to be important.

"What is it?"

Amelia climbed on the bed and Joanna quickly shifted her position to protect the book.

"I'm to exhibit my work at the London Art Academy."

She widened her eyes. "What? When?"

"The final week of June. They decided to open the final week of their season to female artists, and they asked me!"

Her heart filled with joy and she pulled Amelia forward, hugging her tight. "I'm so proud of you." She set her sister away, but held her shoulders. "You did it. Lady Amelia Mabry, London's foremost painter of people and places. I can see the placards already."

Amelia laughed. "Not quite yet, but it will happen. I'm not going to stop until my skill is the best it can be."

Joanna dropped her hand, her eyes stinging with tears of happiness. "You deserve this. You've worked so long, even put off your first season for it."

"It was worth it. If Aunt Mabry hadn't taken me to Paris and Florence, I would have never learned so much." She giggled. "I'd still be painting father's puppies, each with two tails and five legs."

"And don't forget the flowers for ears."

Loved filled her at Amelia's burgeoning success. "I always knew you were born for wonderful things."

Amelia sobered. "I have a lot of work to do. They want a dozen paintings to display."

"You have nearly five times that many."

"But they aren't all good enough." Amelia slid from the bed. "I need to focus on my theme. Yes, I paint people and places, but what do I want my artwork to portray? I need to examine what I have and make a decision on which I will display based upon my theme. Then I must add new paintings to complete the impression."

Joanna scooted off the bed. "I understand what you mean. Do you want me to help you decide?"

"Not yet. Let me ponder it a bit."

She nodded. "I'm happy to generate ideas when you need them. Do Mother and Father know yet?"

"Yes, I told them last night, but you and Mariel were gone. I must have been in my studio when you came home. That's where I'm headed now to make some decisions. Thank you for being happy for me. I was afraid you wouldn't be."

Surprised, she frowned. "Whyever not?"

Amelia shrugged. "Well, it's a special week with only female artists. I thought you would be disappointed my work wouldn't be shown with male artists as well."

"Oh, Amelia. I would never fault you for the narrowmindedness of men and their antiquated thought processes. I'm so pleased for you that my heart is full."

"That means so much." Amelia gave her a spontaneous hug. "What new book is that you're reading now?"

Joanna froze as her sister pulled away. Looking over her shoulder at her bed she could see the duke's book had been halfway uncovered by the blanket. Turning back to Amelia, she waved her hand. "It's an illustrated treatise on what women should learn. I just started it this morning. I'm fairly certain I'm not going to enjoy it."

Amelia pouted. "Poor Joanna. An opened book is a finished book for you. I hope it's not too tortuous."

"I hope not as well." She grimaced.

Amelia strode to the door, her step quick with her excited energy. "I probably won't see you the rest of the day, but I'm still planning on attending the lecture with you on Friday. I hear that Sir Davy is a most charming gentleman as well as an intellectual." She smirked before slipping out the door.

Charming? In other words, a pleasure to gaze upon. Joanna shook her head and turned back to the table. Pouring herself more tea, her pleasure over Amelia's news dimmed. That her sister thought she'd be disappointed bothered her. Had she become too militant? Her whole purpose of discussing women's equal intelligence was to open minds, not cause nervousness or fear. Her sister's revelation had her revaluating her approach. From now on, she would refrain from speaking about her favorite subject when among those who knew her views well.

Pleased with her decision, she added cream and sugar to her tea and took a sip. If Belinda had still been alive, she would have pointed out such a flaw in the gentlest of ways. Joanna sank into the chair. Bea's death at only twenty had hurt them all. She had been the heart of their family. She smiled fondly. The four of them had determined their roles at a very young age based upon their interest. All of them sitting on the floor in the parlor, waiting for Mother to read them their favorite Christmas story.

She had quickly claimed to be the intellect of the family, though at barely ten years old, she was hardly such. Her father, in her estimation, truly held that place of honor. Amelia spoke next, telling them all that she would be the creator because she could draw. Though at the time, her drawings were much like any seven-year-old's. Mariel, as the oldest, and already twelve, decided that she must be the practical one to keep the creator and intellect in check. They had laughed at that.

It was then that Belinda had asked what she should be. Even at the age of eight, she worried about them all and thought she had no strength that defined her. There was silence as they all pondered what her designation should be as if their whole world hung in the balance.

At that moment Mother strolled in with the Christmas story and asked what they were about. When they explained they still must decide on Belinda's role, Mother smiled. "Why, she is the most obvious of all of you. She practically shines with her strength. Every one of us gravitates to her for it." They stared at Belinda as if she were more a mystery than the Sphinx in Egypt.

She'd been determined to solve Bea's mystery. After all, she'd claimed to be the intellectual. As she gazed at Belinda, it finally made sense. "Love!" She'd burst out with it, pleased she's been successful.

Mother nodded. "Indeed, Belinda is the heart of our family."

Joanna would never forget the look on her younger's sister's face as she accepted that she was of such key importance to them all.

And yet years later, she had been unable to save her sweet Bea, their heart. Wiping at her moist eyes, she took another sip of tea. "I wish you were still here."

As the scattered sunlight dappled through the wispy curtains on the widows to the south, Joanna rose. Mother had said there was no use focusing on the past when much awaited them in the future. She moved to her dressing table to pull her hair from its braid and face the day. About to sit, she caught sight of the book on her bed in the mirror's reflection.

Her interest in it had cooled, but she did need to lock it away. Dropping her robe, she quickly prepared herself. She brushed her hair, braided it, and twisted it up with a ribbon, leaving one long curl to lay against her collarbone. Donning her chemise and stays, she tugged them tight enough before taking a petticoat from the shelf of the armoire and putting it on, followed by her bright peach morning dress.

She had much planned, from helping Mariel embroider a wedding gift for a friend to accompanying mother to the milliner for the purchase of a new hat. There would be very little time for reading until later in the evening…maybe. Taking one more look in the mirror to make sure she was presentable for her family and any callers they may receive, she grabbed up the book and headed down stairs.

As it was still fairly early, she doubted anyone would be about. Stepping into the family library, which was half of their collection, she started across the room toward her special cabinet.

"What do you have there, my Joanna?"

Startled, she placed her hand to her chest. "Father, you surprised me."

Joseph Mabry, Marquess of Wakefield, unfolded himself from the wingback chair in the bay window. His thick chestnut hair liberally streaked with gray had been combed, and his rounded chin shaved for the day. His gray eyes lit with curiosity as he stood and held his hand out. "Come, let me see what new precious treasure you have discovered."

She swallowed, her face heating at the thought of him opening the duke's book. As hard as it was, she feigned nonchalance and started toward him. "I'm not sure it would be of interest to you. In fact, you may have already read it." She stopped before him and held out the book.

Her father took it, holding it close to read the title. *"Educating the Feminine Species?"* He looked at her. "Does the author not know that 'female' is not a species?"

She shrugged. "That's what I thought. I plan to read it later this week if I have time." She held her hand out for the book, hoping her father would hand it back. "Until I know whether it will add to what I know or not, I thought I'd put it into my cabinet." She grimaced. "If it's terrible, I'd rather no one else be exposed to it."

Her father chuckled and hefted the large tome. "I hope it's not that poor. That would be a waste of good ink and paper."

She waved the hand she held out then dropped it, her heart in her throat. "It could always be used as a base for a plant or a bust."

"That's my Joanna, always thinking."

He handed the book back to her, and she let out an audible sigh as she grasped it once again, her heart finally slowing to a more normal pace. "I will read it cover to cover and give you any new details worth sharing." Holding the book against her chest, she turned the conversation. "How was your Deliberation Club meeting last eve?"

Her father picked up *The Times* from the table next to his chair and held it up. "The paper was far more interesting. I'm afraid Lord Hennings couldn't stop talking about a new bill being discussed in parliament and Lord Randolf became fixated on the color spectrum." He shook his head. "I fear I may need to invite more gentlemen to join us if I am to have any stimulating conversation whatsoever."

She nodded. "I understand what it's like to be about those who fixate on a single topic. It can be utterly boring and I—" She stopped. She had just promised herself not to discuss female equality among those who had heard her talk of it before. Had she bored them, as well as made them nervous she'd pass judgment?

"And you what?"

Bravely, she met her father's gaze. "And I am determined not to be one of those. I am turning over a new leaf."

His lips quirked. "Another one? My dear, I think you've turned over a whole tree by now."

Though she flushed because he was right, she wouldn't back down. "One can always improve oneself."

"Ah, yes, I do agree with you there. But why do you think you bore people by fixating on one topic?"

She rolled her eyes. "Have you not noticed that I often discuss the need for women to be treated more as equals?"

"Of course. It is something you are passionate about. I'm pleased that you have a strong interest in such a noble subject."

She silently sighed. Her father's lack of social awareness could be a failing at times. "Yes, but I should not speak to everyone about it every time I'm in their company. I would be much like Lord Hennings was last night, boring."

Her father raised his brows in understanding. "Yes, I see how that could become tiresome. Though I cannot imagine anyone finding you boring."

She smiled. "Thank you. I'd best get this book put away and find Mariel. She's expecting my help today." She turned and strode toward her cabinet. Pulling a key from her pocket, she unlocked it and set the book on a half-empty shelf. The cabinet had been a gift from her father after the burned book incident with Amelia. It still held many keepsakes, including a miniature that Belinda had made her of the two of them. Touching the small amateur painting briefly, she quickly closed the cabinet and dropped the key back into her pocket.

When she turned back, her father had resumed his seat, his newspaper held close to his face. She headed for the door then stopped. She'd almost forgotten. "Father?"

She waited a few moments. It always took him time to make note of where he left off.

The paper lowered. "Yes."

"Would you be interested in escorting Amelia and I to the Royal Institution on Friday evening to see Lord Davy speak on his new design for a safe coal mining lamp?"

"Coal mining lamp? Are those not the ones that explode on occasion?" He shook his head. "Such a violent way to die down there in the darkness."

"Yes. Lord Davy has a new design that is expected to keep that from happening."

Her father grinned. "Couldn't get Teddy to go, could you?"

She grimaced. "The only way he would have gone was if Lady Elsbeth was attending, which she isn't. In fact, he will be dancing attendance on her and her cousin who are attending the Worthington ladies' recital that evening."

"Then I would be happy to escort you. I'm very pleased that

Amelia has taken an interest in such mechanical progress."

Not wanting to disappoint him, she kept Amelia's reason for attending to herself. "I can't imagine having a more dashing escort than you."

"Flattery will get you anything from me, so be off before you turn my head."

She chuckled, before striding toward the door. By the time she'd closed it, he was already back to his paper.

She looked forward to attending the lecture. It may not be in an area that she was well-read in, but that made it more beneficial. With Amelia and her father along with her, she couldn't think of a more enjoyable evening. She could even be confident that the Duke of Northwick wouldn't be there since he was otherwise engaged.

CHAPTER SIX

JAMES GAVE HIS cane and hat to the man at the door and escorted Caroline and her father into the Royal Institution. It had been a fairly easy task to beg off from the recital and offer instead the theater the following night. Elsbeth had been excited, though his aunt was in a bit of a dither about clothing and whatnot. By switching outings, he could both accomplish what he wanted and disappoint one of Elsbeth's suitors. Pleased with his success on that front, he'd invited Lady Caroline and her father to accompany him to the lecture. When they entered the large, tiered room, he discovered everyone had already taken their seats, so he stopped before the empty back row on the main tier. "It appears they are about to start."

Lord Holburn nodded and preceded his daughter, leaving her to sit between them. Pleased with the arrangement, James slipped into his seat, giving Lady Caroline an encouraging smile. "If there is anything you have questions about, I will try to answer them after the lecture, but I admit this is not my area of expertise." He kept his voice low to avoid drawing attention.

Astutely, she took her cue from him and leaned toward him, the scent of roses filling his nostrils from either her perfume or her hair, he knew not which. "I'm sure I may need you to interpret the entire discourse as I had never thought about how coal was made until you mentioned this outing."

He nodded. "I understand."

She straightened, her posture exceptional, her alabaster skin unblemished. Her pale blonde curls framed her head, and a small loose bun contained miniature white roses. She would make an excellent duchess.

Turning back to the room, he scanned the audience for his quarry and true reason for attending the night's lecture.

Being tall did have its advantages as he could see everyone in the audience, of which there must be over a hundred. He hadn't thought a new design for coal lamps would be of such keen interest. He took a methodical approach, studying people in each row, looking for two women, one with thick dark brown tresses and one with chestnut seated next to an older gentleman. It was more difficult than he anticipated since there were far more women than he'd expected to see at a lecture. Did they really find the safety of coal miners or the mechanical working of their lamps so interesting?

He finished his perusal of the room, but had only two possible prospects. Neither of which seemed exactly right. Lady Joanna usually wore her hair in a braided knot with a single long curl that came over her shoulder and Lady Mariel wore hers pulled back in a knot at the base of her neck, with wispy curls of hair about her face. If he remembered correctly, neither lady sported extravagant accessories. He only found one lady who appeared to have the braided knot, but the woman next to her had golden hair loosely knotted and many curls on the sides, much like Lady Caroline's.

Had the Mabrys eschewed the lecture for a livelier entertainment? If he had attended alone, he would have considered leaving since the lecture was of little interest to him. He was primarily in attendance to discover if Lady Joanna was his thief. An older gentleman stepped onto the dais, upon which was a table with various items that would no doubt be explained in the lecture. The older man welcomed them all, explained there would be refreshments in the other room afterward so that people could talk further with Lord Davy, then he went into the man's credentials. Despite his lack of interest, James admitted Lord Davy seemed to have a significant background to speak on it.

Finally, Lord Davy stepped upon the dais. The younger man, or at least younger than James expected, smiled as he explained how excited he was by his new design, then proceeded to detail the origin of his thought process. James could not fault him for his logic and by the time Lord Davy demonstrated the lamp, he found himself clapping with the rest of the audience. There was something so simple in the principle yet genius in its application.

As the audience filed into the other room, he remembered his purpose. Standing to the side, he allowed his companions to precede him. "I will join you in a moment. I wish to ask Lord Davy a question."

Lady Caroline nodded and continued forward while Lord Holburn leaned in to whisper. "A tad dry to me, but to good purpose, I suppose." The older man took his daughter on his arm and followed the people slowly leaving the room into the next one.

James studied each group of people. A small number milled around Lord Davy, and that was there he found her. She was with the blonde woman and an older gentleman. Joining the group of no more than six, he waited patiently as Lord Davy finished answering a question, and two young men moved off. As the lord gave his attention to the last young man, James spoke quietly, so as not to alert Lady Joanna to his presence. "My Lord, may I inquire? Are you Lord Wakefield?"

The older gentleman turned around, a smile of welcome on his face. "I am. And who do I have the pleasure of addressing?"

"I am James Huntington, the Duke of Northwick."

The older man's eyes widened. "Your Grace, it is an honor. I did not know you were in London."

He raised his eyebrows at that. "I apologize. I thought you would be aware as your two daughters and nephew attended a dinner I hosted earlier this week."

The man looked over his shoulder before turning back, his bushy eyebrows knit in confusion. "This I was not aware of. Which of my daughters attended?"

It was his turn to be surprised. "Lady Joanna and Lady Beaumont. Do you have more?"

The man's smile returned. "I had four. If you have met Joanna, I must introduce you to Amelia." Lord Wakefield turned, waiting for Lord Davy to finish his answer to the blonde woman, who must be another Mabry.

It was then that Joanna noticed him. Her eyes widened in surprise before narrowing in calculation. Not one to play ignorant, she approached. "Your Grace." She gave the barest of curtsies. "I was under the impression you were otherwise occupied this evening."

He gave her his most haughty tone. "My plans changed."

"Obviously. My question is why?" Her hazel gaze, which looked more blue next to the aqua-colored dress she wore, didn't waver.

"I believe that is rather obvious. I determined that a lecture on miner's lamps would be more interesting than a recital."

She clearly didn't believe him. "And what of Lady Elsbeth? I'm sure she was hoping to attend the recital." She scanned the now empty room. "Unless you brought her with you?"

The question sounded hopeful. Why would she think Elsbeth would be interested in coal lamps? Then again, why was she? "No, she did not deign to accompany me. She preferred to attend the theater tomorrow night."

Before she could reply, her father brought a lovely blonde who was clearly related to Lady Joanna, but in every instance where Joanna was dark, the woman was light. "Here she is, Your Grace. This is my youngest, Lady Amelia."

She curtsied. "It is an honor to meet you, Your Grace."

He nodded. "And I you. I was not aware that Lady Joanna and Lady Beaumont had another sister."

Lady Amelia gave a soft chuckle. "I'm afraid that's my fault.

I'm so rarely out and about that I think they may forget about me."

Lady Joanna grasped Lady Amelia's arm. "We never forget her." She looked fondly on her younger sister. "She is our pride and joy. The most talented of all of us."

The warmth with which Lady Joanna delivered that caught him by surprise. There was true affection in her gaze. Something in that look triggered a long-forgotten memory of his older sister holding his hand and gazing at him in the same way.

Confusion filled him, and he stiffened.

"Oh, one moment, Lord Davy." Lady Amelia disengaged her arm from her sister's and winked at her. "Excuse me, Your Grace." She joined her father in following the speaker from the lecture hall.

"Is something wrong?" Lady Joanna stared at him.

He mentally shook himself. He hated memories from his childhood. "Not at all. Shall we follow?" He opened his arm to indicate she accompany him.

For a moment, she continued to study him, but finally she started forward.

She was far too observant. He idly wondered if others thought that of him. "Did you enjoy the lecture?"

She slowed her pace to allow him to walk beside her. "I did. I think his motivation is admirable and his science is credible. I just wonder…"

"What do you wonder?"

She stopped and faced him. "I wonder what affect the moisture in the mines might have upon his iron mesh." She shrugged. "I'm sure he will test it in all types of environments before sending it down beneath the earth."

As she started forward, his mind jumped on her comment. She was right. Moisture would slowly corrode the iron, which could eventually lead to the deterioration of the mesh. Not a little impressed by her thought process, he hastened to walk with her. A woman with that much knowledge must enjoy reading, which made her more suspect in the theft of his book. Maybe if he enticed her back to the location of the crime, she would give herself away. He was about to invite her to his library when they stepped into the room with refreshments.

Lady Caroline approached. "There you are. Father and I had thought you may have left."

Having forgotten he'd invited Lady Caroline to the event, he nodded to Lady Joanna, and quickly gave Lady Caroline his full attention. "I was just discussing the lamp's construction. Did you have any questions about the lecture?"

She looked up at him from beneath her lashes. "Yes. I'm curious as to why you found this topic so interesting. What I mean to say is, I thought your interests were more in the area of philosophy."

Pleased that she had remembered his conversation in the parlor the other evening, he smiled. "You are correct. However, I have never attended a lecture in London and thought to broaden my knowledge. I will admit that philosophy is still my favorite subject."

Lady Caroline returned his smile. "Then I must know which philosopher you prefer to read."

As he engaged Lady Caroline in conversation, quickly steering them away from philosophy and into subjects she was more familiar with, he kept his eye on Lady Joanna. While her sister flitted about the room, she remained with her father. That might be the way to find out if she took his book. If she felt obligated to being truthful around her father then—

"Your Grace, I think Caroline and I will be taking our leave now and allow you to pursue your conversations with the lecturer." Lord Holburn nodded toward Lord Davy who stood behind Lady Joanna.

Caught not attending to those he'd invited, he immediately switched his focus. "I'm sure Lord Davy will be here until the last person leaves. He does seem to enjoy conversing about his work."

Caroline laid her gloved hand on his arm. "That may be, but we would not want to keep you from your interests. Please, enjoy this experience."

She was not only kind but gracious as well. As if checking off a list in his mind of what characteristics would make the perfect duchess, he found Caroline to be excelling. "Thank you. May I call upon you tomorrow?"

She gave him a shining smile. "I would enjoy that very much."

"Good." Her father took her arm. "We shall see you tomorrow then." With a quick nod, Lord Holburn led his daughter from the room.

As soon as the two were out of sight, he turned to observe Lady Joanna and her father. They were talking to another gentleman, or rather Lady Joanna was speaking in a rather animated way. Strolling over to her father's side, he addressed the older gentleman. "I see that your daughter takes a keen interest in mechanical workings. I think with the progress we're making, she will have many new inventions to keep her occupied."

Lord Wakefield turned to face him. "Your Grace, I did not realize you were there. Actually, Joanna is fascinated by anything new whether it be mechanical, medical, philosophical, or literary." He puffed with pride. "She's very much like myself."

That the man was proud his daughter followed his own intellectual pursuits showed him to be lacking in understanding what a determent it was to her chances of marriage. But since that had no bearing on his purpose, he encouraged the man. "Where do you find these new avenues of learning? Is it only here?"

Lord Wakefield waved his hand. "Oh, no. We find it everywhere. From the latest book to the newest play to a conversation with an expert in a particular field. While just last week, I was conversing with a few of my friends on the possible reason for so much rain and cooler temperatures this summer."

"I have seen a few articles on this in the papers. What is their theory?"

"Sunspots." Lord Wakefield voiced the single word with a quick jerk of his head and the utmost authority. "Trust me, it's sunspots."

He had read about that, finding it amazing that learned men now had instruments that could see spots on the sun, but it was not the only theory. "Is it? I had read that it was due to the eclipse we had."

The older man shook his head adamantly. "It's sunspots. We've had many solar eclipses, but none have affected our weather."

Enjoying himself, he offered another theory. "I have a geological treatise that states quite clearly that the polar ice caps are growing, causing our weather to cool."

Lord Wakefield's gray eyebrows rose. "Ice caps? Now that I haven't heard. A treatise you say on the topic? I would be most interested in that."

He smiled. It was the perfect opportunity for his plan. "Would you and your daughter enjoy a visit to my personal library at Haven House? It's quite extensive. You could read the treatise there, and maybe Lady Joanna might find something of interest."

"Do you have any books on medical treatments or nature's effect on the body?"

Medical treatments? Why would she be interested in those? "I do. In fact, I have a number of volumes on those and related subjects."

Lord Wakefield touched his daughter's arm to gain her attention. "Joanna, the duke has invited us to see his library."

He watched her closely as she excused herself from her conversation and turned to her father. "Who has invited us?"

Her father stepped back as he gestured. "The Duke of Northwick."

Her gaze met his, and she cocked her head. "Really? That is quite magnanimous of you, Your Grace. Whatever prompted such a kind invitation?"

Instead of appearing guilty, she seemed to take umbrage at the fact he'd made the invitation. Again, he was struck by a feeling that she didn't want to be in his presence. "Your father wishes to see a treatise I own, and he told me you are interested in medical science. Since I have numerous books on that specialty, I would welcome your perusal of them. Mayhap you know of a book I'm unaware of."

She opened her mouth to reply, then closed it, instead turning to her father. "I think that's a wonderful idea. I'll discuss a time with the duke if you'd like to take this opportunity of Lord Davy being alone to ask him any further questions you had."

Lord Wakefield's gray eyes lit with excitement, making them appear silver. "Yes, yes. You decide upon the details." Then without excusing himself, he strode toward the lecturer who had finally made it to the refreshment table.

James returned his attention to Lady Joanna. "Would Tuesday be convenient?"

Her head snapped to him and this time there was no denying her anger. "Do you always invite women to explore your library?"

Surprised by both her tone and look, it took him a moment to respond. "I'm not sure what you're implying. You will, of course, be chaperoned by your father." Did she think he'd make advances upon her person? The notion was absurd.

She waved off his answer. "That is not my concern. At your dinner, you implied that women need know very little beyond the social graces. You also made it clear that women's minds were only able to comprehend certain knowledge and certainly not what men comprehend. So I ask you, why invite me, specifically, into your private hall of learning?"

Clarity washed over him, and he grinned. "You thought because of my statement that I would not allow a woman in my library?"

Her brows rose. "Am I not correct?"

He chuckled. "No, you are not. In fact, you only had to ask

my cousin or aunt, who often make use of the books I've collected over the years. My remarks were simply based upon observation."

For the first time since meeting Lady Joanna, she appeared unsure. She almost didn't look like herself as her gaze shifted away. "Then am I to assume that Lady Elsbeth and Lady Astor only read about embroidery, dancing, and painting?"

Her voice had lost its volume and assuredness. It made him uncomfortable. He much preferred it when she was on the attack, which was rather odd and something to ruminate on later. "For the most part, that is their interests in addition to music, poetry, and some select novels."

Straightening her shoulders, she met his gaze. "Then I owe you an apology, Your Grace. I was under the misconception that you opposed women being educated on subjects beyond those you mentioned. I erroneously assumed that you also did not feel women should have access to such knowledge. I am sorry."

Now *he* was in a quandary because what she stated also wasn't true. How could he accept an apology if it wasn't warranted? "I must clarify that I am happy to share any knowledge that may be found in my library. However, I do not believe women should be educated on the same subjects as men."

Immediately, the fire was back in her eyes. "Why?"

An odd relief swept through him as she resumed her former bearing. He smirked, "Then what would men do? If women learn what men learn then there is no division of labor."

"Of course, there can be a division of labor. It can simply be divided differently."

"What? Are men then to learn embroidery? I'll have you know I have no interest in learning that particular task."

She grimaced. "And you think I did? I'd rather do anything instead of that."

The idea that a woman wouldn't find decorating clothes enjoyable surprised him. "What would you do with your time instead of embroidering. I mean something else that may be just slightly more pleasing?"

Her gaze darted to the side and her tongue came out to moisten her lips, her concentration complete. Finally, she gave a quick nod. "I'd rather choose the food for a dinner party of fifty. What task do you dislike the most?"

Her question was fair. If he thought back to his studies, there had been subjects he wished he didn't have to know, one in particular. He gave a brief nod. "Numbers. I despised learning them, and to this day, I must schedule my solicitor to force myself to review my ledgers."

"You don't like mathematics?" She sounded as astounded as he had that she didn't care for embroidery.

He lowered his voice. "I absolutely despise them and would do anything else instead."

Her lips quirked up and the colors in her eyes seemed to dance. "And what would you rather do?"

How could he truly communicate how he felt about numbers? What would be the worst possible task—he grinned. "I would rather muck out my entire stable."

"Oh." She squinched up her nose. "That is truly worth avoiding. But as it happens, I thoroughly enjoy numbers and find it a pleasure to work on an estate's books. So you see, if both genders were taught the same subjects, we could all enjoy our daily tasks. Imagine how much happier we all would be."

Her debating skills were quite extraordinary, but so were his. "Then would you have us men embroider the sheets? No, I'm afraid just as we must all have some tasks which we prefer not to do, it is best we leave things as they are."

Her smile disappeared. "Why?"

"Why, because what women and men learn is based on centuries of figuring out what best works for our society. Surely, you cannot believe that it is this way by happenstance."

The long dark curl that lay upon her collar bone twitched. He followed its length to where is started just over her ear. It twitched again before she spoke. "I'm fairly certain that our division of labor and learning between the genders is the way it is because those who have taken control, men like you, simply wish it to be so and do not care for progress."

He opened his mouth to object to such a blanket statement, but she held up her hand.

"No, no need to defend your ancestors. I understand. It is much easier to be complacent and keep long held traditions than risk expending your energy on change for the betterment of all. Some people simply can't see beyond what they already know."

Affronted by her assumptions, he stood silent. Where to begin to educate her on her numerous argumentative fallacies?

"Now if you'll excuse me. I'd best be saving poor Lord Davy from my father. I'm sure even Amelia is growing bored. Good night, Your Grace." She gave the shallowest of curtsies and strode across the room, her hips swaying forcefully as she made haste to desert him.

Insulted and not a little angry, he thought to rescind his invitation. Taking a calming breath, he reconsidered. If he was to discover if she was his thief in truth, he needed to allow it to stand. However, a strategic plan was in order for when she did visit with her father. One that would make it very clear that she was guilty or innocent.

And then what?

CHAPTER SEVEN

JOANNA ONLY HALF-LISTENED as Lady Dulac related her daughter's success so far this season to her mother. Where did her mother find her patience?

The soothing colors of the room with its walls of ivory and tiny roses on pale green vines, did little to slow down her racing thoughts. At least here in their own parlor, she needn't worry about the Duke of Northwick arriving. Yes, her behavior towards him four nights ago had bordered on rudeness, but she hoped that might mean no forthcoming invitation to his home. What bothered her even more was that she wanted to rail at him for not being able to see the legitimacy of her arguments. Why was it so important to her that he admit she was right?

It had to have been that glimmer of hope she had as he engaged in real debate. He acknowledged her points were valid while making one himself. For just a moment, he seemed to transcend his boorish personality as his blue gaze brightened and he'd given her a rakish smile. But then he'd had to return to the weakest of all arguments – that society was as it was because it always had been. So disappointed in his final reasoning, she hadn't even bothered to take his book from her cabinet to explore it any further. She would have to categorize him with all the others who—

"Joanna, did you hear that?"

She blinked as she looked at her mother who sat in a chair with fabric that matched the wall. "I'm sorry. Did I miss something?"

Her mother smiled knowingly. "Lady Dulac said that a new panorama scene is opening next week. This one is of Paris. We really must go."

Oh dear, and they would probably include Amelia, who would not only point out any flaws in the Parisian view, but also would be sure to explain where the team of artists had missed a stroke. She pasted on a smile. "Of course."

Her mother sighed. "I was so young when I visited Paris. I know it will bring back wonderful memories. I was quite popular back then among a number of charming gentlemen." She lifted her fan and eyed them over it coquettishly.

Thinking of her mother as a young woman who enjoyed flirting was difficult. It did beg the question why she'd married father, but the tale was that he'd solved a serious dilemma, and she'd fallen in love with him. Her mother was still quite handsome. Her chestnut hair showing very few strands of white, and the wrinkles at the corners of her eyes and lips attesting to the many smiles she'd given. In her blue morning dress that matched her eyes, she looked the perfect hostess.

Her mother addressed Lady Dulac, who sat in a pale pink chair opposite in a sage green dress that matched the vines on the walls. "Will you and your daughter be visiting?"

As the lady answered, Joanna tried to listen, but her thoughts wandered back to her debate with the duke. These types of conversations, like the ones her mother and Lady Dulac were having, had to be why men thought women limited in their capacity to think. Yet, when she'd brought up more socially motivated topics among gentlemen, they were quickly dismissed. The duke had been one of the few who had actually listened to her. That might mean that he could be swayed. Maybe she just needed to be persistent. But how could she do that if she avoided him because she stole his book? While convincing a duke of women's ability to become equals in life would be an accomplishment to boast of, it was not worth the risk.

The parlor doors opened, and Teddy strode in dressed in tan pantaloons, a white waistcoat and blue wool coat. "Oh, I apologize. I would have had Channing introduce me if I'd known the lovely Lady Dulac was present."

Lady Dulac rose. "I was just about to depart. I have an appointment with the seamstress." She turned back to mother. "This cooler weather has necessitated new cloaks."

Teddy bowed. "A missed pleasure on my part."

The older lady puffed. "Lord Mabry, save your charm for younger women. I am impervious to it." Did she not realize the color that rose in her cheeks denied her claim?

Teddy walked the lady out before returning and slumping onto the settee next to Joanna. He stretched his long legs out in front of him and crossed them at the ankles, throwing one arm over the side support.

"Theodore, do sit straight, or pretend to at the least." Her mother's admonition had little effect upon her cousin.

Joanna nudged him with her elbow. "Really Teddy, why so dispirited?" He usually saved such dramatic displays for her and her sisters only.

He gave a heavy sigh. "In the last four evenings, I have been to a recital, a ball, a play, and a dinner, and not once was I fortunate enough to encounter Lady Elsbeth. It's as if she's hiding from me." He sighed again and let his head drop back so he could stare at the ceiling.

Her mother, who rarely saw Teddy's theatrics, tsked. "If this is how you conduct yourself around the lady, I wouldn't be surprised if she's avoiding you."

His head snapped up. "Have you spoken to her? Have I done something wrong?"

"No, I have not, at least not since we met her and her mother at the seamstress two weeks ago."

"Two weeks? I couldn't bear to not see her for two weeks. I

pray it doesn't amount to that." His head fell back again.

Joanna rolled her eyes. "She hasn't even come out yet. What about the other ladies you've met this season?"

"Other ladies?" He spoke to the ceiling. "There are no other ladies for me. She is the one I will wed."

The dramatics had taken a melodramatic turn. "What if she determines someone else would make a better husband...someone less emotional."

Teddy sat up and glared at her. "Don't ever say that. I thought you wanted me to be happy."

"We do, Teddy." Mother spoke in a soothing tone. "But this." She gestured toward him with her hand. "This is far too much passion. It is not healthy."

He slumped forward. "I know. I just feel so much."

Her mother shook her head. "Do you not remember Mariel when she lost Lord Stratton?"

"Yes." Teddy's voice was soft. "You are right, as usual, Aunt."

Hoping to distract him, Joanna started a new subject. "Which play did you see and do tell me if I should behoove myself to also see it?"

To his credit, he sat straighter. "I was with other gents, so I can't say that I watched much, but it did have a rather large battle scene. Then again, it may have been a dance, I'm not quite certain."

She chuckled. "That was terribly helpful."

He gave her a lopsided grin. "I wasn't there to enjoy the play."

"No, obviously not." She was about to say more but Channing opened the doors.

"Lady Astor and Lady Elsbeth, my lady."

Joanna heard the sharp intake of breath as Teddy jumped to his feet. She rose as well to allow the ladies to have the settee. "Lady Astor, Lady Elsbeth how lovely to have you call. Please." She indicated the settee.

"Lady Joanna, I so hoped you would be home." Lady Astor

took her hands before releasing them and turning to her mother. "Lady Wakefield, I hope you do not mind this unexpected visit."

"Of course not. It is a pleasure to see you again." Her mother held out her hand. "Please sit. Channing, have tea brought."

As they all sat, Joanna took the chair next to her mother, forcing Teddy to stand, or pull over another one. He did just that, setting it next to where Lady Elsbeth sat on the settee, her white morning dress complementing her pale features.

Joanna didn't miss the blush in Elsbeth's cheeks as Teddy settled in. She hoped that meant his feelings were reciprocated on some level.

Lady Astor smiled. "Elsbeth and I had such a lovely evening when Lord Mabry, Lady Joanna, and Lady Mariel joined our small dinner party that we decided we wished to further our acquaintance."

Her mother gave a gracious nod. "I'm so pleased that my children and nephew made such a favorable impression."

"Indeed, they did." Lady Astor patted Elsbeth's arm. "My daughter was quite insistent that we make a call."

Elsbeth placed her hand on her mother's as she looked at her. "To be fair, it was not just me."

Lady Astor nodded. "Yes, that's true. When my nephew, the Duke of Northwick, heard that we thought to visit, he practically insisted."

Joanna's breath caught. Had he figured out that she had the book?

Her mother placed her hand on her chest. "The duke?"

"Yes," Lady Astor continued. "He wanted us to extend an invitation to Lady Joanna and Lord Wakefield to visit tomorrow afternoon." Her gaze moved to Joanna. "I'm to understand he spoke of this with you at a lecture?"

She let out her breath as relief flowed through her, but her tension did not leave. "Yes, he did. Father was quite excited to read a treatise on the polar caps extending."

Elsbeth gave a tiny chuckle. "Oh, that does sound like something James would have. Were you also interested in polar ice caps, Lady Joanna?"

"While I have read a bit about them, I have no interest in this particular theory."

Lady Astor's gaze turned thoughtful. "I wonder why he asked for you then."

Oh, she recognized that look, that *could she make a good wife for my son, nephew, grandson* thought process. She waved her hand. "It's no mystery. Your nephew and I were having a debate on the education of women. He thinks he has a book or two that will sway my opinion."

"A book or two?" Lady Elsbeth chuckled, hiding her mouth with her hand. "I'm sure my cousin has an entire bookcase on it."

It was Joanna's turn to be surprised. "A whole bookcase? Is it of great interest to him?" This could indicate the duke might actually be open to further debate on the subject.

The young woman sighed. "Only as it pertained to my schooling."

"Yes, I'm afraid my nephew took an inordinate interest in Elsbeth's cannon of knowledge." A sorrowful look crossed over the lady's features. "His mother's education was not typical of most young ladies of the *ton,* and he wished to see my daughter did not suffer from the same unusual background."

The vagueness with which Lady Astor spoke had Joanna's mind spinning with possibilities. "Do you know what kind of schooling she had?"

The woman stiffened. "I only know it was American. It matters little now. She has passed on and my daughter has had only the best instructors." She smiled at Lady Elsbeth. "I do think she will make a wonderful wife."

Joanna opened her mouth to give her opinion on that, but Teddy found his tongue. "I know she will."

The young woman blushed prettily, the color in her cheeks giving a faint rosy tint to her pale skin.

"When is Lady Elsbeth to come out? Will it be soon?" Her

mother didn't even look at Teddy, which meant he'd be hearing a few words from her later.

Lady Astor sat a little straighter. "Actually, that was the primary purpose of our visit. We would like to invite you to Elsbeth's coming out ball at the end of the month. We left an invitation with your butler."

Teddy rose and bowed. "Of course, we will attend."

"Lord Mabry, sit down." Her mother's stern tone brooked no disobedience and Teddy resumed his seat.

Quickly, Joanna drew the lady's attention. "It is so kind of you to come in person to invite us. We are honored."

Her mother chimed in. "Yes, I know that we would very much like to attend." She turned to Elsbeth. "Are you excited?"

The young woman thought for a moment. "I am. There is much to remember, but I think I'm ready now. Mother would not allow it, if I wasn't."

As the ladies began to discuss the preparations for the ball, Joanna cringed. First, a visit tomorrow and then a ball, all at Haven House. How was she to avoid the company of the duke if his family kept inviting them? She glanced at Teddy, who hung on every word Elsbeth spoke. And what would the Huntington family do if it came to light that she stole a book from them?

Then again, it may not be the kind of book they would want discussed. New ideas surfaced, the most prominent one being that she needed to read *Educating the Feminine Species* as soon as possible. After all, *ipsa scientia potestas est*, or knowledge itself was power, as Sir Frances Bacon wrote. If she knew what the book was about, she would have the power.

CHAPTER EIGHT

JAMES DRUMMED HIS fingers on his desk. All was ready. His plan to catch his thief was laid out. Now, all he needed was the thief herself. Would Lady Joanna walk into his trap or would she beg off? He didn't expect her to let her father arrive alone, but if she were smart, which his gut told him she was, then she wouldn't come. He pulled out his pocket watch and checked the time. His muscles tensed. He hadn't been this excited since he'd readied for his final debate at Oxford. It hadn't been easy, but he'd led his team to victory. Anything easier would have been a disappointment. Would Lady Joanna disappoint him or challenge him?

The doors to his library opened and Harrison stopped just inside. "Lord Wakefield and the Lady Joanna have arrived, Your Grace."

He rose, his blood pounding at the fact his quarry was within his very walls. "Show them in here and have tea brought."

"Yes, Your Grace." Harrison turned and strode out, leaving the doors open.

He quickly moved across the room. He wanted to see her expression when she first entered. That would tell him much.

The swish of skirts announced their arrival.

His pulse raced as he grinned, his anticipation strong.

Harrison stepped aside and his guests strolled toward the open doors arm and arm. Both stopped. Lord Mabry's mouth dropped open and Lady Joanna's eyes rounded.

He moved forward. "Welcome to the Haven House library, Lord Wakefield, Lady Joanna."

Lord Wakefield just stared, but Lady Joanna scanned the room before resting her gaze on him. "Your Grace. This is magnificent."

He didn't miss the sincerity in her voice.

She let go of her father's arm and moved toward him before turning around to view the entire room. Her violet skirts swayed as she turned. She grasped her hands to her chest, her voice coming out in a breathy sigh. "Truly wonderful."

A stab of desire at the sound had him tensing. That was completely unexpected. He hadn't invited the woman for a dalliance. He'd invited her to catch her, possibly entice her to confess. He studied Lady Joanna, but that made his desire flame hotter. Her eyes were alight with pleasure and that one long lock she always wore had settled beneath her hands and against her chest. It was so inappropriate that he forced himself to move toward her father. "Lord Wakefield, do step in." He took the man's arm and guided him in while nodding to Harrison, who discreetly shut the doors. "I've ordered tea, but if you prefer, I have some brandy."

The older man nodded, and he guided him to a chair in the bay window where he could view the whole room. After pouring the older man a brandy, he handed it to him.

"Go ahead, Father. Take a sip." Lady Joanna's voice came from behind him as she strode closer.

As if used to doing what she told him, Lord Wakefield sipped.

She gently took the glass from his fingers and set it on the table next to him. "Tell His Grace what you think of his library."

"I have no words." The man turned his gaze to look at him. "How?"

For the first time since building his library, he felt humbled. Wakefield appeared about to cry with happiness. This was a man who could appreciate his collection as much as he did. His throat felt tight as he tried to answer the question. "A good architect and many years of acquisitioning." He refrained from letting the man know he had a larger collection at Burhleigh Park.

"I think my father needs to adjust to so much wealth of knowledge." Lady Joanna laid her hand on her father's shoulder.

"Of course. I'm pleased that you can appreciate what I have built here." Though he spoke to Wakefield, his gaze went to his daughter of its own accord. "If you would like, I can give you a tour."

"I would like that very much." She turned to her father. "Would you like to sit here and read that treatise on polar ice caps?"

At her mention of the treatise, James quickly strode back to his desk to fetch it. He'd already forgotten the reason for them coming. It was Wakefield's reaction that had him off balance. Bringing the treatise over, he handed it to the man. "Here you are. It is the second one in. If you'd like to discuss it when you've finished, I'd be happy to oblige."

"Have you read everything in here?" Wakefield's voice still held awe as his gaze darted to the second-floor balcony.

Heat crept up his neck at Wakefield's blunt appreciation. "I have, but I don't remember every word." He pointed to the book he'd shared. "I skimmed that last night to remind myself of its contents."

Wakefield finally looked down at the volume in his hands and opened it.

"I'm excited to see your collection." Lady Joanna moved away from her father. "Do you have it arranged by pressmark, size, title, or field of study?"

Remembering his strategy to coax out a confession, he stepped away from Wakefield and moved to where she stood, awaiting her promised tour. "It's by field of study and then alphabetical by author, though many in my collection bear old pressmarks inside."

"Ours is arranged by author, but I have seen some organized by title. I would think it would be difficult to find a book if one forgot the title, don't you?"

"I don't forget the titles of my books." At her look of surprise, he softened his tone. "I simply find my arrangement makes it faster to find what I want. I prefer not to take an hour gathering three books on the same subject from different areas of the room."

She held her hand out to encompass the library. "Do you mean to tell me you know every title in here?"

Pride filled him. "I do. I read every book I purchase, so remembering the title is not difficult."

She turned away at that, moving to a bookcase. "These appear to be about ancient Greece."

He followed to stand beside her as he held his hand out to the right. "Yes, and these are on ancient Rome."

Her face lit with excitement. "Let me guess." She pointed to the following bookcase. "Are those on Egypt?"

She learned quickly. He barely kept from smiling with pleasure. "Indeed, they are."

She strode past the next six sections then stopped. "Oh my, we are only in Anglo-Saxon times." She skimmed the shelves and those in the next section. "But where are the *Beowulf* verses? Surely you must have a copy of Turner's literature." She looked over her shoulder at him, her lock falling over the bare skin of her back and past the neckline of her dress to rest at the top of her shoulder blade.

Alexander Pope's question in his comic poem *Rape of the Lock* in which a gentleman did indeed desire a woman so much that he cut off her lock, suddenly made sense to him. *Say what strange motive, Goddess! could compel A well-bred lord t' assault a gentle belle?* The answer could not be expressed in words and was perhaps why he always thought the poem not worth the time. But now he understood how a simple lock could bring a man to great wanting.

"Your Grace?"

What were they discussing? Pope? No, *Beowulf.* He must stay focused. He raised his brow. "I do. In fact, I have those verses as well as the more recent translated ones by Professor Conybeare, one of my former teachers at Oxford. Those are in my literature section."

She turned fully around at that, "You have more verses? I would so enjoy reading those. I found the ones by Turner to be rather a tease. I was unaware that more had been accomplished. Are they in English or Latin?"

Her enthusiasm was rare, even among the few scholars he'd met with. It triggered a like response in himself. "Conybeare translated them into Latin and English. I have the Latin, but he's promised to send me the English version, if you'd like to wait."

She shook her head. "I couldn't bear to wait. The Latin version is fine."

Of course, she'd said she read Latin. Stifling the urge to run up to the second floor and pull the pamphlet from the shelves, he forced himself to remember his plan. He pointed across the room. "On that side I have geography, flora and fauna, mechanical science, medical science, chemical science, and some mathematics," he grimaced. "On that wall is astronomy, philosophy, and religion." He purposefully strolled toward his desk, watching her to see if she'd shy away from the obvious space where his book had been.

As they approached, her eyes scanned the shelves. "This is twice the size of the rest of your shelving, but it has an odd assortment of subjects. Are these books waiting to be shelved in their appropriate place? We have a small table at home that often has four or five books that need shelving, but not nearly this many." Her perusal didn't appear to be any more or less interested than the other shelves she'd seen.

Either she was an adept actress, or she hadn't taken the book. He stopped before the open space on the shelf to explain, never taking his gaze off her. "You are partially correct. These on the lower four shelves still need to find a permanent home. The ones on the upper four shelves are ones I use often or enjoy rereading."

She lifted her hand to touch a book in front of her. Her brows raised. "You enjoy rereading *Pamela*?"

His gaze snapped to the intricately designed leather volume. "No. That's Elsbeth." He sighed. "I have told her that is not fit reading for her, but she fancies herself a Pamela."

Lady Joanna smiled. "Don't be disappointed in her. Though I'm surprised Lady Astor allowed her to read such a salacious novel, there are far worse heroines for her to fancy herself. At least Pamela is virtuous. When I was young, I was positively sure I wanted to be like Robinson Crusoe."

"But that's a man." He didn't refrain from revealing his shock.

She laughed, a full-throated sound that had his body reacting to her very womanly pleasure. "That's exactly what my mother said. I assure you, I did not want to be a man, but I did want to create my own living conditions and prove I could survive." Humor danced in her hazel gaze. "Don't worry. I soon realized that no respectable woman would have the capability to survive that long alone without books to read." She laughed again.

A chuckle escaped him, her laughter contagious. "Now that you point out that particular detail, living on a deserted island is off my list of adventures."

She grinned. "I'm glad I could assist in shortening your list. Is it a very long one?"

"No." He shrugged. "I was never really the adventurous sort." He gave her a sly smile. "I always had my head in a book. There were plenty of adventures there." He sobered. "It's less dangerous." And deadly, as his mother discovered.

"I agree wholeheartedly." She turned back to the shelves and touched the empty spot. "I see the treatise on polar caps was to be shelved. I hope it's not an inconvenience that my father is reading it." She looked down the room to where Lord Wakefield sat.

His mood changed as he watched her, but her head was turned. Even her lock of hair wasn't in sight. For some reason, that bothered him. "Tell me, do you like The Butterfly?"

She faced him again. "Butterflies? I adore them. Why?"

The innocent response was not what he'd expected. One of the first illustrations in the stolen book referenced The Butterfly position. It would at the very least engender a blush from any lady. Recovering quickly, he pointed across the room. "I have a number of books on butterflies."

She lowered her voice as if to impart a secret. "Actually, I would love to see what you have upstairs."

He swallowed hard, the blatant anticipation in her eyes had him thinking of a much more intimate reward. "Yes, well, then let us ascend."

"Wonderful. This is quite exciting."

Her genuine happiness at the prospect struck a like feeling in himself. That's not what he'd wanted to accomplish with the visit, but he wouldn't acknowledge he didn't like it. He didn't have friends, only acquaintances. Life was better that way, no disappointment that someone didn't live up to his expectations. Yet he guessed that what he felt with Lady Joanna was what a friendship would feel like. He was lucky that he didn't have to worry about a woman being a friend.

Holding his palm out toward the stairs, he allowed her to precede him. Once at the top she stilled, staring at the shelves across the room.

"Lady Joanna?"

At his question, she turned a shimmering gaze on him. "Is this a dream? This place? If it is, I don't want to wake."

For the second time during the visit, he found his throat closing as love for his library shone in her eyes. "No, it's not a dream. It's real." He had to force the words out, and he coughed to clear his throat. "It has been a lifelong achievement of mine. I started collecting books when I was seven."

Her eyes grew wide. "Seven? And here I thought I was an early bird at the age of nine." She chuckled awkwardly. "Please excuse me, I'm just overwhelmed by your success."

The inclination to lean in and whisper that Burhleigh Park

had more of his collection was so strong, he gritted his teeth and turned down the eastern balcony. "On this floor, I house the literature, art, architecture, music, dance, folklore, pedagogical books, as well as oddities and rarities. The last are kept in a locked, old book press cabinet."

When she didn't answer, he halted and turned around. She still stood staring at the walls of bookcases on the second level. Doubts assailed him. Why would someone who treasured books as much as she did, steal one? What if it hadn't been her? His mind raced, searching for other possibilities. Now that he gave it some thought, the gentlemen had been in the library while he was still outside speaking to Lady Joanna. But if they had taken it, how had they carried it out of the house without him noticing? He'd bade farewell to each individual person.

She moved toward him, a small smile playing along her lips. "I do believe I'm going to dream of this room when I go to sleep tonight. I never imagined anything so wonderous as this."

At her statement, an image of her in a shift crawling into bed filled his mind and he jerked his head to be rid of it. "The Houses..." he cleared his throat, his words coming out gruff. "The Houses of Parliament have an extensive collection."

She reached him. "That may be so, but for a private library, I'm sure this is the most exceptional anywhere in England."

Heat seemed to suffuse him at her passionate praise, and he pulled at his cravat. "I do not know. I'm sure there are many scholars with a much larger collection."

She walked past him, the scent of cinnamon-vanilla filling his nostrils. "Do not be modest. It doesn't become you. This is grand on the grandest of scales." Her fingers trailed over the leather bound and hard paper volumes on the shelves. "You did say you had books on women's education, did you not?"

He smirked. That wasn't exactly what he'd said. "I have many on education in my pedagogical section and a few that focus on women. One is downstairs waiting to be shelved, but the rest are past the reading area on this level." Did she pause when he mentioned the book to be shelved? The devil take it, he wasn't sure.

"Reading area? How did you fit that among all these bookcases?" She dropped her hand as she hastened her step. "Oh, this is perfect." She stood before the small area that had two red armchairs with a small table between them.

He had sacrificed a bookcase to make it possible. He didn't want to miss her reaction when she saw the view, so he moved closer before speaking. "Please, have a seat. Tell me if it's comfortable."

She gave him a sly smile. "Oh, I'm sure it is." Turning to sit, her face changed, her mouth forming a small "o" as she abruptly sat.

He had to admit that seeing his space through the eyes of newcomers who could truly appreciate it humbled him. His love of books had started with stories whose characters kept him company during his lonely childhood. They were his friends, and he felt as if he had visited so many places with them before he grew old enough to appreciate more factual knowledge. Though his aunt had moved in at that time and tried to interest him in other children, he had far surpassed them in maturity and thought their games tiresome. Everyone at Burhleigh Park knew where to find him if they needed him from the lowest maid to his aunt. The only one ignorant of his whereabouts was his father, who wanted it that way.

"Your Grace, this is breathtaking. I didn't know there was still a view such as this in all of London."

Lady Joanna's soft whisper reminded him of the voices he heard in his head when still a boy reading his books. But that time was past. He turned to face the round window on the western wall that revealed rolling hills and fields being encroached upon by buildings to the south. "I fear it won't last. Soon even Haven House will be swallowed up by new construction as more and more move to Town."

She rose and looked at him, her gaze soft and open. "Yes,

that's true. It happened to Craymore Hall, but we have our country estate for views such as this. In Bedford, we have no theater, no panoramas, no confectioners, and few shops. I think there are advantages to both places."

He liked that she didn't try to deny the encroachment of the city onto Haven House. "That may be, but I will never find London to my liking. I'm only here for the season so as to see Elsbeth well settled."

Her features hardened and her gaze took on the intense look he'd seen at the lecture. "When you say settled, you mean marrying well, do you not?"

He gave a short nod. "I do. She has learned all she needs to know to take over as the mistress of her own home. I'll allow her the choice of husbands among those I feel acceptable."

He hadn't thought Lady Joanna's posture lacking, but at his words she seemed to straighten, gaining at least an inch in height. "So Elsbeth has been groomed much like a racehorse to bring in the best purse."

The analogy was too fitting, and he latched onto the differences with force. "I think not. She is a woman of fine..." his thought was to say *breeding*, but that added to her analogy. "Qualities. She deserves the best in a..." he'd been about to say *mate*. "Husband. A man with a good name, who won't squander her dowry or his fortune, and who will give her the children she deserves."

"And *does* she desire children? If she does, at what cost? Does the man's character, looks, or interest in her matter? Or is she to bed an old man desperate to gain an heir? What if the men you find acceptable are not to her liking? Then where does her choice come into play, Your Grace?"

Her chest rose with her breaths, her argument having turned passionate. The subject had become personal for some reason, and he was curious to find out why. "I would not force Elsbeth's hand. If she does not find the men I deem acceptable to her liking, I will be forced to return next season. There is no need to worry on her behalf. I would not allow her to be used in any fashion, especially not by an old lord simply for an heir. She is, after all, one of the few family members I have left."

"I'm pleased that Elsbeth has a somewhat reasonable cousin as the head of the family."

His statements seemed to calm her, which left him disappointed. He wanted to know more. Had her sister been forced to marry Lord Beaumont? He did not know the man, but it could be the situation. Yet, he didn't see Wakefield as a man that would force his daughters to do anything. Or maybe that was just with Lady Joanna. "And what of you?"

She took a deep breath as if finding her balance once again. "I? I wish to see what you have in your education bookcase." She quickly turned and strode to the spot he'd indicated earlier.

He'd wanted to hear what she wanted in her husband. From what he understood, this was her fourth and final season. Surely there had been men interested in such a vivacious and obviously passionate woman. He imagined her passion would be just as strong were she to find the bedroom of interest.

Despite, or perhaps due to his body's reaction to that idea, it reminded him of his stolen book. Was that why she took it? Did she wish to learn and experience physical passion as well? It was a titillating thought. And discussing this particular subject was the last piece of his trap. So far, he'd not been completely successful in confirming she was his thief. Now was his final attempt.

CHAPTER NINE

JOANNA MOVED TOWARD the designated section of books. Just when she thought her initial dislike of the duke was confirmed, he changed her mind again. Guilt was now riding her hard. The night at his dinner party, she had been so sure he would have forced his cousin to marry who he wanted, but she was wrong. Now, she was conflicted. Had he invited her and her father to his library to see if she'd taken his book or to share his pride and joy with people he thought could appreciate it?

Oh, and she did appreciate it. She hadn't lied. It was magnificent. It was more than that, but she had no actual word for what it was. She needed to create one like she used to do when she was young and didn't yet know the word for what she wanted to say.

On the other hand, he did mention that he knew every title in his library which meant he was well aware the book was missing. Yet he hadn't mentioned the theft. Even when he'd stopped at the exact spot where she'd taken the book. Was that coincidence? Why would that spot have remained empty unless he wanted her to see it? And why wouldn't he tell her the book was stolen? She'd been ready to show surprise at the information, but he didn't say anything. Did he suspect her or not think she needed to know? All she could do was continue as they were, watching for any indication he thought her his thief.

She stopped in front of the bookcase he'd directed her to.

There were many books she had read, but not all. She scanned the shelf for her favorite. The book had spoken to her very soul. She turned her head to find he'd joined her. "It appears you are missing a seminal text on the subject of women's education. I do not see *A Vindication of the Rights of Woman* by Mary Wollstonecraft."

He pointed to the next section. "It's there. As I said, I have more than one bookcase on *education*. It's on the fourth shelf from the bottom, ninth book from the left."

She faced that case to hide her sudden swallow. A man who knew every title and where every book resided in such a vast library, knew he had a book missing. The Wollstonecraft book was the first printing, the same one she kept locked in her cabinet. Carefully pulling the book from the shelf, she opened it. Just having it in her hands had her feeling more confident. She faced him again, glad he hadn't moved because when he stood too close, he made her feel small. "And what did you think of it? You did read it, correct?"

He nodded. "I did. It has some interesting points but doesn't pertain very much to women of our class."

"Just because it doesn't directly discuss the higher social classes, the arguments are no less pertinent and can be applied forthwith."

He folded his arms as he leaned his hip against the balcony railing. "If it could be so easily applied, then why did she not apply it? The answer is obvious. It doesn't apply."

She felt her heart skip a beat. "That's a logical fallacy. She didn't apply it because the audience she wrote for was the gentry and poor, respectively. She knew better than to waste much time on the aristocracy."

His brows raised. "So then she did not think her book would do well among the aristocracy. Is that not a testament to the fact she didn't believe her ideas about equal education would be successful?"

There was nothing she enjoyed more than discussing her

favorite book, and it had been so long since she'd been able to do so. She held the book to her chest with one hand as she put up her other index finger. "No, in actuality it does not. Since she grew up as part of the gentry, only with little to no financial support, her strongest argument would be among her own class. That was where it was most critical. However, that does not mean it cannot be applied to the aristocracy."

She waited, almost breathless, anxious to hear his agreement or next argument. He remained still, obviously thinking about what she said. Having grown used to people dismissing her or actually yawning in her face, she felt quite heady as she waited for him to speak. She studied him and had to admit he was a handsome man in a classical fashion. She hadn't noticed before, most likely because she had judged him upon very little evidence, committing a logical fallacy herself.

He gave one of his truncated nods. "I acquiesce to your point that it may be applied. However, if it was applied, I'm certain it would fail."

Her mind spun with possible rejoinders. Landing on one, she shrugged. "Of course it would."

His eyes widened. "If you think it would, then why debate the possibility or for that matter, why read and obviously endorse the ideas?"

She waved her hand. "Just because education for women of my class would not be accepted today, that doesn't mean it isn't something we should be striving for in the near future." She hugged the book with both arms. "This is the future. Most life changing, no, society changing, ideas are rejected at first. For example, we have Galilei Galileo. He tried to tell his society the world rotated around the sun, but they wouldn't listen. To me, the fact that Wollstonecraft did not address the aristocracy proves she was intelligent enough to understand the historical pillars that would need to fall. She determined that was a battle for another generation and focused on an area where her ideas could do the most good."

He pushed away from the railing. "By that logic, we would all believe that fire is made of Phlogiston because scientists decried Becher for it."

She shook her head. "Galileo was only an example, but the point that the aristocracy was not ready for these ideas when this was published," she held out the book, "is still valid." She turned to reshelve it, not wanting to damage it in her exhilaration over the debate. "But that was almost twenty years ago, and it is time for change." She turned back to find him studying her.

"Does she not posit that women are too emotional? Like you are at the moment?"

"Enjoying a good debate is not being emotional. But to your point, she does explain that women are encouraged by men to be emotional." She cocked her head. "Is that the kind of woman you would like for a wife?"

His gaze shifted away from hers. "I'd rather an emotional wife than an erroneously educated one."

She didn't answer, not sure if he'd meant that as an insult, but her instinct told her his comment was not part of their debate. He had moved from their intelligent conversation to more personal matters. As much as she wanted to know more, she recognized the change for what it was and let it lie. Turning back to see what other books he might have that would be of interest, she noticed a pamphlet sticking out among those on the second section as if it had been hastily added. "What is this?"

"You probably don't want to read that."

She bristled at his tone. "If it's about education, I certainly do." She read the title out loud. "*What Women Need to Know to Please their Husbands.* I hope there is a companion to this one about what men need to know to please their wives."

He coughed. "I don't believe there is."

"At least Wollstonecraft wrote *A Vindication of the Rights of Man* as well." She looked down at the pamphlet to find no author. "Hmph." Turning to the first written page, she read aloud. "A woman must allow her husband free use of her body whenever he wants it. To submit to him at anytime and anywhere will make her more treasured. She must—" Her veins suddenly felt as if molten lava flowed through them. She snapped the pamphlet closed and fanned herself with it. "That is highly inappropriate."

A slow smile spread across his face. "I thought you wanted to learn everything men learn." He pointed to the pamphlet. "And that is actually for a woman to read."

Caught tangled in her own arguments, she turned away from him and slipped the pamphlet back where she'd found it. She wasn't sure how to answer his legitimate counter. She paused. If it was for women, then why was it here? She looked at him, but pointed to the document. "Why did you buy that, then?"

He held his palm out. "To know what was written in it. I do not limit myself only to information written for men. I read books for women, children, the educated, the uneducated, the scholars, and the artisans."

Back on firmer intellectual ground, she countered. "And so women should be allowed the same freedom." He pointed to the pamphlet she'd returned and opened his mouth, but she raised her hand. "I said the freedom, meaning they would be given the opportunity. If they don't want to read about certain topics until say, they are married," her cheeks heated even as she made her point, "then they should have the choice."

He moved closer, forcing her to look up at him. "But what if they want to read pamphlets like this and it is inappropriate as you determined, then what?"

She had no answer. "It is a possibility I had not thought on yet."

He reached past her, his unique fresh bergamot scent filling her nostrils as he pulled the pamphlet out again. "Perhaps to make a clear decision, you should read this." He held the pamphlet on his palm like the servants offered glasses of wine.

Either he was standing too close or the pamphlet itself had her flustered. She lifted her hand to wave off his offer and knocked the pamphlet to the floor. "Oh, I apologize."

He crouched to retrieve it. Looking up at her from his position he offered it again. "Do you not wish to be educated on this topic, or do you already have a book on it?"

A wave of heat filled her at the realization that the book she'd stolen was of the same vein as the pamphlet he so willingly offered. The small smile that played about his lips and the carnal knowledge in his crystal blue gaze had her dress feeling far too heavy. "Please, Your Grace, do get up."

He rose like a tiger she'd seen at the Royal Menagerie, uncurling himself in one graceful movement, his gaze never leaving her face. Somehow though, in doing so, he seemed to have moved closer. He didn't say a word, just held out the forbidden literature, the socially forbidden literature.

Part of her wanted to take it, just to prove her point, but then he might wish to discuss it and that was a topic she'd discuss with no one. "I will decline for now. When you said I could borrow a book on feminine education that wasn't what I had in mind."

"No, I'm sure it wasn't."

The arrogance in his voice and the grin he gave her almost had her changing her mind. His eyes told her he knew everything while she remained ignorant. She hated ignorance.

She took a deep breath as her sister Belinda had taught her to do whenever her emotions were overruling her intelligence. Though it did calm her, she didn't miss the change in the duke's face as he stiffened. Maybe he was having second thoughts about allowing her the privilege of borrowing a book. Quickly, she turned to scan the shelves. "Is there something else you would recommend that specifically discusses education for women?"

He cleared his throat. "I do, but I doubt you would enjoy it as it supports my opinion on the matter. Then again, it might behoove you to learn more about where your opponents stand."

As much as she disliked it, he did have a point. She continued her perusal of the volumes before her as she spoke. "Which would you recommend that best supports my argument and which that best supports yours?"

She sensed more than heard him step behind her. His hand appeared next to her, lightly brushing her shoulder as he pointed. "This is an excellent discussion on why education should be separated by gender."

His proximity made the conversation feel far too intimate. She bent to retrieve the book, expecting him to step back, but he didn't. To dispel the feeling, she read the title aloud in a sing song cadence. "Progression of the Intellect by Age. If I had seen this in a bookseller's window, I would have thought this a philosophy text."

He chuckled, his breath brushing the side of her neck. "That's exactly what I thought. It's one reason why I read each before it gets shelved. You can't always gauge the subject by the title."

Clasping the book to her chest with both arms, she looked over her shoulder and up at him. "And the text that would best support my position?"

His lips quirked up. "Allow me."

Before she knew what he was about, his arm lifted and he leaned into her as he pulled a volume from an upper shelf. She felt entirely surrounded by his large body and the bookcase. The sentence she'd read flitted through her mind. *A woman must allow her husband free use of her body whenever he wants it.* Her own flesh suddenly understood exactly what that might mean, and a strange craving started deep inside her.

The duke lowered the book and held it once again on his open palm as his arm encircled her. "I believe you'll enjoy this one much more."

She took it, trying to remember what they'd been talking about, her mind filled with his presence. She forced herself to read the title. *"The Quandary of Female Intellect."* Her train of thought returned. She examined the binding. "It's a rather brief study, is it not?"

The duke stepped back and chuckled. "That observation does say much about your position."

She turned to face him and lowered her brows. "Not at all. It is only one book. And I doubt that you've made it a personal pilgrimage to find more with this point of view."

"A valid point." His grin was back. "Then again, I saw no reason to spend more time searching out such a minority perspective."

"At the moment." She grasped the book to her chest with the other. "But I'm confident the body of work on this topic is growing. I'm anxious to start reading this." She pointed toward the small nook with the beautiful view.

He stepped aside. "Of course. Be my guest while I return to your father to see if he has any points he'd like to discuss."

She walked past him. Now that her equilibrium was back, she could be magnanimous. "Thank you for inviting us. I know he won't stop talking about this visit for weeks. It's rare he finds someone who is as well-read as he."

"And what of you? Are you enjoying your visit? I'm sure there is tea below if you'd like to partake."

She stopped in front of the two inviting, very wide armchairs. Whatever she may have thought of him, and still thought of him, it did not take away from the experience he'd given her and her father. "Your Grace, I can't truly express what a wonderful encounter this is. Your generosity in sharing your collection with us is humbling."

His polite smile faltered. "Don't be too humbled. It is rare that I also find others who can appreciate what I have amassed here. I have always been willing to share it."

Something in his look reminded her that she had a book of his. A treasured book that he knew was missing. Guilt permeated her chest. A sudden need to confess filled her.

"I will leave you to your reading." After his usual truncated nod, he turned and strolled along the balcony to the stairs. When he disappeared from view, she fell back into one of the chairs. She was the worst, immoral, depraved, reprehensible—no, that would be she was the most depraved, immoral, reprehensible, worst guest ever in the nineteenth century. No, since the battle of

Hastings. No, since Julius Caesar!

Her lips twitched. She was so much better at berating herself now as a twenty-four-year-old than she had been as a nine-year-old. "Bea, you'd be so disappointed in me."

She may not agree with the duke's stance, but he didn't deserve to have a book stolen. She'd just have to find a way to return it with none the wiser. Feeling better about her error in judgment, and her plan to rectify the matter, she placed the larger book on the small table between the chairs and opened the one that supported her position. Having never heard of it, she was anxious to see what further arguments it might make.

CHAPTER TEN

JAMES TIPPED HIS hat to an acquaintance who passed him as he strode along Oxford Street, not wanting to tarry. Hatchards booksellers had sent him an invitation to see their newest acquisitions. He never failed to purchase one or two new volumes. He was still undecided on whether to replace the book that was missing with another false covered book or to ask for his book back.

Unfortunately, his plans to determine if Lady Joanna was his thief had been inconclusive. There were moments when he was sure she had his book, but others when she'd shown no knowledge of what he referenced. His last effort, to have her find the pamphlet on a woman's sexual responsibilities to her husband had been set so as to gauge her reaction. He'd never expected her to start reading aloud from it. Not only had it flustered her, but it had made his own body react inappropriately. It was the only explanation he had for moving so close to her. It was as if her voice had spoken to his body, completely bypassing his own mind.

Not that he found her unattractive. In fact, he found her quite stunning in a very unpopular way. That she eschewed the usual white and pastel dresses common among the ladies, showed she recognized that brighter colors brought out her own dark beauty. He couldn't help but feel a certain admiration for her confidence and independent spirit. She was the only woman he'd met where he found an inseparable connection between her physical appearance and her intelligence. One could not think about one without the other.

His stride slowed. Perhaps that uniqueness could be of benefit to him in discovering the truth. If she had started reading the book, then her knowledge of the bedroom will have increased. If he were to suggest that a woman's primary purpose should be to please her husband, his true opinion on the matter, but keep his arguments to the physical aspects, he may be able to entice her to admit she'd taken the book and prove his own position at the same time.

Pleased with his new strategy, he increased his pace. The weather was cold once again despite it being April, and he found it invigorating. There was nothing like a brisk walk to clear the head and keep one's mind sharp. Which meant, that in the advent he was incorrect on his supposition that she had *The Illustrated Pleasures of Seduction*, he should enlist the help of Lord Mabry in determining if any of the gentlemen in the library that evening had wandered over to his desk. He was positive that the young man would be more than happy to oblige him with the truth. If no one had, then he'd firmly ruled out everyone but his staff. That would be a quick remedy by having Harrison investigate the matter surreptitiously. Since half his staff at Haven House were from Burhleigh Park and the other at Haven House for years, he had doubts that his thief lay in that direction.

Rounding the corner onto Bond Street, he stopped as Lady Caroline and her mother exited a shop up ahead. Part of him wanted to duck out of sight, anxious to avoid any delays to the bookseller, but this was a prime opportunity to further his acquaintance with Lady Caroline. As he drew closer, he anticipated the light tone of her voice and the scent of roses.

Lady Holburn spotted him first. "Lord Northwick." She waved her hand, causing Lady Caroline to look up from handing packages off to a footman. When she saw him, she smiled warmly, her pale lips lifting. She wore a pretty ivory pelisse of velvet and a light pink bonnet.

He gave a nod and made his way toward them.

The older woman beamed. "How wonderful to see you, Your Grace." She curtsied. "My daughter and I have just been about purchasing new material for your cousin's ball. Thank you kindly for the invitation."

"It was my pleasure." He turned his gaze on Lady Caroline. "I'm very pleased that you will be attending."

The young woman lost her smile, proving she thought the subject very important. "I wouldn't miss it. I only just had my first ball two months ago. I remember clearly being very excited." She cocked her head. "But you were not yet in town, were you?"

"No, we only arrived six weeks ago. I'm sorry I missed such an important event."

She lowered her gaze, her cheeks coloring. "That is very kind of you to say."

"Your Grace, would you be interested in joining us?" Lady Holburn looked to her daughter before turning back to him. "We were about to step across the way to Monsieur Armand's lovely shop. He has the most delicious sugar biscuits, and I must admit to a love of macarons. We'd be honored if you could join us."

As both women looked at him with hope in their gazes, he had to squelch the desire to be on his way. His priority for being in London was to find himself and Elsbeth a spouse, so he'd never need participate in the social whirl again. That Lady Caroline had not been spoken for yet was very lucky. Or she may have turned down an offer. Something to look into. "I'd be delighted. I have only had Monsieur Armand's ice cream. I did not realize he also made other sweets." He offered his arm to Lady Holburn then offered his other to Lady Caroline and turned toward the street. He waited until there was a short lull in the carts and horses traversing the popular roadway before leading them across. When they reached the other side, he didn't see a confectioner's shop.

As if she sensed his confusion, Lady Caroline pointed to the right. "It's just down here once we cross the street."

"Thank you. I hadn't known it was near here."

Her blonde brows puckered slightly. "Did we keep you from an errand then? I would not want to delay your afternoon."

He smiled down at her. "Not at all. I was just on my way to purchase another book for my collection, but I have no doubt it will be there tomorrow as well." That would be true only if he sent his footman to let them know he'd been delayed.

"You collect books then?"

At her question, he was reminded that she had not seen his library. "I do. I read them as well. Do you read?" He recognized the hope behind his question.

"Oh, I did read aplenty during my youth."

He swallowed a chuckle because she was clearly at least ten years younger than himself.

"But I've been so busy with preparing for the season that I haven't picked up a book since."

He ignored the disappointment that followed her statement and ushered both women into the small shop they'd come to with simply Armand's on the sign. The small space contained four petite tables each with four chairs. At the moment, no other patrons were present. He wasn't surprised considering the weather had turned so unseasonably cold.

They settled in at the table closest to the window that looked out upon Oxford Street. A young man came over and quickly took their order. Macarons weren't his favorite, but he wasn't going to say so.

Lady Holburn loosened the ties of her own cloak before folding her hands on the table. "So you must tell us who else is coming to Lady Elsbeth's ball. Will it be a grand affair or small and intimate?"

The question wasn't one he'd contemplated. "I have left all the details to my aunt. She is far more versed in these matters."

Lady Holburn patted his hand. "Of course. I don't know what

you men would do without us to arrange all the details." She beamed at her daughter. "Caroline is an absolute expert at details. I hardly had to arrange anything for her ball. She knew exactly what she wanted and who to invite."

"Mother, I couldn't have made all those arrangements without you." She turned to him, her pretty light blue eyes holding his gaze but briefly. "Learning about such events is very different from actually putting them in practice." She put her hand over her mother's. "I would have been lost without mother's council."

As the two took turns telling him about the grand ball they had arranged and complimenting each other on their ideas, his mind wandered. It wasn't that he didn't wish to be bothered, so much as it wasn't of great import to him since it had already passed.

"—was the beautiful butterfly."

His attention returned at the mention of that particular insect. "A butterfly?"

Lady Holburn nodded. "Yes. The pale blue glass wings set off the blue glass beads in her dress, making her sparkle."

He gazed at Lady Caroline who blushed. "The hair piece was a beautiful creation made by Rundell and Bridge." Have you heard of them?"

He shook his head, his mind quickly reverting to The Butterfly illustration he remembered in the stolen book. He couldn't see Lady Caroline being willing to try something quite that...creative. But marriage was not about creativity. It was about having a wife who could run the household and produce heirs. Unlike his own father, he planned to actually live in the same house with said heir.

"Tell me, Your Grace. Are you enjoying the season?" Lady Holburn leaned in as if she were sharing a confidence. "I understand this is your first season as well as Lady Elsbeth's."

Enjoying would be giving it far more credit than he would allow. "It has been both interesting and educational so far."

Lady Holburn twittered as she leaned back. "Educational.

What a unique way to look at such a variety of activities. I admit that I, for one, enjoy every last moment until we must leave Town."

Lady Caroline gazed sympathetically at her mother. "Father did say we could host a few more balls this winter now that I'm out in society." She looked over at him from beneath her lashes. "That is if I'm still unmarried by then."

The hint wasn't subtle though the look was. He appreciated her candor, no matter how it was related. "I doubt very much that a young woman of such fine qualities like yourself would be unspoken for by the season's end. I'm surprised you have not had any offers."

"Oh, but she has." Lady Holburn unclasped her hands and laid one on her daughter's arm. "You've had three, have you not?"

"Yes, Mother, but I'm sure that his grace would not be interested in my—"

"Piffle. I'm sure he is." Lady Holburn looked straight at him. "I'm afraid that all three were lacking in something. We expect that Lady Caroline's husband will be well-bred, well set-up, and well-placed. Is that not what you are expecting for Lady Elsbeth?"

The woman was shrewd. "It is. The gentleman also must be to Elsbeth's liking, so it may take a bit of time for us to agree."

Lady Holburn gazed at her daughter with motherly pride. "My daughter always agrees with me."

He glanced at Lady Caroline to catch a mutual look of adoration. It triggered a memory of his older sister and mother, the look of knowing so similar. The image sent a chill up his back. Why think of them now? His aunt and cousin didn't agree like these two, so why would he remember his deceased mother and sister? Suddenly uncomfortable, the need to escape grew. Searching for some excuse, he was thwarted by the waiter coming with their sweets.

Anxious to leave, he took advantage of the young man's presence and bumped him at just the right moment so the macarons fell in his lap.

"You clumsy fool." Lady Holburn looked about. "Where is Monsieur Armand? This should not go unpunished."

"No, it was my fault. I moved at the wrong time." He lifted the macarons from his lap and set them on the plate that had made it to the table. "Do not search out Monsieur Armand." He stood, wiping the crumbs off his tan pantaloons. "But I'd best leave and change."

The waiter apologized for the third time, so he turned to him and pressed a shilling into his hand. "No harm done." He gave the man a wink.

The young man visibly relaxed, having figured out his ploy.

He couldn't manage a smile, so he motioned with his head. "Please tell Monsieur Armand to send the bill to the Duke of Northwick at Haven House." Turning to the two ladies, he bowed. "It has been a pleasure."

As they said goodbye, he was already headed for the door. Stepping on to the pavement, he paused to allow a couple to pass by him before he retraced his steps, back to his waiting coach still another street away. Every sound hurt his ears from the whinny of a horse to the call of a flower girl to the chatting of the two men behind him. Weaving between those out for a stroll, he was almost at a run by the time he reached the coach. Not waiting for his footman, he opened the door himself and jumped in. "Haven House!"

Within seconds the coach started to move, the din of the street muffled by the walls. He closed the curtains to block out the sights as well.

"I hate London." His voice broke the relative quiet of the coach, making the statement hang in the air as if a tangible thing. To him it was. Old memories of his mother saying goodbye as she left him at Haven House with his father, lying to him and telling him she'd see him soon when she'd planned to be gone for three months. His older sister holding their mother's hand, her confidence in their mother's love as great as his own...then.

Until…

He spread his knees and lowered his head, focusing on taking deep breaths. It had been years since this had happened to him. He'd thought himself far beyond the age of his panophobia hysterica, not having had any panic terrors due to vapors in nearly a decade. It was the city. He hadn't stayed more than a sennight before this year. He should have found a wife in Peterborough, then he could have remained at Burhleigh Park.

Even as he thought of the vast pastures and full forest of his ancestral estate, his heartrate slowed and his chest loosened. It might be time to go home and find his equilibrium again.

Sitting up, he rested his head on the back of the seat and closed his eyes to better concentrate on home. It had always been his home except for the few years when he'd been sent up to Oxford for his studies. That too had been an adjustment, but not too difficult. His classes and activities had filled his days until he fell into bed after studying, completely exhausted. It had been an exciting time for him.

He grinned at the memory of finding a pamphlet on sexual positions hidden in an old book he'd bought. That pamphlet had made the rounds and then some. It was the first piece of reading material he'd ever thrown away, but not before experiencing every position illustrated. It wasn't nearly as civilized as the pamphlet Lady Joanna had pulled from his stack.

He opened his eyes, the humor of winning that particular argument raising his spirits. She had wanted to learn everything men learned. Next time he was in her company, he would have to teach her more. Only by doing, did one fully understand all the concepts in that area. As a gentleman, it was his duty to enlighten her, within certain limits, of course. Whatever her views on education, she was still a lady.

CHAPTER ELEVEN

JOANNA WALKED ARM and arm with Mariel down Fleet Street toward their coach. She scanned the people on the other side of the road.

"Joanna, whatever are you looking for?"

She turned her head back to Mariel. "I'm just looking."

"No, you're not. You're looking for someone. Who is it?"

She chuckled. "You're very observant. Yes, I'm looking for the Duke of Northwick."

"What makes you think he might be here. Did you receive a note from him?" Mariel leaned in closer. "Are there feelings you'd like to confess in confidence?"

Joanna whipped her head back. "Not at all. I'm looking for him so as to avoid his company."

Mariel's brows lowered in confusion. "I don't understand, then."

She patted her sister's arm. "Yes, I'm being rather obtuse. Allow me to explain. Over the last few weeks, whatever public outing I was about, the duke also attended. You remember at Vauxhall?"

Mariel nodded.

"Then at the lecture Amelia, Father, and I attended, he arrived, when he'd specifically said he would be at a recital."

"Did he give a reason for changing his plans?"

"He did, but they were suspicious. Lady Caroline was there as well. It could be that he heard she was attending and so changed his plans, but we still argued."

They stopped at the coach, and the footman opened the door and set down the steps. She waited for Mariel to situate herself before following. Once inside, she continued. "I'm relieved that today we never happened upon the duke." The fact was, now she felt guilty. She hadn't confessed while at Haven House. Her father and the duke had engaged in a long debate about the polar ice caps descending into civilization, which had allowed her to finish the smaller book she'd started. But since her father was in their company, she'd never had a chance to tell the duke she'd taken his book. Her father would be more than disappointed in her if he knew, and she hoped to avoid that.

"You won't be able to avoid him for long. We have Lady Elsbeth's coming-out ball in less than a fortnight. Mother is quite taken with Lady Astor and pleased we are all going as a family."

She grimaced, having forgotten about that. Though she doubted she'd be able to discuss her issue with the duke there, she was pleased for Teddy. "You mean all of us and Teddy. I do hope he conducts himself appropriately instead of like a besotted fool."

Mariel gave a soft laugh. "He really is taken with her. I wouldn't be surprised if he called the next day and asked for her hand in marriage."

"Oh, I hope not. I know he has a passion for her, but how well could he possibly know her?"

Mariel's gaze drifted to the street outside. "A great passion is not always about the intellect, Joanna. Sometimes the heart just knows."

She knew that look in her sister's eyes. It was a mixture of love and loss. Only Mariel, of all of them, had given her heart completely. Reaching across the carriage, she touched her sister's knee. "Was it worth it?"

A soft smile lifted her sister's lips as she met her gaze. "Loving Marcus? More than I can put into words."

Her heart constricted and she sat back. Though she often considered herself brave, she did not think she could ever give her heart to a man. Losing Belinda had been too difficult. Yet Mariel had lost not only the man she loved, but the older man she married as well. She was truly the most courageous of the family. "Do you think then that Teddy feels a great passion for Lady Elsbeth?"

Mariel clasped her hands, one thumb rubbing over the other as she thought through her answer. "I think he may. I also think that Lady Elsbeth looks kindly on him as well."

"It is odd to think of Teddy as a husband." She chuckled. "I still think of him like the baby bear we watched at Vauxhall last year, curious, excited, and awkward in his environment."

"Yes, but baby bears grow to be ferocious bears. I think Teddy would protect his future wife with every breath."

She tried to imagine her cousin scaring off other suitors, but couldn't do it.

The coach came to a halt before Craymore Hall. They alighted and hurried into the house, the wind having gained strength since they left Fleet Street. The clouds had also covered the sun once again. If the season continued to be so cold, she may just have to take another look at that polar ice cap theory. Once inside, Channing took their cloaks and Mariel headed off to rest.

She, on the other hand, headed for the library. Stepping inside, she scanned the room to be sure no family members were present. Satisfied she was alone, she strode to her cabinet and taking the key from her reticule, she unlocked it and pulled out the duke's book. Quickly, she locked her cabinet and went straight to her room.

The house was quiet as it darkened outside. It was time to spend a few hours reading. She was more than a little curious as to the knowledge she would gain from her pilfered tome. Once upstairs and in her room, she set the book down on her settee. Then she locked her door. She didn't want any surprise visits. Lighting the oil lamp near her reading corner, she grabbed up the book and stretched out on the settee. She quickly flipped past the pages she'd already viewed. She clearly remembered the parts of the male and female anatomy with the large illustrations that labeled each area on pages three and four.

Lifting the next sheet of paper, she stared at the illustration on page five. There was no question what she was looking at. Her mouth went dry and her body heated. Pulling the neckline of her green day dress from her skin, she blew down on her chest, but never took her gaze from the page. Before her was an illustration of a naked man on top of a naked woman in what was labeled The Missionary position. After reviewing the initial pages and with her knowledge of how animals procreated, it was clear what was happening in the drawing.

So *this* is what men learned? She continued to blow on her chest as she turned to page six. It showed two clothed individuals, the man standing behind the woman, his head bent. Was he kissing her neck? The caption below stated, "There's this." That didn't make sense. She turned back to page five. Below the drawing, the caption read "Before this." Now it made sense. Turning to page six again, she studied the illustration. He was definitely kissing the woman's neck, just below the ear. She could almost feel the touch like when Northwick had stood behind her and reached for the book above her. His breath had touched very close to that spot.

She snapped the book closed, her chest suddenly feeling very sensitive. Standing, she set it on the settee and moved to her dressing table where she'd left her fan from earlier in the day. Picking it up, she paced the length of her bedroom, cooling herself as she walked.

There was no question as to what the rest of the book would contain. She was only on page seven, but it was clear the illustrations would show how a man seduced a woman. It might even show the mechanics of mating. The question was, would it be better to remain ignorant? She didn't plan to marry, so the knowledge would be of little use to her. Then again, she had learned about safety lamps for coal miners the other night, and she'd never have a need for those. The week before, she'd read a book of poems by William Wordsworth. Those she thought emotionally fulfilling at the time, but they weren't *needed*.

That meant her argument that she wouldn't use the information was irrelevant. She stopped and narrowed her eyes at the book. It called to her like forbidden fruit. If she read it, would she be cast out of Eden like Adam and Eve? Would her innocence be gone, despite her still being innocent? She dropped her fan on her dressing table and set both hands, palms down upon it, staring at her reflection. "Mother and Father would be horrified. Teddy would think it a fine joke. Amelia would want to read it, too. Would Mariel already know all of it?" She didn't like the idea that Mariel knew more than she did. Her father would call that hubris, and it was, but she couldn't help her competitive nature in this one area.

She examined her face. "Are you ready to lose your innocence?" Would she look or feel different? Did it matter?

I thought you wanted to learn everything men learn. As Northwick's words echoed in her mind, her resolve solidified. She would stand by her principles. Knowledge itself was power as Sir Francis Bacon had written.

Standing straight, she took a step toward the settee then halted. Turning, she pulled her fan from the dressing table then returned to the book. She reclined and put it on her lap. Maybe it could teach her how to avoid being seduced. Now that would be very practical. She flipped to page seven and found half of it was writing, the other half small pictures showing places to kiss a woman. She studied each one, determined to learn it all. Even having never been kissed at the crease of her elbow, below her ear, or at her temple, she found herself flushing with a mild heat. The explanation of these sensitive spots gave her pause. They were all so accessible. On the following page was another large illustration of the couple, the backs of the man's fingers were on the woman's cheek. She brought her own knuckles to her cheek.

It didn't feel any different than when she propped her head with her hand as she pondered an idea.

She moved on to page nine, which again had a lot of explanation and a number of small illustrations. Besides the fact a gentleman should never touch a woman's skin unless she was his wife, none of the touches appeared particularly seductive except one. She studied the small illustration of a man's fingers on the woman's collarbone. Now that was a place that caused her to giggle as if she were nine again. For some reason, the spot tickled, so not a very advantageous place for a man bent on seducing her. Not that any had tried, but it was good to know what a touch like that was supposed to mean.

Turning to page ten, she viewed the full-page profile of the man and woman locked in an embrace, their mouths sealed to each other, his hands on her behind and hers encircling his neck, the fingers of her near hand splayed in his hair. The artist had their bodies touching their full length even though still dressed. She felt warm again, but didn't pick up her fan. Northwick was lean and so much taller than her. He'd radiated heat as he stood behind her, the scent of bergamot and leather clearly filling the space. She'd never witnessed a couple kissing like this. Her mother occasionally kissed her father on the cheek, but nothing more. Then again, their days of seduction had probably ended after Amelia was born.

This page had no caption, but there was an explanation. *If there is no fire in the kiss, no position, whether it be The Rider, The Butterfly, or any other will be satisfying.*

Her breath left her. The Butterfly?

Northwick's question whistled through her head. *Tell me, do you like The Butterfly?*

He knew!

Northwick knew she'd taken his book. Embarrassment washed over her, even as she sucked air back into her lungs. She pushed the book away, and it fell to the soft rug on the floor. Grasping her fan, she used it rigorously. Why else would he have asked her for no reason if she liked butterflies, no, not plural, one – the butterfly. He thought she'd read his book!

She jumped to her feet and stalked to the other side of the room where she turned to glare at the offensive tome on the floor. Not only did he know she took it, but he knew what it contained and assumed she'd read it. She spun around to face the wall. What must he think of her?

She clapped her free hand over her mouth. And she'd read from the other pamphlet out loud in front of him!

If only she could faint right now. A respite from her spinning, unrelenting mortification would be welcomed, but she had never been one to lose her senses. Besides, she'd probably hit her head on the dressing table if she did. She turned around again and leaned against the wall, fanning herself as she wallowed in self-flagellation. Belinda always warned her to harness her emotions and focus them on what was worthwhile. She did try, but she failed more than she succeeded.

"Belinda, I needed you to live. I know it's selfish, but selfless, too, don't you think?" Despite how carefully she listened, all she heard was the silence of her room and the steady fall of the rain against her windows in response. The scene was the opposite from the beautiful day in May two years hence when her beloved sister, under her own ardent and unrelenting care, slipped away from her. She had tried everything, even after the doctors shook their heads and walked away. She'd been so confident after Belinda made it through scarlet fever that she would live.

But she hadn't. The heart of their family had died and left her floundering.

"Now look at what I've done, Bea." She threw the fan down on the dressing table and dropped into the chair, shaking her head at herself in the mirror. There was no putting the book back now. No confessing she'd taken it. She'd just have to avoid Northwick. That hadn't worked until now, so she'd just stay at Craymore Hall until he left London again. Yes, she'd remain here for the season. If he arrived for some unknown reason, she'd claim a migraine. She would be a hermit. No one would miss her. It wasn't as if she had any marriage prospects or wanted any.

She closed her eyes, imagining staying at Craymore Hall for the next two months. She could read. Father would be happy to purchase more texts. She could help Mother with running the house and Father with his books. But what would she do after the first four days? She stood again. "Think, Joanna. There is always a solution. If not readily seeable, look deeper." She started pacing again. It was so much easier to think when pacing. Her mind spun with possible paths out of her predicament. She halted. If Northwick knew she had the book, why hadn't he requested it back?

That gave her pause. She grinned. Because he didn't know for sure if she had it. That had to be it. If that was true, she must continue as she was, doing what she always had done, so he wouldn't suspect anything and neither would her family. Mariel knew she had taken a book, but hadn't mentioned it, nor would she. Mariel never said anything about any of the volumes she'd borrowed.

Guilt sprinkled through her conscience at hiding her theft from everyone else, but she had no choice. Even if Teddy married Lady Elsbeth one day, and they were all related, she'd just have to keep her secret. She halted in front of the book. She'd been right. It was the apple that banished man from Eden, and it was this book that banished her from her ignorance as well as innocence.

Bending over, she scooped it up. If she had to keep this secret, she might as well know all of it. Settling onto her settee, she opened the book to where she left off and turned the page.

JAMES SMILED LIKE an Indian tiger spotting his prey as he stepped into the building. Lord Mabry had been quite forthcoming in his eagerness to help him. Not only had he learned from the young man that none of the gentlemen had wandered near his desk the night his book disappeared, but he'd also ascertained quite a bit about the Mabry ladies' schedule for the week. Their various activities had him discovering more about Town than he had on all his past visits combined. The Mabry family appeared to enjoy all London had to offer, but he wasn't at the Weeks's Museum of Mechanical Curiosities to delve into its exhibits. He hadn't even been aware there was such a place. His sole purpose in this visit was to teach Lady Joanna that there was much of a man's world that she would prefer not to know.

Spotting his quarry in a strawberry-red dress standing before a mechanical hawk that opened its wings to scratch before closing them and looking at the bystanders, he walked through the light crowd to stand behind her. "I find the real ones much more impressive."

Lady Joanna whirled around. "You. I mean, Your Grace." She gave a quick curtsy. "I didn't know you had an interest in mechanical motion."

He grinned. "Much like you, I have an interest in many things."

She flushed. Now *that* was different. "Actually, I'm fascinated by the mathematics that goes behind every movement."

He grimaced. "I find the creation of the parts to be the most interesting." He pointed past her to the breast of the bird. "Finding just the right color metal, for example, to make this hawk's feathers to best emulate the natural bird takes an artist's eye."

Lady Joanna gave him a lopsided grin. "Then you'd do best to tour this museum with my sister Amelia." She scanned the crowd then shook her head. "She's most likely off viewing the Bird of Paradise." Her gaze returned to him. "She's an artist and a rather good one at that. She has also studied the paintings of various genius artists while she was on tour with my aunt."

"I would posit, then, that if you and your sister were to work with a man who knows his much about metals, you could create something far more impressive than this bird."

She cocked her head. "I would prefer to work with a woman like Rebecca Emes, the silversmith, because then I wouldn't have to argue every nuance. But even if the three of us were to undertake such a task, to what end?"

He raised his brows. "To what end does a painter paint, or a builder build, or a chef cook? For man's enjoyment."

"Man's enjoyment? What of woman's enjoyment?"

Bringing her into a debate was far too easy. "I would assume that women enjoy gazing at paintings, walking into buildings such as this, and eating mascarpone ice cream as well as any man."

"Exactly. So why not say that the purpose of such creations is for man and woman to enjoy?"

He shrugged. "It is assumed that women are included in that case."

She raised her index finger. "Then by that logic, Brooks's should be opening the doors wide for me to become a member."

He hadn't expected that argument. A man would have mentioned far more mundane avenues such as seats in Parliament or appointments to the church. Her mind worked far differently than any man's. "That would be a moot point as Brooks's is a *gentleman's* club. Many men are not allowed to be members. I would suggest that Almack's is a similar instance as only certain ladies and certain men who are approved by the *female* patronesses are allowed inside its hallowed doors."

"Do you wish to enter?" She gave him a sly smile. "I'm sure I could have my mother suggest your name to one of those fine ladies."

He didn't engage her on that subject. She was far too good at distracting her opponent, but he'd noticed that before. "Why your mother and not you?"

Her eyes rounded. "Me? Surely you know that I'm not married." She leaned closer and lowered her voice, "nor am I in a quest to be."

When she straightened, he was left with the scent of sweet spice in his nostrils. It was unusual enough to remark upon, yet familiar in a comforting way.

"My mother is of one of the finest families and is well respected in the *ton*. I, on the other hand, am…"

He waited as she searched for the right word. It couldn't be that difficult – accepted would work. "You are what?"

She lifted her hand palm up. "I'm tolerated."

Now that was interesting.

"Though I daresay I'm also laughed at, ridiculed, and pitied."

He lowered his brows. "I don't believe I understand."

"No, I'm sure you wouldn't." She waved her hand before turning to stroll toward the next exhibit.

His curiosity was far too strong to let the conversation end. He moved up next to her before a mechanical boy who sat at a desk and wrote on a piece of paper. The boy, which looked like a puppet, was so far from looking lifelike that any interest he might have found in the machine itself disintegrated at once. The inner workings of Lady Joanna's mind were far more riveting. "For one who is focused upon knowledge, it would appear you are in no haste to enlighten me."

She turned at that, obviously startled by his accusation. "Not at all, if you wish to know?"

"I do."

She scanned those nearby. "Walk with me, and I'll be happy to educate you."

A woman did not invite a man for a stroll, but instead of remarking on it, he offered his arm.

Taking it, she pointed. "I understand there is a silver swan at the other end of this room. Shall we view it?"

He angled them toward the middle of the hundred-foot room which remained empty since people gathered by the exhibits set up around the outer walls. "Now then. You were going to explain why you are laughed at, ridiculed, and pitied."

"So I was. It's not done in front of me, of course, but I hear comments I'm not supposed to, as do my sisters. I am what is considered a bluestocking. A woman of intelligence, and therefore with no marriage prospects. The marriage issue is the one for which I'm pitied."

His gut tightened as anger swirled within it. Yes, Lady Joanna was not typical of most ladies he'd met, but he didn't see her as unmarriageable nor a bluestocking. "That is ridiculous."

She turned a startled gaze up at him. "Thank you for that, but there is no need for alarm." She gave his arm a slight squeeze. "I don't mind. I'm actually rather flattered that many in the *ton* think I'm very intelligent." She leaned in and lowered her voice again, though no one was near. "I think they are a tad afraid of me to tell you the truth." She pulled back and wiggled her brow.

He wasn't sure what to make of that.

"And as to the marriage issue. I'm quite well set up. My aunt kindly left her estate to me upon her passing." She raised her hand as if he were about to interrupt. "And yes, she had an excellent solicitor who was able to insure that the property remains mine even if I should choose to marry. So you see, the thoughts of others about my person are of no consequence, but I do try to follow society's dictates as much as possible for my family's sake, especially Amelia and Teddy."

A piece of the puzzle of Lady Joanna suddenly slipped into place. "And that was why you didn't speak your mind the first night we met at my dinner party. You didn't want to make a poor impression upon me because Lord Mabry is enamored with my cousin."

She laughed softly. "I knew that very night that you were intelligent."

As she smiled up at him, a wave of self-satisfaction flowed through him. He'd had many a woman flatter him. As an unmarried duke, he was forever a marriage prospect, and so praise, deserved or undeserved, was heaped upon him regularly by the fairer sex. But Lady Joanna's praise felt like a gift. Somehow in their talks over the last weeks, he'd come to admire her, especially her mind.

He returned her smile. "And here I thought I had done so well to hide it."

A laugh escaped her, causing a few people to turn around, but they lost interest in seconds. "Don't try to be humble. You did your best to intimidate the other men at your dinner party. You clearly wanted them to know that you were in charge."

Her observation was uncomfortably correct. "I was so obvious then?"

She nodded. "But no need to worry. It is quite expected of a duke, and as you are new to the London season, it's an important distinction to make." She paused as if not sure how to continue. "Is there a particular reason that you have avoided the season until now?"

If she had meant to be subtle, she'd failed miserably, but he found he preferred she be straightforward. It was refreshing. "I despise London."

At that her eyes rounded, and her steps halted. "That is rather harsh. I do agree it has its drawbacks such as nasty smells, noisy docks, and clogged streets, but I wouldn't dislike the entire city because of that. Is there something about Town that causes such strong feelings in you?"

Yes. It's the city where I lost my mother forever. The feelings of anguish and anger that seethed beneath the surface of his consciousness whenever in the city bubbled up once again. He was an expert at controlling them, but for once he didn't want to. "It was the last place I saw my mother before she left us." He gestured to a tall window. "Here it's quite easy to board a ship for America and be lost forever."

He could still hear his father's shouts, ranting at fate when the news had reached them before all talk of her stopped. Pressure on his arm made him look down and he recalled himself and his surroundings at the sympathy shining in Lady Joanna's gaze.

"I'm sorry. If my mother…if that had happened to me, I would hate the place where it happened as well."

He jerked his head in a short nod, acknowledging her unique understanding. He appreciated that she didn't ask more questions. It said a lot about her character. It also said a lot about him because he *wanted* her to know more. There was a strange relief at telling her. He'd allowed the gates of his past to open, but he forced himself not to walk through. "It was a long time ago. I was barely seven. All that is left of that event is my dislike for London." Even as he said the words, he knew them for the falsehood they were.

"So then it really is a sacrifice for you to be here for your cousin's season."

He grimaced. "Yes, but it's a bit hard to play the martyr when I've combined it with my own hunt for a wife and business affairs that need to be tended to."

She nodded. "Lady Caroline. She would make you a fine wife."

He agreed, but was curious as to why she made her opinion known. "Do you think so?" He started walking them forward again as he waited for her reply.

"I do. She is the epitome of what every duke wishes for in a wife. She is accomplished in French, dancing, running a household, and playing the pianoforte. Even more important, she comes from a good family, she's gracious, and she has an excellent reputation."

He smirked. "In other words, no scandal dogs her heels."

She shook her head. "None at all."

"You don't mention her looks." He admitted, if only to himself, that he found Lady Joanna much more attractive, but not for a duchess.

"Is that important to you?" She raised her brows, clearly skeptical. "I didn't see a man of your intellect being limited by certain aesthetics, but if that is the case then I would suggest that she is of the typical coloring highly sought after by males in the *ton*. Much like the lighter plumage of the North American Oriel is sought after by the male of its species."

He was both flattered and insulted by her phrasing. His instinct told him she had meant it to be so. "You do not feel outward appearances are important in a husband or bride?"

"To be honest, I have not considered it since I have never been on the same quest you are. I imagine it would be preferable to have someone pleasant to look at while sitting across the table at breakfast, but as far as one coloring over another, I don't see how that should matter. We are not paintings after all."

As much as he wished to argue the point, he found himself failing to find a legitimate counter.

"Oh, but now this, this is stunning." Lady Joanna slipped her hand from his arm and moved forward to view a three-foot high swan made entirely of silver.

Stepping up behind her, he easily viewed the mechanical creature over her shoulder. It was indeed lifelike as it sat straight in what appeared to be an illusion of water beneath it. Then it started to move.

He sensed more than heard her intake of breath as the swan lifted a wing off its back and scratched itself before straightening. It then lowered its head to the water illusion below and came up with a fish in its beak before swallowing it. The movements were so lifelike and graceful that when it finished its pattern, those around them quietly applauded as if afraid to scare the bird. Not much in the mechanical realm impressed him, but this was quite remarkable. "Did you enjoy its movements?"

Lady Johanna looked up at him over her shoulder, her ever present lock dangling upon her chest. "It was far more beautiful than I expected."

Her appreciation for the scientific artform shone in her eyes, which appeared in the light to have their own silver flecks. He had the urge to compare her to the swan and tell her she was far more impressive, but he stifled it.

She turned back to the creature, who remained still, its mechanical pattern waiting to start again. "It is quite an unusual swan."

That was an understatement. "Because it's silver or because of its mechanics?"

She looked up at him, a twinkle in her eye. "Because swans don't eat fish intentionally and they would never seek out such a big fish." She moved away to view another exhibit.

He laughed. The sound as unexpected to him as to the people around him, who gave him curious glances. Only Lady Joanna would make such an observation, and she was absolutely correct. The fish the artist had chosen was far larger than swans would ever eat, since they ate minnows by accident while feeding on water vegetation.

He followed to where she strolled, viewing the various oddities.

She stopped in front of a clock that wound itself through barometric pressure, or so the sign claimed. Though she didn't turn at his approach, she addressed him. "I read about this theory, but haven't seen it put to purpose."

"All knowledge has purpose, though I would not have thought of this particular application for barometric pressure. That is such an unpredictable phenomenon."

"You mean like the cold summer we're having? I don't think we've had more than a handful of days that have been pleasant." She leaned closer to the clock, studying it. "I wonder if that has had an effect on this machine."

He pulled his pocket watch from his waistcoat and compared the times. "Doesn't appear to have caused any inaccuracy." He held it out as she turned to look.

She noted the time then looked back at the automation. "You're right. It seems a shame that someone can figure out how to create a perpetual clock, but we still can't even diagnose illnesses correctly."

That was an odd statement. Curious, he probed. "Knowledge is far more than reading and calculations. It also means experimenting and applying theories in concrete ways."

That engendered her full attention. "Of course, that is how

progress is made, yet despite our medical profession's rejection of the four humors, they still find reason to bleed people. Loss of blood can lead to death, so why they insist on that as a way to cure anything is beyond my comprehension." Her cheeks had become flushed and her brow furrowed. She'd jumped from reason to emotion, but why?

He opened his arm toward the middle of the room to entice her to move away from those nearby. She strode forward in that direction, not giving her surroundings a thought as she continued. "If they can dissect a cadaver, then surely they should by now, understand how the body works and be able to fix it."

"I'm not sure what you mean. They have learned quite a lot about our bodies and can set broken bones and even extract bullets. I understand there was some miraculous work done by the doctors during the Peninsular Wars."

She waved off his comments. "I'm not talking about bone and tissue. I'm talking about blood, pulse, breathing, digestion."

She had a point. "I believe those areas as well as the brain are still being discovered, but we have made progress. We aren't as easily discoverable as metallic elements or various gasses."

"Why not?" She stopped and faced him. "Since we are so far advanced above all other creatures, why have we not discovered our own inner workings? Why must people die of consumption, small pox, or scarlet fever?" She pointed at him, her voice rising. "Men of learning should know this by now. Maybe if women had been able to have the same educational opportunities, we all could live longer lives today."

Her chest rose with her quick breaths. A few people in the room had turned to look at them. Normally, that would concern him, but her obvious distress had him searching for ways to soothe her. The problem was, she wasn't like Elsbeth or even his aunt. In unchartered waters, he chose a more forthright path than normal. "Has the medical field failed you that you feel so strongly about this?"

She snorted. "Failed would be a kind way of expressing it.

They were utterly useless." She threw both hands up before dropping them to her sides. "No, actually, they were a hindrance." Suddenly, her shoulders slumped and air whistled through her lips in one long exhale. "Your library would have been far more help than they were. At least I might have applied some of its knowledge to some success."

She'd obviously lost someone dear to her. Lady Beaumont's comment at Vauxhall came back to him. *I'm afraid we are far too close for most families to understand, but with the death of our sister, all formality was lost.* The pieces fell into place and understanding flooded him. Gentling his tone like he would with a nervous horse, he put his conclusion into words. "You cared for your sister before she passed."

She nodded. "I did. I was the only one who had caught and survived scarlet fever, so I nursed her." She lifted her gaze to meet his. "And Bea survived. But then she couldn't seem to gain her strength back. She couldn't walk very far without having to stop to catch her breath, and she said she had pain in her chest." Lady Joanna's hand came up to cover her own chest as if from memory. "Eventually, she stopped trying to leave her bed unassisted. That's when I noticed that her body would jerk on its own."

Even as he listened, he wished they were in his library, a particular book coming to mind where he was certain he'd read of a similar malady. "Those are very specific symptoms and yet the physicians had no suggestion for treatment?"

Her brows lowered. "Oh yes, they had plenty of suggestions. They thought to bleed her, which I refused to allow. They said it was consumption, which it clearly wasn't, so they felt there was no hope. One suggested fresh country air, another no outside air at all. And one..." Her hands tightened in her skirts. "One suggested it was hysteria and that she be put in an asylum."

Despite not knowing Lady Joanna's sister, even he was appalled at that last course of action. "That man should not be called upon as a physician."

Her hands relaxed. "That was my thought as well. But as you can see, they were of no use, except to exhaust me. I had to fight them and reason with my family."

"But if the physicians, learned men who have focused on curing the human body could not aid your sister, why do you think you could have?" Maybe if he pointed out the obvious, the sense of guilt he felt emanating from her would dissipate. It was also a logical question, which he'd found her quite adept at.

She snorted. "Because I'm a woman, that's why. I have common sense, something these supposed learned men have no experience using in combination with their knowledge. If I could have just found one that would converse with me as an equal, the two of us could have surely found a cure, but as they were judgmental and pompous, I had to find the information myself." She shook her head, the sorrow in her eyes too vivid to look upon. "I ran out of time."

An unfamiliar feeling crept up his spine. Those physicians sounded a bit like him. Could simple attitudes and beliefs have determined whether a young woman lived or died? The responsibility of that deduction left him grateful he'd never taken an interest in the application of medicine.

She continued, oblivious to his self-reflection. "All the while, Bea was content, happy with the time she had. She told me her time after the fever was blessed, because without me tending to her, she would have never had it."

The relationship between the Mabry sisters awed him. He felt the loss of his older sister more keenly. Could they have had a similar relationship? "She sounds like she was a special kind of person."

"She was. She was the heart of our family." A bittersweet smile formed before she straightened as if recalling where they were and what they'd been conversing about before. "But back to your point. So I do know what it means to apply knowledge in concrete ways."

He gave nod to accept her assertion as he gestured back to

the swan, which was currently in motion. "As do I, though there is much I haven't tried, such as mechanical silver swans."

She gave him a mischievous grin. "And the waltz."

He found himself chuckling at that. "Yes, and the waltz. Though I have read about it."

"And was reading about how to ride a horse as satisfying as actually learning how to do it yourself?"

"Yes."

Her eyes widened. "Yes? How can that be?"

"Let's just say that I took my fair share of falls." He grimaced both at the memory of the falls and the old stableman who had taught him at his own insistence. "Reading about it was less painful."

Her soft laughter filled his ears, generating a sense of pleasure that he'd been able to bring her mood around. A sudden idea took root, and instead of debating the positives and negatives of it, he trusted his instinct. "Teach me to waltz."

"What?" She looked askance at him.

"Teach me to waltz. Elsbeth's ball is coming in less than a fortnight, and I'm sure the guests will expect me to know how. Since you have obviously been through the pains of learning it, I think you would be an apt teacher. I assure you, I will review all I've read about it."

She cocked her head and smirked at him. "You want me to teach you how to waltz."

He shrugged. "You were the one who pointed out that it is knowledge I have not applied yet. And you must admit that it would look poorly upon my family if I haven't mastered this new dance."

"And what of Elsbeth? She would need to know how to as well as I'm sure there will be many suitors there who would ask her."

He hadn't thought of that, but it would be appropriate. "Then perhaps your cousin, Lord Mabry could join us, and we can learn together."

"Oh, I know Teddy would be happy to. After all, I do believe Elsbeth will be much lighter on her feet than I was." She paused as she contemplated his suggestion.

He had no doubt that she was weighing all sides of the proposal, like he should have, but for once, he just wanted her to agree. "I will of course, include my aunt as an appropriate chaperone."

"I'm sure that would disappoint Teddy, but I find Lady Astor delightful. I do have some experience having taught my sisters how to dance and being the lead. Yes, I would enjoy the challenge of teaching you to dance." She winked. "We'll see if we can't hone your skills well enough to leave Lady Caroline in a dither."

That hadn't occurred to him, but she was correct. It would be in his favor to dance the waltz with Lady Caroline. At least if he could execute the dance with some skill, it would be an option. He gave Lady Joanna a short nod. "I will appreciate your tutelage. Is Friday convenient for you? Our ballroom at Haven House would probably make Elsbeth feel the most comfortable, if you wouldn't mind."

"That will be fine." Her gaze moved from him to something past him. "Oh, I see Amelia has returned from viewing the Bird of Paradise. I should join her if only to allow her to critique to someone who won't be offended."

He raised his brows at that. "Indeed."

She dropped a short curtsey, murmured a quick farewell, and left him.

Surprised by her quick exit, he turned to see her link her arm with her sister and steer the petite blonde toward the exit. He remained staring, ruminating on the strange family of Mabry and one Lady Joanna in particular. He'd dreaded coming to the museum, usually unimpressed with such trivial mechanisms, but his stay had been rather enjoyable. Not only had he seen knowledge applied, but he'd had an interesting conversation, and learned something else about the lady. Her drive for erudition was clearly based upon what she viewed as her past failure in keeping her sister alive. What would she have been like if that event had not occurred?

That was one of those philosophical questions that needed far more thought than he planned to give. Having no further interest in the museum, he started toward the exit himself. As he stepped onto the sidewalk outside, the Mabry coach passed by, the Lady in question clearly in a lively conversation with her sister. As the conveyance turned the corner, he strode in the opposite direction toward his own coach, carefully dodging other walkers. It wasn't until he'd entered its comfortable interior that he remembered his purpose for braving the throngs of London civilians in the first place. A purpose he'd completely forgotten.

He leaned his back against the cushioned seat and contemplated his next steps, for steps they would be and in his own ballroom. For some reason, when he was with Lady Joanna, their conversations centered around their environment. If they continued along that path then his ballroom, a place where men and women decided upon their lifelong mates, should be the perfect place to bring up the topic of what women's primary purpose should be and how a pleasant bedroom led to a pleasant society. Next time, he would not allow her to lead him astray as it were.

CHAPTER TWELVE

J OANNA SQUEEZED TEDDY's hand. "That's enough."

Teddy finished their turn and stopped, his smile wide. "The man who invented this dance really should be awarded a medal."

Elsbeth clapped her hands. "I think I understand the turn now."

From where Joanna stood, Northwick in his brown pantaloons, white shirt, and paisley waistcoat looked ready to battle Napoleon, not like he was ready to try to waltz again. She walked over to him. "What part of the dance has you confused?"

He shook his head. "The dance is logical in its four-step pattern. It is not confusing." He glanced over at Teddy, who had started moving Elsbeth across the floor to the music Lady Astor stroked on the pianoforte.

"Then what is it?" His demeanor had changed considerably the moment they had started to learn the turns, and she found it rather puzzling.

"It's nothing. Let us try it again." He stepped closer and wrapped his right arm around her waist. His height made the space between them acceptable until he lifted his left arm above his head.

"Remember to curve your left arm, otherwise your shorter partners won't be able to reach it." She lifted her left hand up to prove her point.

His lips quirked. "But if you were closer…" His arm around her waist pulled her toward him. "Then you could reach." His upper hand clasped hers.

The position had her breasts actually touching his waistcoat and her gaze centered on his neck for to raise her head would cause her chest to be crushed. She could practically feel his heartbeat. It was bad enough that the scent he wore seemed to entice her senses, but in this proximity, her skin began to tingle. Forcibly, she yanked his hand down and pushed back against his arm. She might as well have attempted to hold up London Bridge. "Your Grace, you need to allow light between the partners, or it makes movement difficult."

"Truly?"

Something in his tone had her glancing upward. His eyes were closed, his lips slightly raised as if he were having a pleasant dream. She couldn't imagine why he'd think they could move—a drawing in *The Illustrated Pleasures of Seduction* appeared in her head and heat filled her body. Their position might not be exactly the same, but it was close enough for her to feel both titillated and uncomfortable. She dropped her arm from about his waist and pushed against his ribs.

He stepped back immediately. "I can see I need more practice with this."

Since his brows were lowered once again, she had to find fault with herself for imagining there was more to his hold than he'd intended. "Just be patient. Once you get used to the position and steps, it seems easy."

"Come, cousin." Elsbeth grinned as she and Teddy twirled around them. "If I can conquer the turn, I know you can."

The duke didn't appear to share her confidence. "It is always harder to lead than to follow."

She laughed. "You are far too serious. Dancing is to be enjoyed just as much as reading." She moved her gaze to Teddy. "It's also rather energetic. I would like to see exactly how cool it has become outside."

Teddy stopped their movement and in one move had tucked her hand in the crook of his arm. "The sun has broken through, so let us investigate."

As the two headed for the closest set of French doors leading into the gardens of Haven House, Lady Astor stopped playing. "Not without a chaperone."

Teddy halted. "But of course." He held out his other arm. "It wouldn't be half as pleasant without you with us."

Lady Astor didn't fall for Teddy's charms. "An excellent reply."

Joanna covered her mouth to keep from laughing out loud. Lady Astor's ability to know Teddy's thoughts had been a hurdle for him as he'd confided, but he was all the more up for the challenge.

Once the three had strolled out of doors, she turned toward Northwick to remark on what a delight his aunt was, but her words died on her lips at his gaze. If she didn't know any better, she'd think he'd been studying her and found that she passed muster. His blues eyes seemed to appreciate and admire, but in a puzzled fashion.

Since her "chaperone for propriety's sake," her father, was well ensconced in Northwick's library, she didn't want him to conclude anything about her either flattering or otherwise. She was simply here to teach him to waltz. "Would you also like to rest?"

"No." The word was pronounced with the utmost certainty.

"Very well. Then as I was explaining, your position will need to be adjusted based upon the height of your partner. As you saw, Lady Elsbeth and Teddy are close in height, and so it is easy for them. But you are quite tall and even Lady Caroline will need you to bend your arm much more so that there is space between you to allow for movement."

He stepped up to her again and his arm curved around her waist.

She in turned laid her hand around his back and lifted her arm over her head to a comfortable spot. "Now lift your arm and curve it to grasp my hand."

He did as she bade him.

"How does that feel?"

He grimaced. "Awkward."

"Tsk, tsk. These are the machinations you must complete to impress the ladies. For Lady Caroline, you won't have to curve it quite that much as she is a bit taller than I am."

"She is?" He'd raised his brows as if surprised by that fact.

She wanted to roll her eyes, but she refrained. "Yes, she is, and as one of her suitors, you should know this."

"She has other men interested in her hand?"

Until this point, she had considered James Huntington, Duke of Northwick to be a very intelligent man, but in matters of the heart and the *ton,* he appeared to be sorely lacking any kind of knowledge. "Of course she does. I have heard that she's already turned down two earls and a viscount. Though to be fair, one of those earls was old enough to be her father."

The doubt that flitted across his face had her hastening to add encouragement. "But you are a duke, who is well established, and more importantly, she does seem to find favor in your looks."

Now his lips moved into a smirk. "That one item you think is of no consequence."

She shrugged the best she could considering one of her hands was above her head and the other around his waist, which recalled her to their purpose. "I don't think the ability to dance the waltz is of particular concern in a mate and yet here I am helping you."

"Yes, you are. So tell me truthfully because I do know that you can be truthful. Do you think my appearance acceptable for someone like Lady Caroline?"

Could the arrogant, self-assured man in front of her really not know he was remarkably handsome? She studied his face for any kind of subterfuge, but saw none. "Your appearance is more than acceptable. I'm sure many more ladies in addition to Lady

Caroline would think you well put together."

He chuckled. "Well put together?"

"Yes." She warmed to her subject. "Aristotle said that beauty was about symmetry. Your eyes are equally spaced about your nose, which is straight. I'm sure we could measure and find it was a certain degree that Aristotle would consider appropriate. Your mouth is centered below said nose. Your cheekbones likewise are well spaced and even the jut of your chin lines up perfectly with the center of your forehead. I also believe that Aristotle would approve of your sky-blue eyes contrasting with your dark hair."

At first, he didn't say anything, then he broke into a laugh, his arm about her waist tightening, pressing her once again to his chest. "Lady Joanna, I don't believe there is anyone else like you."

Having been caught off guard by his movement, she found herself looking into happy smiling eyes. It was such an unusual visage that he took her breath away. Luckily, he set her back and grasped her hand tighter. "Very well, since my appearance is well put together according to Aristotle. It's time I finish learning these last steps of the waltz."

She didn't say anything, still surprised by how much she enjoyed looking into his eyes when he smiled. Instead, she nodded.

The next ten minutes had her complete focus on instructing Northwick. He wasn't awkward, nor did he stumble, but he hesitated, losing the beat in his effort to place his foot in the right spot. Nothing was natural. Looking up at him, she realized what was wrong. "Stop."

He did so immediately and stepped back. "It's not right. I know my steps are right, and my arms are right. Could it be the lack of music?"

She shook her head. "That's not it. You are so focused on the steps that you're missing the joy."

"I'm not sure I understand." His lips quirked up. "Will you give me another lesson, perhaps one on joy?"

She grinned. "I'm sure you are well aware that Socrates had

much to say on the subject, but no, I will not give a lesson on joy. What I want you to do is look at me when we dance. It will force your mind to think about two tasks at once, and I believe your natural grace will emerge."

"You think I have natural grace?"

The man couldn't hide his own smile. She was tempted to hit him on the arm like she did Teddy. Wouldn't he be surprised by that? "Oh, don't try to tell me not a single lady in your country life who danced with you ever remarked on your fluidity of movement."

He opened his mouth to reply.

"Liar." She laughed at his stunned expression.

"I was just going to admit that you were correct in your surmisal, but if you insist that I am lying then you must be incorrect." He tried to hold his stern look, but it lasted a mere second before he chuckled.

"As I thought." She pointed her finger at him. "Now stop asking for compliments and let us see if we can't get that legendary gracefulness back."

"Yes, your majesty." Though his words were mocking, the laughter in his eyes belied their meaning. "I am at your service."

"I'm quite sure I'm the one in service here. Now come." She waved him to her.

Without hesitation, he wrapped his arm around her waist yet again and took her hand above her head, but not too high, leaving space for them to move.

She counted. "And one two three, one two three." As they moved to her beat, she stopped counting. "Now look at me and focus."

As he lowered his gaze to hers, there was a slight catch in his steps, but then what she hoped would happen did. They began gliding around the room, flowing as one. She beamed at his success, beyond pleased that she'd been a part of it.

He laughed aloud even as he traversed the large room, his blue gaze alight with pleasure. "I see now why the waltz is so popular. It is like throwing away all of life's woes and sharing a moment of…of joy." His smile was wide as he gazed down at her.

Before she realized it, he had slowed their pace until they came to stop on the far side of the room.

"Joanna, thank you." He pulled her closer and kissed her forehead.

His actions sent a thrill into her chest. She titled her head. "I am happy you feel confident now. See how well a man and woman can get on together if they both have learned the same information?" She'd hoped with her change of subject, he would release her, but he didn't. In fact, he held her closer.

"There are many activities men and women do together because they have the same information." His gaze became almost predatory as it roamed over her face and neck.

The illustrations from her pilfered book popped into her mind, and she understood what he implied. Heat suffused her cheeks as she desperately tried to force her mind to focus. "Why yes, I'm aware of that." She looked past him, avoiding the eye contact the book had discussed. As Shakespeare had written, the eyes were the windows to the soul. She was not about to bare her soul to him, no matter how flustered she felt. "For instance, there is shopping, eating, attending the theater, and riding."

She felt his back muscles stiffen and his breath on her cheek whooshed by.

"Do you enjoy riding?"

The silkiness of his voice had her body responding in most inappropriate ways. Unfortunately, because of how far she'd read in his book, she knew exactly why. She also recognized his reference to riding as a position in mating, though she hadn't seen that particular illustration yet. For that she was grateful. She dropped her arm from around his waist and tried to lower her other one, but he held tight.

With her heart beating a staccato in her chest, she found it difficult to take deep enough breaths, and the air she took in was scented of him. With brutal force, she made her mind focus. "I have to admit I would rather travel by boat as opposed to riding. It's so much more comfortable. Don't you think?"

"Boat?"

She grinned, thankful she read nothing about boats in the purloined book. "Yes. Granted, I've only been on small ones on lakes and those types of waters, but the feeling of floating was quite pleasant." She moved her gaze to his. "I believe you can lower your hand now unless you planned to practice the turns some more. If so, I suggest we try it with the music when Lady Astor returns."

As if he'd forgotten they'd been standing chest to chest, he dropped her hand and stepped back quickly. "No, I believe I have it now."

"Excellent." She pulled her gloves up, keeping her focus on them and not him. "I admit, I was rather curious as to how they stay afloat and even took a few lessons in rowing." She finally met his confused gaze. "I have quite a knack for that."

"For what?"

"For rowing." She waved her hand. "Of course, I only did it for a short while, but it did intrigue me, and I set to reading all about rowers from history to present day. It's not only an art, but quite an exercise." She was rambling a bit, but as long as the subjects were not covered in *the book*, she would go where her thoughts took her, and hopefully him.

He leaned his shoulder against one of the half-pillars that jutted out on the wall and crossed his arms. "Rowing is far more than quite an exercise. It's hard labor. Definitely not something a lady should undertake on anything besides a calm pond."

Based on her sore arms the next day, she silently agreed. "Of course, that is just an example of women and men sharing at task." She warmed to her favorite subject. "Can you imagine how pleasant it would be for those in the aristocracy to be able to equally share the responsibilities of life?"

He opened his mouth, but she shook her head at him and started pacing, her yellow dress swishing each time she turned.

"While I admit that not many of my female peers share my interest in the many subjects usually regulated to the hallowed halls of Oxford and Cambridge, I do believe they should at least be allowed to pursue such interests when they arise. If my father had thought as you do, I'm afraid my family would be living in a cottage in Bedford with no servants." She stopped to see how he digested that piece of information.

He remained there, coolly watching her. "You will have to explain your logic on that."

"Of course." She resumed pacing. "As you know, I have quite a skill with numbers."

"I did not know this. You said you enjoyed them, though I still find that rather odd."

She grinned. "I stand corrected. Enjoying something and doing well at it is not the same thing. In my case, however, it is. I not only enjoy the logic of numbers, but I am very, very good with them. So that being said, I will explain the situation our family found ourselves in, and if it wasn't for the women, you would not know us today."

"I'm still deciding if that is a positive."

"What?" She halted again, but at the sly smile on his face, she relaxed. "How could you not be happy to have made our acquaintance? I'm positive that we provide you with a type of entertainment you have never encountered."

He gave his signature nod. "I can agree with that."

"Good." She resumed pacing. "My father is like you. He does not care for digits and so had hired a man to handle our financial affairs. Of course, Father reviewed the ledgers and was involved in the investment decisions, but…" She paused, not wanting her story to reflect poorly on the man who had taught her so much. "But he was easily distracted. As the numbers were not of interest to him, he found it difficult to concentrate, and thinking he'd hired a well-learned man in that area, did not apply himself perhaps as he should."

Northwick dropped his arms. "Was the man he hired not as

skilled as he portrayed or was he unscrupulous?"

"The latter. Father was confused when he received a missive from his tailor about a bill that had gone unpaid. He tried to review the ledger, but eventually gave up and asked for my assistance. To this day I'm thankful for that tailor. My father's man had been moving money out of our investments and into his own. We were close to losing everything."

"The devil take him." The curse from Northwick had her turning back in her stride. His brows were lowered and it looked like he was about to throttle someone.

It warmed her heart that he already appreciated her father enough that he could be angry at what had happened. "I sincerely hope that is what occurred, but we don't know. As soon as I figured out what was happening, I had Father remove him from all our business and add me to it." She grimaced. "That was no easy task. The first few balked so much that my father stopped giving my name as Joanna and just put down Jo. That helped tremendously, which in my opinion is ridiculous."

"Jo?" He ruminated for a moment. "Yes, it fits you somehow. And I can see your point."

Had she scored yet another victory in her favor? Excited now that he was truly listening, she continued. "But the damage was done. There was so little in the investments that to recoup the money would take longer than my father would be alive. That's when Mariel came to our aid."

"I did not know that the Lady Mariel had your talent as well."

She shook her head. "Oh no, her talents are far different from mine as are Amelia's. However, what Mariel did provide was a personal sacrifice. You see, the man she had planned to wed, was killed in battle against Napoleon. Since she no longer could have the man she loved, she immediately set out to marry a wealthy man who would offer us a stipend. My parents tried to dissuade her, but she was adamant."

"I must conclude she was successful because you introduced her as Lady Beaumont."

She stopped pacing, her heart squeezing at her sister's sacrifice. "Yes, she married George Walford, Earl of Beaumont. He was older than my father, but desperate for an heir. The marriage was more of a business transaction."

"They always are."

"Yes, well this was a document the size of *The Canterbury Tales*. Myself, through my father and our new solicitor negotiated well for Mariel. In the end, she was widowed two years after her marriage. Part of the settlement was that all financial assets would go to her in the event of her husband's death, with the estate and lands kept in trust for any children. If no children survived birth, then the rest went to a distant cousin in Scotland."

He strode toward the double doors that led to the gardens. "And so your family's wealth was restored. What Lady Mariel did is what many a young maiden does for her family. There is no knowledge beyond loyalty needed."

Sometimes, he could be so incredibly ducal. Fisting her hands, she spoke to his back. "That may be true for families who do not care about the feelings of their children, but that is not our way."

He looked at her from over his shoulder. "Yours is an unusual family. The norm is to ignore the feelings of the children." He turned back to continue his perusal of his gardens.

She took exception to his statement, but two things were true. Her family was unusual, and she was absolutely certain he spoke from experience. For the first time, she wondered at how he'd grown up. With his mother leaving him, it must have been difficult. As an only son, his father most likely expected great success from his heir.

Shaking away her thoughts on his past, she refocused on her point. "While Mariel did keep us from having to give up the life we were used to, it was my stewardship of our investments that has put us back in a position of comfortable wealth."

He turned at that. "You? You said you had a new solicitor."

She nodded. "We do. However, I continue to control the

ledger and all investments. I am the one who has the skills, so why not me? Because I am a woman? Can you not see how women could bring their own expertise to aid in making a comfortable life?"

He strode purposefully to her. "But many women, as you stated, have no interest in such subjects."

Something in his gaze told her she may be persuading him. Now her heart raced for an entirely different reason. "True, and for them life is just as they would like it. But there are others in the aristocracy, younger women, who long for subjects beyond what they are taught."

His skeptical façade returned. "And you know this how?"

Too excited to be deterred, she smiled. "I've spoken to them, at length. At dinner parties, balls, in theaters, even while shopping. It's all in whispers for the fear of being labeled a bluestocking, but their young minds are thirsty for math, science, literature, philosophy, and Latin."

He raised his brows. "Latin?"

She chuckled. "Very well, that was mine. But with all the other subjects I have had conversations with them. Did you not see how many young women were at the lecture on coal lamps or at the mechanical museum? They are hungry for topics not provided to them."

He was smiling now. "Did you talk to these women just to be able to prove your point to someone?"

"No, the conversations were unexpected. While many women my age shun me for not wanting to be considered a compatriot, the younger women searched me out, though with the utmost caution. I was elated I wasn't the only one. It was they that made me realize we need to expand the education of women." She found herself out of breath, too excited at the prospect that she may have finally reached him, but she needed him to know one more fact. "Even Lady Elsbeth sought me out apurpose."

"Elsbeth? What topic could she possibly talk to you about

when she has the full use of my library?"

She smiled. "It appears your library is lacking in the area of geology."

"Geology? I didn't know she wished to learn about rock." He held his chin in his hand, contemplating her information.

She didn't want to interrupt, hoping he would admit her argument was sound, yet fearful he'd find fault with yet another aspect and dismiss her argument. If she were honest, his acceptance meant more to her than anything she'd yet done in her life. If the Duke of Northwick agreed, it would validate her beliefs, something that meant more to her than she realized. When had her father's agreement stopped being enough?

He dropped his hand. A slow smile lifted the corners of his mouth. "Your argument has merit. I didn't see it originally, but you have empirical facts. Granted they are few, but they are a start."

Joy rifled through her like nothing she'd ever felt. She should be stoic and accepting, but that wasn't her. She spun in circles, her arms thrown wide. "Yes!"

He chuckled. "You're going to make yourself dizzy."

"I don't care." She continued to spin, her triumph too great to shorten the celebration.

"You're going to make *me* dizzy." His good humor came through in his voice. He was such a good sport at losing.

Finally, out of breath, she stopped, only to have the room tilt precariously. As she lost her balance, he caught her to him.

"Look at me and don't stop until the room ceases to spin."

For once, she was happy to obey him. He really did have a very handsome face. Aristotle would be pleased. He seemed even handsomer now that he agreed with her. She was sorely tempted to kiss him, like one of the illustrations in *the book* had shown. She licked her lips.

His gaze moved to her mouth and his pupils dilated. He really did have the most beautiful sky-blue eyes. His head lowered.

Unable to think, she watched his lips come closer and the

feeling of anticipation inside her built. Without conscious thought, she licked her lips again.

He blinked and pulled back. "How are you feeling now?"

Oddly disappointed, she answered. "Winded, but I think my balance has returned."

He slowly set her back.

She stumbled a bit, and he grabbed her shoulders. "Maybe you should sit down." He scanned the area around them. "Come." He guided her as if they were in a dance, one hand holding hers, the other behind her and resting on her shoulder.

When they reached the outside doors, he let go of her hand and opened them. There was no furniture outside, but he led her down a few steps, and she sank down onto the top one. "Thank you." The air was crisp like autumn, though it was the middle of April. Still, it felt good on her heated skin. She took a few deep breaths, her stomach now starting to scold her. She placed her hand on her abdomen. She absolutely refused to be sick in front of him.

"Shall I send for water?" His concern was genuine.

She looked up, but the light was behind him, and it made her stomach queasier. "No, if you could just sit?"

He turned and seated himself next to her. "The cooler air should help."

That's what she was hoping. How silly to have spun so long. She knew better. She was just so bloody happy. Even with her stomach still rolling over, her lips quirked. She would tell her father as soon as they were alone, and then she would tell...no one else. While her family supported her ideas, except for her father, none of them would truly understand the significance of having convinced Northwick. A bit of the joy seeped away, but she stubbornly held onto the rest.

CHAPTER THIRTEEN

J AMES KEPT HIS gaze on Joanna, fearing she may give up her afternoon meal. One moment she sounded so mature and wise and the next she was spinning like a child. He'd never encountered a woman like her. There was something very natural about her that appealed to him beyond her intelligence. Maybe it appealed too much. He frowned at how close he'd come to kissing her. That would be highly inappropriate. But even as he scolded himself for his behavior, his body reminded him of how enjoyable it had been to pull her close.

He shook his head to get rid of his lustful thoughts. Joanna was far from the wife he sought. Not that he didn't think her capable, just not conventional enough. He simply enjoyed debating with her. She didn't prattle on about parties and fashion, and heaven forbid the weather. He looked up at the gathering clouds. Though that topic this summer did seem to warrant some attention.

She moved her hand from her stomach and laid it on the step next to her.

Hopefully, that was a good sign. "Better?"

She nodded, though she was still taking slow deep breaths, her gaze on the top of the fountain directly down the path in front of them. She pointed at it. "Is that a gargoyle or a very poor rendition of a baby cupid?"

He turned to look, and a half-dozen or so birds that had been sitting beside it and on it suddenly took flight.

"Oh, it's a cupid, and not a bad one at all."

He grinned, now that he saw how she could have thought it a gargoyle, though why she'd think a gargoyle would be on a garden fountain was a question he wouldn't ask. "Yes, it is. It wouldn't have been my choice, but it wasn't one of my priorities for changes when I inherited my title."

She turned her head to look at him. "Cupid is perfectly acceptable. What would you have wanted, Poseidon?" Her lips quirked up as if she were ready to laugh at his answer.

It seemed as if she was always ready to find the mirth in a situation or the opposing view. How contradictory. "No, if I had to choose among the ancient gods, I'd choose Athena, goddess of wisdom."

"A female deity?" She raised her brows. "I think she would have been a bit too large for that fountain."

He smiled. "You're right. In that case, I'd choose Medusa's head."

Her round eyes widened. "Oh, whyever for?"

"When I was a boy, I was fascinated by snakes." He couldn't take his eyes off her, anticipating her reaction.

She rolled her eyes. "That says quite a bit about you. I could see you staring at someone until they turned to stone."

He slapped his hand to his chest. "I? I am anything but intimidating."

"Must I remind you of your dinner party and your dominance of all the men there?"

He smirked, dropping his hand. "Point made."

She waved toward the fountain. "And what if the statue didn't have to be an ancient god of old. What would you choose?"

Now that wasn't something he'd pondered before. He sat in thought for quite a long time, staring at the fountain. Unlike other women he knew, she did not feel a need to fill the silence.

Finally, the answer presented itself. "I think a swan." He turned to look at her. "Of course, this one wouldn't be very realistic as the fish spouting the water around the edge of the basin are far too big for a swan to eat."

She laughed. "Yes, it would have to be a giant swan. I was thinking a heron myself. Those are very large fish."

"Very practical." He very much enjoyed the paths her mind brought them down. "Would you like to try to stand again?"

She nodded.

Rising, he offered his hand. She took it and stood, not moving right away. "I do think my equilibrium is stable now." She let go of his hand. "Yes, I'm fine now, thank you."

"Would you like to inspect the fountain any further?"

She shook her head and turned toward the glass doors. "No, thank you. I'm starting to feel cold."

Though she wore no ball gown, her bright day dress couldn't be warm and the clouds had shut out the brief interlude of sun. "Of course. You have no shawl today, like the night we met."

At his words, she almost tripped, and he grasped her arm. He stifled his shout of triumph. He hadn't meant to reflect on that night, but her reaction was all the evidence he needed. The shawl must have been her excuse for being at her coach where she must have hidden his book. It was the logical thing to do. He barely refrained from smiling. Her trip meant she may be suffering a guilty conscience. There was only one reason for her to feel guilty from his perspective. She was his thief.

He opened the door for her. "Maybe I should send for tea."

She nodded, but didn't speak. To him, that was more evidence against her. Once inside again, he tucked her hand in his arm and walked her toward the pianoforte where a set of settees and chairs were set up for recitals. He deposited her on a settee. Then he opened the inside doors to the ballroom and gave directions to Harrison.

When he turned back to rejoin her, he found her watching him.

"I feel accomplished for the day. Not only have I convinced you, a duke, of the need for access to a wider education for women of my peer group, but I also taught you to waltz."

He stopped at the chair opposite her. "I admit to being surprised at how easy it was for you on the first and how difficult for me on the second."

"You think convincing you of my argument was easy? I would not care to debate with you then when you decided to be stubborn."

He chuckled as he sat in the chair and crossed his ankle over his knee. "I had Harrison send tea to your father as well. I expected him to search us out by now."

She shook her head. "If you keep feeding him, he won't emerge from your library for at least eight more years."

He gave her a soft smile, pleased at her father's almost worshipful view of his library. "I enjoy allowing others to share in my collection when they can truly appreciate it."

She clasped her hands in front of her. "You don't know what a boon it is to him to be able to wander your library and read to his heart's content. I can't thank you enough for allowing him the privilege. The moment he heard that Teddy and I were coming to Haven House, he made it a stipulation that he join us." She paused. "It means much to me as well. Books are his bliss."

He tapped his fingers on his knee and shifted his gaze to a point beyond her. That she enjoyed his collection as well was obvious, especially since she'd absconded with his book. It had been clear to him from the start that she felt free to pursue her varied interests, which meant he may have missed a flaw in her argument.

He moved his gaze back to her. "If as you say, some women of our set wish to study subjects normally left to the male domain, why do they simply not do so?"

"That is a legitimate question." She paused. "It is my belief that there are a number of reasons, first and foremost their mothers. Mothers can be rather domineering when it comes to what their daughters should know. From the day of their female child's birth, they are planning what to teach her so she can make a good match and be a fine wife."

He raised his brow. "I find that difficult to believe. I'm sure my aunt thought of other topics besides making my cousin marriageable."

She shook her head. "I suggest you ask her when she comes in."

Surely, a female child being born meant more to the mother than that. "I will. But I will concede in the meantime for argument's sake. Are there not other ways to search out the knowledge these young women wish to learn? You said yourself that they were at the lecture and the museum, which must mean their mothers do not mind their experience with additional subjects."

She laughed, but he scowled, and she sobered her countenance to an indulgent smile. "I forget that you are not used to Town life and then you reveal your ignorance of it."

As much as he was loath to admit it, he was rather unfamiliar with the norms of society beyond country life. He had not deemed that a shortcoming until now. "I cannot know all, so enlighten me."

"These young ladies do not tell their mothers they are interested in the mechanics of safe coal lamps. They tell their mothers that a very handsome and eligible peer is lecturing at the Royal Institution, and it would be a great opportunity to be acquainted since so few other women will be there."

"Are you saying they use the lecturer's marital status as a ruse for attending?" He hadn't thought women quite that devious.

She nodded. "They do. And if you might have noticed, there were no older ladies there. The mothers choose to send their daughters with their father, who would have much more interest in such things."

"The devil you say." He grasped his ankle and leaned forward. "The subterfuge is ridiculous." There were far deeper undercurrents beneath the *ton* than he'd ever suspected.

"Yes, but necessary if those who are determined to learn more want to gain the opportunity. Those who are interested but cowed by their mothers, who to be fair are simply complying with rules set by our society for generations, go without." She held both hands out, palms up and dropped them in her lap.

He narrowed his gaze. "Then how did you manage to acquire so much knowledge. I had classmates at Oxford that weren't as well-read as you."

A light blush filled her cheeks. "I was quite a disappointment to my mother, but I was fortunate in that she loved me anyway. That and my father took up my cause simply because he enjoyed teaching me."

That made sense. She did come from a rather odd family life. He began to tap on his knee again. "What do you plan to do then?"

Her brow furrowed. "Do? About what?"

He stopped tapping his fingers and waved his hand. "About the fact that some of your peers wish for learning that goes far beyond what they have access to now?"

"I don't think I understand." Her head cocked as she stared intently at him.

He rose to lean against the pianoforte. "If ladies learning more than simply how to play the pianoforte," he laid his hand on it, "paint," he then pointed to a picture on the wall behind the instrument, "and speak française, then something must be done, *n'est-ce pas*? Surely, your end goal is not to simply talk about such a crucial societal issue?"

The footman entered at that moment with the tea service.

He allowed Joanna to contemplate his question as she poured. His instinct was telling him that convincing others was as far as she'd thought. To be fair, he could understand why. He was far more opened minded and better read than a majority of his peers. He tried to picture Joanna convincing any of his acquaint-ances that she had a point. He couldn't imagine a single one listening to her, never mind agreeing with her. That conclusion bothered him more than he was willing to admit.

Joanna lifted the cream to him, and he shook his head. After taking his cup from her, he waited to drink, too eager for her answer to be distracted.

After taking a sip, she set down her cup. "I wonder where Teddy, Lady Elsbeth, and Lady Astor have gone off to? They have been gone quite some time. It's growing quite dark."

Disappointed that she changed the subject, he shrugged. "I have no doubt my aunt has herded them into one of the other rooms off the garden and is even now having tea served."

She took a sip from her cup. "What would you do?"

He recognized the rhetorical trick as one he'd used when a debate wasn't going well. He raised his brows. "Me? I'm hardly qualified to do anything. I'm a gentleman."

Her hopeful countenance fell and her shoulders slumped. "There isn't much I can do alone."

Just like at the mechanical museum, her sudden capitulation bothered him. "Now, that I don't believe. If you could wear me down and bring me round to your view point, there is much you could do." He contemplated her, trying to guess what she thought. "If there were no impediments in your way, what would you do?"

She squinched up her face as if he'd just asked her to eat snake. "That's very difficult to imagine."

"Try."

He expected her to get up and start pacing again, but she surprised him. Instead, she closed her eyes. He couldn't resist the opportunity to gaze at her while her bright hazel eyes weren't actively watching him. She always gave him the impression of endless energy, but now, there was a softness about her face and a peaceful sense about her. Her lips were neither pursed nor open, but simply closed as if in sweet repose. As for whether Aristotle would approve, he much doubted it. One cheek bone was slightly higher, one eyebrow slightly longer, and her left ear was slightly smaller than her right one. Yet, he found her visage very appealing. That she could make him question Aristotle was something he wouldn't let her know.

Even as he admired the dark curl that rested on her collarbone, he noticed the pulse at her throat increasing. Suddenly, her eyes snapped open practically glittering with excitement. "I could start a school for ladies of the peerage."

Taken aback, he widened his eyes. It was bold, but brilliant. He let a slow smile spread his lips as he gazed at her in admiration. "That is a worthy goal."

"It is!" Her excitement faded as quickly as it rose. "Creating a school would be a dream, but we do not live in dreams." Her shoulders slumped. "I don't see how I could make it happen."

He dropped his leg and leaned forward. "Is that what Lord Davy thought when he discovered miners were dying with the coal lamps they were using?"

"That's not fair. He's a man. Can you give me one good example when a woman was able to do something innovative and succeed?"

He opened his mouth then closed it. He searched his memory of the women who had made it into his books on scientific topics. "What about Caroline Herschel?"

"The astronomer?" She looked away as she thought then returned her gaze to him. "Granted she identified new comets, but that's hardly innovative. If that's all we can think of, I'm doomed to failure."

He didn't want her to give up so easily. He stood then walked to the open doors of the ballroom and back, his hands clasped behind his back. There had to be a woman who had been innovative in a way that helped mankind progress. He discarded one name after another. Twice more he made his path when it came to him. He stopped and met her hopeful gaze. "Eleanor Coade. She invented the new stone composite that is in almost every new statute and column in London." He preened at having found the perfect example.

Unfortunately, she didn't share his enthusiasm. "That *is* innovative, I will admit that. But it hardly challenges old societal beliefs and values. Unless the fact that she is a woman in a building trade is unique, which it might be, but her stone doesn't shake the foundations on which the trade is based." She sighed, obviously giving up before they'd exhausted all possibilities.

He put one hand on his hip. "You did not indicate that as part of the parameters. With this new information I must think again."

She shook her head. "It's a waste of time. There are none. It was a hopeful request, nothing more."

He came to stand next to the chair he'd been sitting in and laid his hand on its back. "There always has to be someone who is first. Did not your favorite author, Mrs. Wollstonecraft, set up a school for women who needed skills. It may not have been for ladies, but it was new and innovative and went against social norms."

"That's true, and it did challenge societal beliefs about women and what they needed to know." She cocked her head and raised her gaze to his. "That is actually a very good example."

He raised his chin. "I know."

She rolled her eyes. "Cockiness does not become you."

"I'm not being cocky. I'm being truthful." He kept his pose, determined to look triumphant.

She laughed.

His lip quirked but he kept his face serious. "And don't forget Lady Mary Wortley Montagu who convinced Princess Caroline to inoculate her children for small pox."

She raised her hand. "Stop." She tried to get a hold of her laughter by not looking at him, but she still chuckled. "I agree with your points. There have been women who have innovated against societal norms."

Happy to see her smiling again, he relaxed his ridiculous pose. "Good. So there is no reason why you can't open a school for ladies of the peerage that is far more than simply the subjects regulated currently to women." The idea had merit and he found himself thinking about all it could entail.

She picked up her teacup and swallowed more tea, her gaze flitting from right to left and back.

"What are you thinking?" He was anxious to hear the many ideas that were obviously running through her sharp mind.

She set down her cup. "I could use my aunt's estate that she left me. It is in the country, but no women would want to attend during the season anyway."

"Fair point. From what I've seen, there is only one goal for them during the season. Find a husband." He grimaced.

She raised her brows. "Is that not why you came, to find one of those ladies to take to wife?"

He gave her a curt nod acceding the point, but the need to play devil's advocate spurred him on. "True. But what if they wish to continue their studies during the season?"

She rose. "That's doubtful."

"But if they are not out yet or if they are already married, they may enjoy the company of like-minded individuals."

She strolled around the settee she'd sat upon and faced him, gripping the back of it. "I could set up teas at Craymore Hall and various outings to the Royal Institution for lectures."

"Or the Museum of Mechanical Curiosities?"

She nodded, her eyes glowing with excitement once again. "There are many museums, productions, and events that would have educational value."

Now he too gripped the back of his chair. "And what about at the school itself? How will you determine what to teach? Will you have required classes in each area of study? Will you allow them to study what interests them most?"

She started pacing again, this time behind the settee. "I would prefer that my students learn what they wish to learn. Perhaps I could have required sessions on each subject so they could best determine what they wished to learn more of. Is that how they do it at Oxford?"

He snorted. "Hardly."

"Really? So they prefer to teach all men all the same subjects."

He shrugged. "Generally speaking, though there is time for following one's interests."

She stopped walking. "Would you be willing to make a list of everything you studied there?"

He backed away from the chair and leaned his ass against the piano. Crossing his arms, he frowned. "I don't know. That sounds like releasing vital information to the enemy."

"What?"

He winked, his lips lifting. "I can make a list for you, but I don't guarantee I'll remember every course."

She relaxed at his teasing. "Thank you." She walked forward and took another swallow of her tea. "I will need teachers, as I'm not an expert on everything. I could use the Socratic method, but with numbers that doesn't work as well." She flopped down on the settee. "This is a significant undertaking." Her brows puckered in doubt. "There are an overwhelming number of tasks to be accomplished." She clasped her hands, studying them.

He pushed away from the pianoforte and sat down across from her. "Start small and start slow. There is no rush to change the world." He chuckled. "Not even London."

She nodded, but still appeared doubtful. "To have young minds molded by what is taught in *my* school is a momentous responsibility. What if I'm wrong. Not about the school, but in what I teach?"

He leaned back, crossing his legs and smirked. "Compared to what they know now? How much damage could you actually do?"

She snapped her head up. "This is no laughing matter."

"I'm not laughing. I'm absolutely serious." He also was absolutely confident that anything she taught would be correct, but she wasn't willing to listen to that at the moment.

"If you're so sure this school I may or may not open is the right solution to the problem I presented to you, tell me, would you allow Lady Elsbeth to attend?"

He turned his head slightly. The answer was obvious, at least to him. "I would, if she wished to attend."

She froze as if stunned by his support. It was obvious, she didn't realize her own assets. She blinked before she sat straighter, her lips forming a confident smile. "So I may have one student. I will need to recruit a few more."

Pleasantly surprised that his support meant so much to her, he was anxious to do what he could. "How many students?"

"I think six to start. It is enough to have a conversation or two without being overwhelming for all involved."

He gave a short nod of approval. "That is a good number."

"There's so much to think about. I often taught my sisters and Teddy as we were growing up, but it never occurred to me to start a school." She rose. "I think it's time for me to gather my father and return home. I have much to do."

Disappointed that she would continue planning without him, he forced himself to stand. It was, after all, her idea and her school. "Of course. Let's see if we can find Lord Wakefield." He allowed her to pass him and followed her out of the room.

She stopped at the closed double library doors and faced him. "If you don't mind, I'd like to keep this a secret until after I have the school running. I have no doubt that I can find five more young ladies interested in attending, but their mothers are another matter. I will not pretend to them that this school is like every other."

In that moment, he felt an odd pride in her. She not only had conviction, but would follow through on her idea. He'd never met anyone, male or female, who had such strength and purpose. "I believe I understand. No reason to cause an uproar and undermine the start of something new. Would you like me to approach my cousin and aunt on the matter?"

She nodded. "Thank you. Now let us see if we can find my dear father." She opened the doors and sucked in her breath. "Father!"

He followed her gaze. Lord Wakefield looked up at her voice.

He occupied James' personal desk.

The older man slapped his hand to his chest. "Do not sneak up on me like that, Joanna."

"Sneak up on you?" Her tone proved she was horrified at her father's behavior, but he was at a loss as to why.

She hurried forward. "Do you know where all of these go?" She waved to the open volumes that littered the desk's top.

"Go? I have them where I want them. Where would they go?"

Now, he understood her concern. He laid a calming hand on her warm shoulder. "It's fine. I know where they belong."

She looked askance at him. "I'm sorry. He probably just forgot where he was."

"Forget where I am? How could I possibly do that?" Wakefield waved with one hand to encompass the whole room. "This is heaven, dear daughter, and nothing less."

He held back a chuckle at the description, though he'd often thought there was something peaceful and redeeming about the room.

"Shh." Joanna ducked beneath his hand and hurried around the desk. "It's time for us to depart."

Her father's eyes grew round. "Already?"

"We've been here over three hours. We really must take our leave."

"Time just speeds by when in a good book." Her father grinned at him.

"Or seven of them." She scanned the books on the desk then quickly started closing them.

He stepped to the desk, not at all concerned. "You can leave them. No harm done."

She shook her head. "One book remaining open could mean another thirty minutes." She continued to close the books.

He looked to her father who was indeed, back to reading from the one directly in front of him. Though he found the entire scene rather comical, he had no doubt she was anxious to return home and take quill to paper with her plans.

He reached over and closed the three books on the far side of the desk.

When she had them all closed, her father's brows lowered. "I can see that no further erudition is in the making for me today." He rose, clearly irritated that his jaunt in "heaven" had so abruptly ended.

Joanna took no offense to her father's attitude. "Perhaps, but you can tell me all about what you have read on the way home."

Her father stepped past her. "I'd rather not. I'm still cogitating upon it."

He bit down on a smile as Joanna rolled her eyes. Lifting the book that had been sitting before Wakefield, he held it out to him. "Perhaps you'd like to borrow this one until I next see you?"

She sucked in her breath. "Are you sure?"

At her question, he understood her hesitancy, since she had his other book. Taking the opportunity to gauge her reaction, he phrased his response carefully. "I have no doubt that one who respects the written word so much, would not allow anything untoward befall one of my volumes."

Her cheeks flushed.

It was all the confirmation he needed. She most definitely had his book.

"Your Grace." Her father took the proffered book with a bow. "I will take the utmost care of it."

Joanna took the opportunity to walk to the other side of her father and link her arm with his. "Your Grace, thank you for allowing my father to enjoy your library."

He gave a slight bow. "Thank you for the lessons in the waltz."

She pulled her father to get him to move toward the door. "Be sure to practice. The ball is less than two weeks away." She didn't look at him, a telling sign.

He leaned his hips back against the desk and watched the unlikely pair. As she came to the open doors, she finally looked back at him over her shoulder. "Good bye, Your Grace."

"I shall send a missive on the subject we discussed."

She gave him a brief smile then ushered her father to the front doors.

He listened as she helped her father, who had already started talking about what he'd read, obviously having forgotten he'd wanted to contemplate it first. When the front doors closed, he moved to the sideboard and poured himself a drink. It had been a very revealing afternoon…in many ways.

Joanna half listened to Amelia's narration of both the positives and the negatives of the new Paris panorama as they ambled in a long lazy circle around the building. That Amelia actually had anything positive to say was a nice change.

Though she enjoyed experiencing each new panorama set up in the round building built for that purpose, it was more her mother's favorite London site. Because the owner had the Paris panoramic view painted on the larger lower floor, meant he was already at work on another slightly smaller view upstairs. But she wasn't looking at the views. She was looking for someone in particular. She had so much she wished to discuss.

"Joanna, what are you looking at?"

Amelia's change in tone caught her attention immediately. "Nothing."

"Nothing or everything." Amelia brought them to a stop, allowing their mother, Mariel, and Teddy to continue on without them. The circular building meant it wouldn't be hard to find them if they decided to leave.

She chuckled. "You know me too well. I'm watching the people who are entering the exhibit."

Amelia looked to her right where the long dark tunnel that opened upon the large circular room revealed a continuous line of people coming to see the newest panorama. "And is there someone in particular you are looking for?"

If she told the truth, it would start Amelia's mind in the wrong direction, so she chose a near truth. "Yes, as a matter of fact, I'm watching for Lady Elsbeth's entrance. I know that Teddy told her we would be here this afternoon, and he is very much looking forward to seeing her again." And she hoped James Huntington was with them so she could share her good news.

Amelia's brows lowered. "Teddy has completely focused upon that young woman, hasn't he?"

The tone with which her sister asked the question gave her pause. "Yes. Why? Do you see a problem?"

Amelia shrugged delicately. "Nothing specific. There is just something about those two together. When I see them next to each other, to me they just don't aesthetically pair well."

"Aesthetically?" She stared at her sister. "What does how they look together have to do with how they feel about each other?"

"It doesn't. It's just how I look at things." She lifted her chin to a young couple not far away. "Now they look well together." She gestured to another couple the age of their parents. "They look well together, too."

She found the whole concept intriguing. Looking about, she searched for a pair that she would think wouldn't be right together. "What about the couple standing before the view of Notre Dame?"

Amelia turned her head to find the people. "The tall slender man and full bosomed woman?"

"Yes."

"Definitely aesthetically pleasing. See how they complement each other? What one lacks, the other fills in. And the couple next to them are also aesthetically perfect but for different reasons. They are so alike as to be one." Amelia smiled, fully enjoying the search for perfect couples.

It reminded her of Plato's split-apart theory. *Love is born into every human being; it calls back the halves of our original nature together; it tries to make one out of two and heal the wound of human nature.* Could Amelia's artistic eye be in accordance with the soul's search for its other half, or were Aristotle's views of beauty in opposition to Plato's views on love? It was a question she wished to discuss. If James were around, she'd seek him out, but he wasn't. It was disappointing.

How strange that she had gone from trying to avoid him to hoping to see him. Of course, that was because they were in full agreement now. She'd hoped to tell him about her student recruitment efforts and the list of topics she'd made thanks to a lengthy conversation with her father that she'd couched in simple debate terms so as not to let on why she was so interested in what he had learned at Cambridge. She wasn't quite ready to tell her family, especially her father, who would brag to everyone he met.

Amelia squeezed her arm to get her attention. "For me, the couple before Napoleon's wooden *Arc de Triomphe* are not aesthetically pleasing."

Joanna studied them. They were of similar height and width, though the woman had blonde hair much the color of Amelia's and the gentleman's was a medium brown color. She didn't see why they wouldn't be considered aesthetically appropriate. She shook her head. "I'm afraid I do not have your eye for such things."

Amelia started them walking again. "Then I'll just have to be your guide in this area, and you can be my guide in, well, everything else."

Embarrassed, she shook her head. "There is much I am ignorant of." As she had discovered in James' library, especially after reading, or rather viewing, more of it. Even as she thought of *the book*, her cheeks grew hot.

Her sister just chuckled. "You know something about everything. I know a lot about a little. So I'd say we complement each other."

She squeezed Amelia's arm. They really did, and so did Mariel. The only area they were lacking was Belinda's. As usual, at the thought of her sister, her spirits waned.

"Now, this view of the Panthéon is very well done." Amelia stopped them before the spot on the curved wall.

It was so unusual for Amelia to compliment the painting done in a panorama that she took note. Unfortunately, she hadn't been to Paris and so could not say if it was well done or not, but she trusted her sister.

Amelia leaned in. "Do not tell, but I saw a forgery of Jean-Baptiste Hillaire's painting of the Panthéon in Lady Spencer's drawing room when I called on her last week."

Forgeries were rather common, but the question was always whether the owner knew she had a forgery or not. "Did she know?"

"No." Amelia shook her head. "She bragged about having the original."

"Whatever did you do?"

"I waited until her other callers had left and then let her know. She was shocked, of course, but angry and embarrassed. She decided to switch it out with another painting which I was able to assure her was original."

"You are such a good friend."

"I just despise it when people are sold a painting under false— what is Teddy doing?" Amelia gestured to their cousin.

Her heartbeat sped up even before she looked in Teddy's direction. Unfortunately, he ran toward the entrance where Lady Elsbeth had emerged with Lady Astor. They were followed by James and Lady Caroline, and finally Lord and Lady Holburn. "He's meeting Lady Elsbeth." The young woman was dressed in a lovely, pale pink dress and matching hat that accentuated her pale skin beautifully.

She couldn't resist asking, "What do you think of the duke and Lady Caroline?" To her they were a perfect couple, almost too perfect. He, dressed in tan pantaloons and a dark brown coat and she, dressed in a seafoam-colored dress with matching-colored leaves in her hair. If there was a couple to aspire to for young men and women, the two of them appeared to be it.

Amelia took her time answering. "I think they may be a new couple. They do not move together well. It would be unfair to judge yet."

She liked that answer. "You're right, they are a new couple, just this season. Shall we go greet them and try to keep Teddy from playing the fool?"

Amelia chuckled, but they started forward. "I do think we'll be too late for that."

She was right. At that moment, Teddy knelt before Elsbeth and had his hand to his chest. They couldn't hear what he said, but Lady Elsbeth blushed, and Lady Astor frowned. Luckily, Mariel and their mother caught up to him and Teddy rose.

"I wonder what that was about?" Amelia kept her voice low.

"I'm not sure. He needs to stop going to so many plays. He's starting to behave like an actor."

Amelia shook her head, but didn't comment further.

As they approached, James noticed them and sent a smile in her direction, but before she could say a word, Lady Astor greeted her. "Lady Joanna, I'm so pleased to see you. I have so much I wish to discuss with you."

She glanced at James to gauge whether it would be a good discussion or not, and he gave her a quick smile. Relieved, she acquiesced and walked beside the older woman. She did enjoy Lady Astor's company.

"First, I want to thank you for teaching my daughter and nephew how to waltz. They've been practicing. Elsbeth is determined that her first dance be a waltz and not the Quadrille. I agreed as the dance shows her off beautifully. She moves so gracefully that I'm sure she will have many suitors after the ball." The woman studied her, clearly looking for her reaction.

She gave her a kind smile. "It was my pleasure. I'm very pleased they have practiced as I instructed. I want Lady Elsbeth to enjoy her ball fully. I know that Teddy has fallen in love with her, but it's important that she make her own choice. I would very much like being related to you, but if she chooses elsewhere, I hope we can be friends."

Lady Astor stopped and clasped both her hands. "I appreciate you saying that because I feel the same way. Having you as family would be wonderful, but if not, friendship is definitely assured. I wasn't sure how you would feel, as I gathered from Elsbeth that your family champions your cousin in his affections?"

She squeezed Lady Astor's hand before letting go. "Yes, we do, but we would also respect Lady Elsbeth's decision and would not have any ill will toward your family."

Lady Astor took a deep breath. "That is a relief as I wished to discuss another matter."

Uncertainty filled her, making her hands moist inside her gloves. Had Lady Astor decided not to allow Elsbeth to come to her school? "Of course."

They started walking again, but Lady Astor leaned closer and lowered her voice. "I must tell you that when James told me about your proposal for a school for young ladies, at first, I was concerned. There are many available from what I understand, and to be blunt, I didn't see you as one who would be successful."

Despite the sting in her heart, she managed a short nod.

"But when he told me exactly what *type* of school it would be, I have to say I thought it a brilliant idea."

Surprised, she stopped. "You do?"

Lady Astor nodded. "I do. I wished for just such a school when I was young, but of course, there were none. There's still none. But now you...I'm so very excited."

Her chest warmed at the thought that Lady Astor supported her. "Thank you. Your endorsement means much to me. Does that mean Lady Elsbeth will attend? Is she interested?"

"She is. Though probably not as interested as I."

Confused, she cocked her head. "You want to attend?"

Lady Astor took a moment to scan the crowd around them, then she lowered her voice. "No, I wish to teach, if you would have me."

Stunned, her throat closed with emotion.

"Now, I admit that I am no good with numbers, but I have been studying philosophy for some time now. James' collection between Haven House and Burhleigh Park is quite exhaustive."

She stammered. "You…you want to teach?"

"Yes. I could instruct in philosophy and literature. I also have extensive knowledge on astronomy. Are those subjects you plan to offer?"

She nodded mutely. Her quest for teachers had yet to begin, because she'd been focused on recruiting students. And here was Lady Astor offering her services. Her heart felt so full, her eyes started to water. "It would be an honor to have you as an instructor."

Lady Astor clapped her hands together. "How wonderful. Thank you. I will, of course, keep this between us. My nephew told me you'd like to start your school before it becomes known."

She blinked rapidly to see better. "I appreciate your continued discretion in this."

"Of course." The lady waved her hand as if it meant nothing to keep a revolutionary school a secret. "I have so many questions for you. Would you mind if I called on you tomorrow?"

Joanna pressed her hand to her chest. "That would be lovely."

Lady Astor leaned in. "James and Lady Caroline approach. I'm sure you and he have much to discuss, so I will be sure to whisk the lady away for a bit."

At that, she turned to see that James did indeed approach with the poised Lady Caroline.

He smiled warmly at Lady Astor. "Dear Aunt, I do hope you are enjoying this lovely panorama of Paris and not simply bending Lady Joanna's ear."

"Actually, James, I haven't even looked at it." She smiled at Lady Caroline. "Perhaps I could impose on Lady Caroline to accompany me in studying it?"

Lady Caroline inclined her head. "I would be happy to accompany you."

Lady Astor took Caroline by the arm. "Have you ever been to Paris?"

Joanna turned her attention to James, dropping a quick curtsey.

As soon as he gave his usual short nod, he spoke. "What did you think of my aunt's offer?"

"I am humbled. I admire your aunt and to have her at my school would be an honor."

He gave her a smug smile. "Then I'm glad I suggested it to her."

"You did?" That he'd gone to so much trouble to help her made her feel twice as guilty about the book currently locked in her cabinet in the library at Craymore Hall.

"I did. I also wrote that list of subjects for you and gave it to her to add to. Did she give it to you?"

"No, but she plans to call tomorrow. You have a wonderful aunt."

He looked past her to where his aunt was pointing at the Panthéon. "She is a unique woman, much like you." He returned his gaze to hers. "When she came to live with me at Burhleigh Park, everything changed for the better."

"Was that recently?"

"No. Her husband died in a coach accident, leaving her and baby Elsbeth alone. His nephew took over the estate and my aunt decided she preferred living with me."

Her mind spun at this new information. "Elsbeth was a baby? Then you must have been not even half a score. I imagine your father was surprised by the sudden change in residence for his sister."

His face became void of all emotion. "He didn't know for months. When my aunt arrived at Burhleigh Park and discovered my father was living at his hunting estate in Scotland, she was so angry that she refused to send him a missive." He finally relaxed, his lip quirking up. "I believe it was the dressmaker's bill that finally got his attention."

She tried to piece everything together. It sounded as if James had been living alone at his home with no more than servants until his aunt arrived when he was but nine or ten. But he'd said he lost his mother at the age of seven. He'd been abandoned by both parents! A lump formed in her throat at the realization.

"When she first arrived, I refused to come out of the library." He shook his head. "I was angry and thought she would try to usurp my little kingdom. But she was patient and kind." He looked to where the lady in question stood. "She was also very calm, unlike either of my parents. She has always had that quiet confidence about her."

She swallowed hard to free her voice. "I think that's why I enjoyed her the moment I met her."

He returned his attention to her. "Have you made any progress on your plans?"

"I have." She gave him a wide smile. "I have recruited all my students."

His eyes widened. "That was quite quick. Did their mothers approve?"

"That was much more difficult. I would have had eight, but two mothers wouldn't be swayed. My reputation is not the best with the parents." She held up her hand as he opened his mouth to speak. "Not in that way. Just by the fact I've been out for four seasons and still have yet to marry." She shook her head. "They don't realize I have no plans to marry, so I distract them with a compliment about their daughter."

His brows raised. "You sound like a worthy negotiator. Perhaps I should have you talk to my neighbor in Peterborough about selling his duck pond to me."

Now that could be fun. "I am at your disposal."

His laugh drew a few stares, but he didn't seem to notice. She liked that he wasn't overly concerned by the opinions of his peers. Then again, he was a duke and a man, so there wasn't much effect a poor opinion could have on him.

She continued with her accomplishments to date. "I've also

alerted the staff at Silver Meadows that I will be in residence this winter with six guests, though now with your aunt, it will be seven."

"Don't forget you may also need more teachers."

She held out her hand and counted on her fingers. "First, I need to settle on my list of required courses. Second, I need to determine who to teach them. Third, I need to plan on activities that apply the knowledge. Fourth, I need to set up a schedule for physical activities. Fifth, I'll need to determine when the women can go home for the holidays and return. Sixth, I'll need to—"

His large hand enfolding hers startled her. "You are becoming agitated. I suggest a list of items that need tending to be done in a more private place where you can pace."

She took a deep breath. She had started to become anxious at the tasks to be accomplished, now that she had students and a teacher. How had he known? She dropped her hand, and he let go. "You are correct. This is not the place, but I do appreciate discussing it with you. It helps me to think out loud, but I definitely do not want my family to know yet." She sighed. "I guess I'll chat with your aunt about it on the morrow. Mother is making calls with Mariel, and Amelia is always painting at that time of day."

He lifted his chin. "Have you thought about when you will allow others to know?"

"No." She grinned. "But I'll add it to my list."

His blue gaze twinkled with humor. "I believe you may need a list of your lists fairly soon."

"And I believe that you just like giving me more things to do."

He shrugged, but the mirth remained in his eyes. "True."

She laughed. Being able to speak freely after the last few days of listening to her own thoughts was a relief and a pleasure.

A bump against her shoulder had her turning to find Teddy, who raised one eyebrow. "What are you laughing at? Is it a painting flaw Amelia pointed out?"

He had Lady Elsbeth on his arm, who seemed perfectly happy to be there. She hoped that their affection would continue. She liked all the Huntingtons now, which was quite a revelation. "I was laughing at a list of tasks Lord Northwick would like me to accomplish, but I think I will be the captain of my own ship."

Teddy smirked. "I'm surprised he'd even attempt any suggestions." He faced the duke. "My cousin charts her own course in all things."

"So I'm learning."

"Cousin?" Lady Elsbeth looked pointedly at Northwick as she gestured with her free hand to her right. "If you need a task, I think Lady Caroline would like a reprieve from Mother."

James' head jerked as if he'd forgotten about the lovely Caroline. "You are quite correct. If you will excuse me."

Lady Elsbeth lowered her voice as he strode off. "I believe my cousin is going to be talking to Lady Caroline's father any day now. He's been calling on them regularly, and we all attended the opera in their box two evenings ago."

Teddy opened his mouth to comment, and Joanna frowned at him, speaking before he could voice his opinion. "They do make a fine couple."

"I know, but she's so…uninteresting." Lady Elsbeth pouted as well as any young lady who was already out this season.

She stifled a chuckle. "Perhaps it is just that what interests her, does not interest you."

Teddy patted Elsbeth's hand on his arm. "I will be happy to interest you. What would you like to discuss? Shall I tell you of the time I bested Joanna in a sword fight? I was the knight, of course, and she the terrible dragon."

Lady Elsbeth raised her brows as Teddy started to lead her away. "Dragons can use swords?"

Joanna smiled at the memory. They had all been so young then. Sometimes Teddy still seemed so, though he was but two years younger than she. Her eyes scanned those strolling around the panorama, and she found James with his aunt now. Maybe

Teddy simply appeared young because she'd spent much time of late in James' company. She estimated his age at about a score and ten. That was far older than her dear Teddy.

"Excuse me, Lady Joanna?"

At the sound of the cultured voice, she turned to find Lady Caroline. "Oh, Lady Caroline. I did not have a chance to greet you properly. Lady Astor whisked me away so quickly. How do you fair?"

Lady Caroline did not smile. "I wish a word with you."

Confused, she nodded. "Of course. Can I help you with something?"

"Yes. It would be a great help if you would stop fluttering after Lord Northwick."

She started to laugh but quickly coughed. "Flutter after the duke?" The woman must be jesting.

But there was no smile on Lady Caroline's face. In fact, she had abandoned her usually serene countenance for something much more shrewish. It definitely did not become her.

"It is rather obvious that you wish the duke's attentions. You happen to be at almost every event he attends. You talk endlessly with him, and you take every opportunity to smile at him. It is clear that you are infatuated with him. You must know that he has absolutely no interest in you. His attentions are elsewhere. You have no hope of stealing the duke away."

Joanna wasn't sure whether to be affronted or simply laugh at the woman. She chose another route for her response. "Lady Caroline, I have no such intentions with the duke. I think you see something that simply does not exist."

The lady tucked a stray blonde hair back behind her ear. "No, I'm quite confident in my observations, not only from seeing you with the duke, but from his talk of you. You are clearly smitten. I'm merely suggesting that you refrain from further interaction." Lady Caroline smiled sadly, even as she set her hand to her chest. "I would spare you any heartbreak. He is not interested in having a bluestocking as his duchess. I do hope you understand."

Her patience with the lady's faulty logic ended. "I don't know how to be more forthright about this. I have absolutely no interest in the Duke of Northwick."

Lady Caroline shook her head. "I think you may believe that. I suggest some self-observation and perhaps a week or so out of society. For someone who is so well read, it truly is surprising that you are so unaware of your own actions. All I can do is alert you that your affections for the duke have been noticed and not appreciated. Trust me, it would be better for you to lower your husbandly expectations."

She scowled at the lady, her muscles tensing as she tried to remain still. "My expectations, or lack thereof, are irrelevant. I have no wish to be tied to the duke or any other gentleman."

"Of course. Believe of yourself what you will. I have done all I can." With those final words, the woman gracefully twirled and strolled toward the duke and his aunt, who had turned to watch the conversation.

Despite being under observation, she fisted her hands within the folds of her dress. Until now, she'd thought Lady Caroline uninteresting at best and insipid at the worst, but it appeared there was an intelligent mind beneath the surface that was wholly limited by her upbringing. That the chit couldn't imagine a reason for conversation or smiling beyond courting was astounding, aggravating, insulting, and infuriating!

No, she needed to rethink that in alphabetical order to calm down, especially because she stood in such a public setting, and Teddy's courting depended on her behavior. That Lady Caroline could think no further than courtship was aggravating, astounding, infuriating, and insulting. There. That was much better. Taking a deep breath, she forced her lips into a pleasant smile and uncurled her hands. Spotting her mother and Mariel, she walked briskly toward them, purposefully avoiding looking at James' party.

"There you are, Joanna." Her mother held out her hand. "Is this not the most beautiful panorama yet?"

She grasped her mother's hand and pasted on a warm smile, not wanting to spoil her parent's experience. "I think you can appreciate it more than I since I have not seen the represented city before."

Her mother patted her hand. "Trust me, Paris is breathtaking. This brings to mind so many fond memories." Her mother's eyes sparkled with happiness before she lowered her brow. "Of course, when I visited, there was no wooden monstrosity called the *Arc de Triomphe*, but the rest is as I remember it."

"I'm very pleased you are enjoying it." She squeezed the hand in hers before letting go. "Amelia seems unusually content with the artistry as well. Based on that, I feel as if I've been to Paris."

Her mother laughed. "The views are only half the city's charm. I hope someday you can travel there."

She had no interest in going to Paris, especially not now that she had a school to start. But even that thought couldn't calm the roiling in her stomach. Her mother continued her stroll and Joanna fell behind, not wanting to engage in conversation when her thoughts whirled about in irritated turmoil. The audacity of Lady Caroline's assumptions had her questioning the woman's fitness to be James' wife. Not that it was her concern, but for all his arrogance, he was intelligent, and she couldn't imagine him being happy with a woman who could be so horribly mistaken.

As her mother stopped before a scene of extended gardens, Mariel stepped back. "Joanna, is something amiss?"

She looked her older sister in her eyes and couldn't lie. She gave her a brief nod. For some unknown reason, the sympathy in her sister's gaze made her eyes sting with unshed tears.

"Would you like to leave? Teddy has his carriage and can bring Mother home when she's ready."

"Yes, I think I've seen and heard enough."

Though her sister gave her a quizzical look, she didn't ask. Instead, she spoke to their mother and in no time, they were both well ensconced in their coach on the way to Craymore Hall.

"We are in private now." Mariel's soft gaze welcomed any

confidence.

She growled. "I'm infuriated and insulted by the Lady Caroline."

Except for a slight raising of her brows, Mariel didn't react. "Tell me."

And she did, everything, even about the school. Everything, that is, except what was in *the book*.

CHAPTER FOURTEEN

JOANNA PACED FURIOUSLY across her bedroom. "The chit can't even tell when someone is teasing her. How dare she pretend to know what I am feeling."

Mariel had taken a seat on her settee and inclined her head. "What *are* you feeling?"

She narrowed her eyes at her sister as she approached. "I think it rather obvious."

"No, not about Lady Caroline. I mean about Lord Northwick."

She stopped on her way back to her dressing table and turned. "What do you mean?"

Her sister took time to smooth out the skirt of her dress before answering. "I mean, what is your relationship to Lord Northwick?"

"My relationship? I don't have a relationship."

Mariel shook her head. "Yes, you do. After his dinner party, you thought him the most antiquated, arrogant, closed-minded man you had ever met." She lowered her head slightly and looked up at her for confirmation. "That is what you said, if I recall correctly."

She moved to her bed and grasped the bed post. "I may have been wrong about him at the time, but that was the impression he made upon me that night."

"So your opinion of him has changed. In what way?"

"For one, I've discovered that despite being a bit antiquated in his thoughts, he is intelligent enough to be open to new ideas."

"So he's not closed minded then?" Mariel's green gaze was direct.

She nodded. "No, I was wrong about that." She held up her hand to postpone any interruption. "But I still believe him arrogant. However, now I see he has reason to be. Not only is he a duke, but he is the most learned man I know." She frowned at her sister. "You won't tell Father, will you? He'd be so hurt."

Mariel waved away her concern. "Don't I keep all your secrets?"

It was true. If Mariel knew a secret, she never revealed it to anyone. It made her the perfect confidant. "He's also very supportive of my school idea. He is allowing Elsbeth to attend." She hopped up on her bed, her feet dangling over the side. "I'm not sure what Teddy will think of that once he learns of it, but that the duke let it be Elsbeth's decision tells me that he is willing to allow her to choose her future husband as well. I will admit, at first, I didn't believe him when he said he would. He did stipulate that the man must be acceptable to him, meaning family, money, and good character, which Teddy has."

Mariel harrumphed. "Maybe he did, but lately Teddy has become ridiculously mawkish."

"You noticed that too?" She clasped her hands. "Maybe I should talk to him."

"No." Mariel leaned back. "Never interfere with affairs of the heart."

She swallowed her reply. She may have much book knowledge, but when it came to art, she listened to Amelia, and when it came to love, she listened to Mariel. "I hope he doesn't put himself in a bad light."

"As do I. But we weren't talking about Teddy. We were talking about you and the Duke of Northwick."

She started at that. "I am not in league with the Duke of

Northwick. Until just recently, when he finally accepted that I had a point about women of the peerage being allowed to learn what they wished, all we did was debate." She threw one hand in the air. "And I can tell you we don't agree on anything else."

Mariel didn't say anything to that. Obviously, she'd made her point.

"That's not to say I don't enjoy debating with someone who has read far more books than I have. Father concedes too quickly, but the duke holds onto his stand as long as possible, using many debate tactics such as appealing to emotion or distracting with related topics. It forces me to be constantly assessing and thinking. It's quite exhilarating."

"So I see." Mariel smiled, staring pointedly at her hands.

She quickly brought them back to her lap. "Yes, I flap my arms about when I get excited. Father calls me a goose when I do that."

Mariel chuckled. "I thought I heard him call you that, but I thought I was mistaken."

"I like it." She shrugged. "He always says it with affection."

"Father does like to give nicknames."

She grinned. "Yes. He even dubbed Northwick's library as 'heaven' in front of Northwick himself."

Mariel's hand came to her chest. "Oh my. When did he do that? Was that when the duke invited you and Father to see it?"

She shook her head. "No. It was when Father insisted on coming with Teddy and me when we visited to instruct the duke and Elsbeth on how to waltz."

Mariel's intake of breath warned her that perhaps that hadn't been the most appropriate gathering, but she didn't particularly care about appropriateness. She waved one of her hands before Mariel spoke. "It was nothing. Though Father was in the library, Lady Astor was there."

Mariel studied her silently.

"What is it? What are you thinking?"

Her older sister rose and walked to her. Then she took both

her hands. "Did you enjoy dancing with the duke?"

"At first, no. The man is far too tall and doesn't take instruction easily."

"But then?"

She wasn't sure what Mariel was trying to discern. "Then eventually he mastered it. I understand he and Elsbeth have been practicing for her ball."

"Joanna, though I dislike immensely how upset Lady Caroline made you, she did make one legitimate point, as you would phrase it."

She very much doubted that. "And that was?"

Mariel squeezed her hands. "You need to reflect on your time with the duke and decide exactly what your true feelings are."

She opened her mouth to protest, but Mariel let go of her hands and pressed a finger to her lips. "No, do not dismiss the idea out of hand. You once told me that only the brave can reflect upon themselves and not shudder at what they find. You need to discern the truth of your feelings. Only you can do that."

When her sister removed her finger, she didn't know how to respond.

Luckily, Mariel didn't appear to expect an answer. She moved to the door. "I promised Mother I would help her with the dinner planning for next week. I hope you will take time to reflect before you next see the duke." With those final words, Mariel slipped out of the room and closed the door softly.

She jumped onto the floor and started pacing. Mariel didn't understand that there was nothing to reflect on. She and the duke currently agreed on something, and so at this moment in time, she enjoyed his company. That he was handsome just made that activity easier. That he moved with grace and smelled exotic made teaching him easier. That her heart thudded when he held her close and she wanted to kiss him…

Halting, a shiver passed through her. Did she simply like James Huntington, the intellectual, or did she like James Huntington, the man and all that entailed? She dropped onto her settee. The answer was as clear as a summer day, or rather a normal summer day.

She liked the man.

Her heart thudded hard in her chest. "I like James Huntington, the Duke of Northwick." Saying it out loud forced her to accept the truth. So what did that mean?

It could mean nothing. She liked Lady Astor, but that didn't change how she would treat the lady tomorrow when she called. So she wouldn't change how she treated James either.

Except it wasn't the same. Not even slightly similar. Her feelings for James were complicated, now that she admitted she liked his mind, his body, his smile, and his scent. No, she should organize that in alphabetical order. Now that she was sure she liked his body, his mind, his scent, and his smile, she would feel differently around him. She also liked his teasing, his dancing, his caring, and his laughter. His tone of voice was exciting too. She also liked having him hold her, and his eyes. She sighed, the sound swallowed by the room.

She jumped to her feet. What was she to do? Heading for her dressing table she sought answers. She would avoid him. But she'd already accepted the invitation to Elsbeth's ball and she had to go. Fine, she would go, but she wouldn't converse with him. No, she wanted to converse with him. What was wrong with talking? She simply wouldn't dance with him. But it would be rude to refuse one's host. They could dance one of the country dances. But what if he asked her to dance the waltz? She twirled in mid-pace, remembering the feel of being in his arms. She couldn't refuse him a waltz. Bloody hell, she didn't want to refuse herself.

Flopping on her bed, she stared at the ceiling. How much did she like him? Would she be willing to give up her independence for him? What about her school? She never wanted to be a wife. Is that what she wanted with him? She groaned and rolled onto her stomach, hugging her pillow. How did this happen?

A knock at the door was her only warning before it opened.

Amelia strode in and flounced onto the settee. "I need help."

So did she, but she doubted very much that Amelia could be of assistance. Happy for the distraction, she sat up in her bed.

"Is something wrong?

Amelia's question almost made her laugh, but she squelched it, not a little afraid of her own emotional state. "No, it's nothing." *It's everything. It's my life.* "What do you need help with?"

Amelia rolled to her side, tucking her feet up on the settee. "I have a delicate matter to discuss with you and only you."

Oh good, something she could focus on. "I promise not to tell anyone."

"Good. I thought about asking Mariel, but she's too…"

"Too insightful? Too discerning? Too practical?" They were all the qualities she ascribed to her older sister in a positive light.

"Proper."

She raised her brows. "Proper? This does sound intriguing."

Amelia lay her chin on the side of the settee. "It's not, but it *is* delicate."

Despite Amelia's statement to the contrary, her curiosity rose. She lay on her side so she faced her younger sister. "I understand. Then what is it?"

"It's my painting. It's not right." She sighed again.

Art was far from her area of expertise, but she could approach this logically. "What about it, isn't right?"

Amelia lowered her voice as if they could be overheard. "It's the men. Their figures are wrong."

"But you've painted men before. What's different?"

"They were always small and in the distance. In this painting, there are two men in the foreground, and there is something not right about their anatomy. I've seen the men painted by the great painters. I've even sketched the statue of David by Michelangelo, but using them as models, isn't working. My men look nothing like earls or dukes of London."

"I see." She didn't exactly because she didn't have an artist's eye. "What would you need to make them look how you want them to?"

Amelia sat up. "What I really need is a nude male model." Her shoulders slumped. "But that would be entirely improper. The next best option is access to sketches of nude men." She looked up hopefully. "Does Father have a book in the library that might contain even one?"

Drat. She wanted to help her sister but that would mean revealing the book. "Why? Are you painting nude men now?"

"Of course not. To do that I would *have* to have a male model." Amelia shook her head in exasperation. "But to paint a man correctly, especially with fashion the way it is today with everything so closely tailored, I need to know what is beneath the clothes."

"Oh." With her sister's upcoming exhibition, she was aware of how important this was to her. But how to explain *the book*. Since she planned to sneak the book back during Elsbeth's ball, it was, in actuality, just borrowed. "There is a book that could help you."

Amelia's blue eyes lit with excitement. "Oh, you must tell me which one immediately."

She shook her head. "No I can't because it's not one of Father's nor is it one of mine."

"I don't understand." Amelia had already begun to pout.

"First, you must promise me that you won't tell anyone about this book."

Her sister gave her a sly smile. "Is this one of those books you borrow from friends without them knowing?"

"What? How did you know?" Her stomach clenched. "Does everyone know?"

"No, of course not." Amelia waved off her worry. "I saw you take one at the Dulacs' soiree two months ago and asked Mariel about it. She didn't want to say anything, but I threatened to tell Lady Dulac."

Hurt, she scowled. "You would have revealed my borrow

just to find out the truth?"

"Of course not. How could you think that I would do that as your sister. I'm hurt that both you and Mariel thought that." She grinned. "But it did get me what I wanted."

She wasn't sure how she felt about that. "You are devious."

Amelia shrugged. "I call it creative."

Hmm, devious or creative, it was not necessarily a positive trait. "But how do I know I can trust you with this book, which is also borrowed and must be returned three days hence."

She could almost see Amelia's mind working as she thought. "Three days, you say? So you borrowed it from the Duke of Northwick. Is it a book of nude sketches from an artist's view or is it one of those tiring anatomy books you like to read? I don't care which, as long as it has at least one very detailed sketch of an unclothed male."

"It's neither. I thought it was a book on feminine education."

Amelia nodded. "Of course. So the author thinks a woman should know what the male body looks like? That's rather forward thinking."

She cleared her throat, not sure how to explain, but she did indeed have to explain if she was to share it and help Amelia. "The cover was misleading. The inside title was different and the illustrations inside are not fit for women like ourselves."

Amelia dropped her feet to the floor and sat up straight, her voice but a whisper. "Is it an illustrated version of one of those racy novels I've heard exist?"

There were illustrated versions of racy novels? Why had she not known this? Did Northwick know of them? "No, it's even more revealing."

"More revealing?" Amelia's lips puckered as she pondered. Then her eyes grew wide. "Oh dear." She leaned forward. "Is it a how-to book on what husbands and wives do to beget heirs?"

She nodded, her body heating at discussing the topic even tangentially with her younger sister.

"Excellent." Amelia jumped up and gave her a hug. "That's

just what I need. Where is it?" She scanned the room as if expecting it to be within sight.

She frowned at her sister's excitement. "It's in my locked cabinet. Amelia, you need to understand two things about this book.

"I'm listening." Her sister had indeed stopped her search and waited patiently.

"First, I must have this back in three days. Second, this book, from what I've seen, contains very explicit illustrations and cannot be allowed to fall into anyone else's hands."

"I see. Would you feel better if I simply borrowed it for a couple days and returned it to you then? I can make sketches of the sketches and keep them hidden. I do have a locked chest in my art studio upstairs."

Though not entirely relieved that Amelia understood the significance of the book she was about to use, Joanna did feel better. However, she'd learned many more facts about her sister in their conversation than she had in the last year. Maybe she needed to spend more time with her. "I would be amenable to that arrangement."

"Good." Amelia wandered back to the settee and reclined on it once again. "I'll wait here."

Oh, so she was to get it posthaste? Very well. She climbed off her bed and went to her dressing table, taking the key out of the small drawer. She'd have to change the key's hiding place now. No reason to have a locked cabinet if others knew where the key was. "I will return."

She slipped out her door and headed below to the library. If her father were present then Amelia would just have to wait. Though she still retained misgivings about lending the book, she couldn't see what else she could do to help Amelia beyond finding her a male willing to pose nude and that was too far beyond propriety, even for her.

Luckily, her father was not present, and she quickly retrieved the book and returned to her room. Amelia was still where she had left her, so she walked to the settee and handed her the volume.

Amelia didn't wait. She immediately unlatched the catch, opened it about midway through, and stared. "Oh, these sketches are very good."

Joanna peeked over the top of the book to find the words The Prisoner and an illustration of a naked man who had pinned the naked woman against a wall. One of his hands held both hers above her head and the other hand—she spun away. "I'm very glad it will help you."

From behind her, she heard the sound of the book being shut, then Amelia brushed by her. She stopped at the door and faced her. "I wonder why the duke owns this book." She shrugged. "It's not important. I'm just thrilled that you have it. Thank you." And with that, she left.

Joanna fell back on the settee, the heat in her body almost suffocating. Had that picture not stirred Amelia at all? Could she really view such sexual activity without it affecting her? Was that what an artist's eye meant, that there could be such a dispassionate connection to what was viewed?

Grabbing her fan that she'd left on the table next to the settee, she tried to cool herself, but in her mind all she could see was that illustration, only in her mind she saw the face of the man clearly and he was James Huntington, and she was the very nude woman. She closed her eyes to erase the image, but instead she saw her and the duke waltzing, slowing, and him bringing her flush against him. Her eyes popped open. For the first time in her life she understood why the waltz was considered scandalous. Now that the image was burned into her mind, how was she to gaze into those sky-blue eyes without remembering it?

She shook her head even as she fanned herself faster. Why had she ever taken that bloody book?

CHAPTER FIFTEEN

JAMES SIPPED HIS drink, the fine brandy sliding smoothly down his throat. If he had any doubts that Lady Caroline came from good stock, they were assuaged throughout the evening.

"Will you remain in Town for the whole season then?" Lord Holburn sat opposite him, enjoying a glass of port.

He found the question odd. "That is my intention. Both my aunt and Lady Elsbeth deserve a full season since I have denied them that for so long."

The older man nodded. "Yes, we do need to indulge the ladies to keep the home a contented place. I like that you have experience with that."

Experience with handling a household of women? Why would he care if—of course, the man was judging him as a possible son-in-law. That must have been the impetus for the invitation to dinner. It wasn't as if Lady Caroline had any brothers with which Elsbeth could become acquainted. He hadn't considered that a lady's parents would need to approve of him as well. It was not a position he was used to being in, and he wasn't comfortable with it.

"Will you be returning for the season next year as well? I know that once the ladies have a taste for it, it seems to be the only reason they are able to live through the winter months in the country. Though I dare say, this season has felt more like winter than summer."

The question caught him off guard. "I'm hoping that Lady Elsbeth will find a suitable husband by the end of this season. That would preclude me from having to venture back to London for another. Of course, if she needs a second season, since this one will be relatively short for her, than I will do what I must. I take my responsibility to her to heart."

Lord Holburn's brow wrinkled. "Do you not think you and your future wife will return often?"

The man's concern made sense. If Lady Caroline were to become his duchess, her father most likely expected to see her during the season. Unless… "Does Lady Caroline enjoy the season as much as you and your wife do?"

The man finally smiled. "She does. Town has so much to offer the ladies. She very much enjoys visiting and shopping and going to the theater. Now that I think on it, I don't believe I've seen you in Town much before this season."

He took another sip of brandy as he contemplated his new dilemma. "No, I have many responsibilities at Burhleigh Park, so my trips to London have been infrequent and relatively short until this year."

As Holburn went on to extoll the advantages of London, his concern grew. Would Caroline expect them to come to London every season? Maybe he could bring her in, and she could stay with her parents. That way he wouldn't be forced to endure all the social gatherings. That might suffice. He lifted his glass once more.

He stilled halfway to his lips. Had he really just thought to leave his wife in London without him, when his own father had done exactly that when he brought his mother to London so she and his sister could take a ship to visit her family in America? He shook his head. How could he have thought something like that?

"You don't think the Thames will freeze over again this winter like it did a couple of years ago?"

At Holburn's question, he tried to refocus. "No, I just don't feel I have the knowledge needed to give an educated answer."

"True. True. Much of this talk about the weather this summer is speculation. I'm pretty sure, though, that it cannot bode well for the harvest."

Now that was a concern he had as well, and being in London when his tenants might need his advice was difficult. Now that it was mentioned, he would plan on a poor harvest and adjust his rents accordingly, though that might not help with food if it was a truly poor crop. Something he needed to think about.

At that moment, the two of them were joined by the butler who indicated that Lady Holburn was not feeling well.

"It must have been the cow's head. I told her not to serve it, but she insisted." He lifted his glass in honor. "She wanted to make a good impression on you." Holburn took a sip then set his glass down and rose.

He stood as well. "Please tell her I have very much enjoyed our evening."

As they strode toward the entry, his aunt, cousin, and Lady Caroline emerged from the parlor. It seemed that Lady Holburn had taken ill quite suddenly and was already ensconced in her rooms. After saying their farewells with much ado about Lady Elsbeth's coming ball, they were finally settled in their coach.

His aunt, who sat across from him, cleared her throat. "So did you take the opportunity to ask Lord Holburn for Caroline's hand?"

He blinked, the topic so far from his mind that he didn't see a connection at first. "Why would you think I would do that tonight?"

"It was the perfect time, and Lady Caroline seemed to expect it, as did her mother. At least until she started feeling poorly."

"I had no intention of asking this evening. Do you think that is why they invited us?"

Elsbeth nodded. "I'm quite sure of it. Lady Holburn wanted to make it easy for you."

Insulted that the Holburn family would think he couldn't call on his own to request the lady's hand, he scowled. "I'm not some young man just out of leading strings. I can very well do what is needed *when* I wish to." And he refused to take away from his cousin's ball by announcing his own engagement.

His aunt cocked her head. "Don't be upset with them. Lady Caroline is the only lady you have been seen to have an interest in. It is not a surprise they expect an offer. After all, she *is* the only one you are interested in, correct?"

"Of course. Who else would there be?"

The two women looked at each other before turning back to him.

Something was afoot. "What are you thinking? No secrets. You know I detest secrets."

"Elsbeth and I were just remarking yesterday on how well you and Lady Joanna seem to be rubbing along lately."

"Rubbing along? You mean like one would with a school chum? That alone proves she is hardly duchess material."

His young cousin crossed her arms over her chest and lifted her chin. "Then I think you should re-evaluate what is duchess material."

"You do, do you?" Now his ire was truly up. "And that must be because you have so much experience in choosing a duchess."

To give her credit, Elsbeth didn't back down. She dropped her arms and took her mother's hand. "My mother was a duchess, so I have had an excellent role model. In my estimation, Lady Joanna would make a fine duchess."

Why did he have a feeling that allowing Elsbeth to attend Joanna's school might cause a shift in her character? Fine. If she wished to debate the subject, he'd be happy to. With such a novice, he was sure to win. "And you think Lady Caroline would not?"

"We were not discussing Lady Caroline. We were discussing Lady Joanna, who is clearly much more intelligent than the aforesaid lady. She also makes you laugh, which I've seen no other woman do. She's far more intriguing and has objectives far surpassing what pattern to embroider on her pillows."

Shocked to discover his little cousin did indeed have a sharp mind, he was taken aback by his inability to distract her. "So far you have only mentioned the lady's good qualities, but what about those which detract from her?"

Elsbeth shifted her gaze to the passing lamplights outside the window. "That is a bit difficult." A secret smile lifted her lips. "Well, there is the fact she is hardly attractive."

"Not attractive?" Affronted on the lady's behalf, he felt obligated to defend her. "True, she has darker coloring than is the fashion among the *ton*, but that hardly makes her unattractive. Her eyes are quite expressive, she blushes as well as any other lady, and she has an energetic grace that is difficult to describe."

"I suppose, if you could overlook her need to discuss such obtuse topics." She brought her hand to her chest. "I, of course, enjoy them, but they are absolutely boring to the average woman." She lowered her voice. "There is reason for this being her fourth season and her designation as a bluestocking. You did know, did you not?"

"Bluestocking?" He despised the word. It had morphed from a positive one among gentry and middle class to making a woman a pariah in his own. "Do you even know what that is?"

Elsbeth gave him a condescending smile worthy of a future duchess. "The bluestocking circles of the last century were led by women of superior intellectual ability and included gatherings where conversation focused on learned topics. They were generally for men and women but very few ladies of the peerage attended. Of course, now, the term is used in a derogatory way to describe a lady who has studied far too much to be marriageable."

He sat for a moment in stunned silence.

She shrugged. "I doubt Lady Joanna would care about the term. She doesn't need to marry, and now with her school…I don't imagine she would be interested in any requests for her hand anyway. So really, it's a moot point."

"A moot point." He echoed her words as he followed her

logic, feeling as if the dinner he'd just eaten had somehow turned into a large stone in his stomach. Turning his attention to his aunt, he found her smiling. "And do you agree with all this?" He waved his hand dismissively at his cousin.

"I do. But it is a shame she's not quite right to be a duchess. I think Lady Joanna would have been a lovely addition to our family."

From where he sat, they already had a young Lady Joanna in their family. He scowled at his cousin. When had she become so smart? "How did you know about the bluestockings?"

She sighed. "Surely you don't think I only visit your library to watch the sun set?"

He shook his head. She may have learned the history of the word there, but she had acquired her new debating skills elsewhere. They lapsed into silence for which he was grateful. As opposed to his cousin, he was of a different mind about Lady Joanna. She would make an excellent duchess, but in a unique way, a progressive way.

He envisioned sitting across from her at breakfast, as she had suggested a married couple might. There would be no reading his morning paper. She would insist on conversation about the day or about whatever was in the paper. He would eventually retire to his library to pour over his ledger. Or would she do that? It would be a relief to have her take that over and then they would discuss various topics of planting, tenant issues, and investments. Then at night they would retire to their separate bedrooms, where he would don a robe and knock on her door. She would greet him with a smile and wrap her arms around his neck.

"Are you coming, James?"

His aunt's voice from outside the carriage jolted him to the present. Stepping from the carriage, he joined her and Elsbeth as they all hurried into the house, the wind having stilled leaving behind a winter cold chill.

Once inside he handed his hat and gloves to Harrison.

"Really James, I've never known you to be one who day

dreamed." His aunt released her cloak.

"I was not day dreaming. I was thinking."

"About Lady Caroline?" Elsbeth's smile appeared entirely too innocent.

"Where did you learn to debate? I have not instructed you in that."

She grinned. "Mostly Lord Mabry. He was forced to learn by Lady Joanna, but yesterday I had the opportunity to debate with her. I just love how her mind functions."

His aunt saved him from responding. "Upstairs with you Lady Bluestocking. I'll have hot chocolate sent up and join you."

Elsbeth clapped her hands together. "Just what I need. Thank you." She kissed her mother on the cheek and ran up the stairs in a most unladylike way.

His aunt laid her hand on his arm. "May I speak to you briefly?"

"Of course." He led her to the library where a fire was ordered every evening if there was a chill in the air. The parlor, the lesser used room in the evenings, would be too cold. He walked to the chairs before the fire and motioned to one.

She declined, but availed herself of the fire by moving before it. "I wish to speak to you about Lady Caroline."

He raised his brows as he moved to the other side of the fireplace. "Not Lady Joanna?"

She smiled. "No. I think Elsbeth did enough talking on that subject." She held her hands out to the fire. "I just wanted to tell you that I was relieved you didn't speak to Lord Holburn yet about his daughter."

"Relieved? Do you not care for Lady Caroline? I thought you considered her quite marriageable."

"Oh, I do think she would make a gentleman a perfect wife one day."

When she didn't continue, he filled in the rest. "But not for me. Could you tell me why your opinion has changed?"

"I don't know how to explain it. She's too perfect, I guess.

Almost to the point where she seems not quite human. There is no emotion, and if there is, it is hidden. You deserve a woman who would be honest with you about what she's feeling. I wish I could explain it better. Call it instinct, but I don't think you would be happy with her."

There was a score of responses he could give his aunt, but this was not a debate. She simply felt a certain way. "I appreciate you confiding in me. I do give your counsel weight, though in this instance the final decision will be mine. Tell me. If I were to marry her, could you accept that?"

His aunt took a deep breath. "Yes, I could. Elsbeth will marry soon, and I'm sure I will be in her household, so my interactions with Lady Caroline would be few. It is not that she is difficult to be around after all."

Though he always knew his aunt would live with his cousin when she married, having it said out loud and as something soon anticipated, startled him into the reality of his future position. Whoever he married would be the only other adult in his home besides the servants. He was so used to his aunt in his life that he found himself unable to imagine it. "I will miss you."

She smiled warmly and placed her hand on his cheek. "Not more than I will miss you. You have been the son I never had. I'm so proud of the man you have become. Though I did little to shape you, I hope I helped make your growing years more comfortable."

Emotion filled his chest. It was such an unusual occurrence that he found himself at a loss for words. All these years, he had railed against fate for first taking his mother away from him, when in fact, he had gained a mother who loved him like he was her own. Without thinking, he stepped to his aunt and enfolded her in his arms. He lowered his head and whispered in her ear. "You have been my true mother."

Her arms tightened around him for a moment, then she stepped back, tears in her eyes. "I'd best get the hot chocolate ordered. I still have one fledging bird who needs to take flight, and she, I'm afraid, is going to need a lot more hovering than you ever did."

He nodded. "I will be happy to help you with that after her ball. My instinct is telling me we will have to combine our efforts to insure she lands in the right place."

"Thank you." She turned and headed for the door. Before leaving she looked at him. "Remember, there is no rush for you to make a decision." Then she slipped out.

He stared at the flames. His aunt was correct, there was no immediate hurry to find a bride, but he didn't want to spend another season in London. Was avoiding another season worth the risk of marrying the wrong woman? Then again, he couldn't be sure that Lady Caroline *was* the wrong woman. Nevertheless, he would be more intentional in his observations of the lady. His aunt would not have brought up her concerns unless they were genuine and disturbing.

As for his cousin, she had obviously been spending far too much time with the Mabry family. He grinned. He felt a certain amount of pride in her debate skills. Did she really feel Joanna was poor marriageable material or was she playing devil's advocate? Though he had no intention of marrying Joanna, he did not like others speaking poorly of her. Any man should consider himself fortunate to have her for a wife. Perhaps he could show the *ton* that the Huntington family fully approved of Lady Joanna.

There was, of course, her own aversion to marriage, but that was sure to dissipate if the right man were interested. He glanced over at the bookcase behind his desk where the space remained for his missing book. Unless she had an aversion to the marriage bed. Is that why she took the book? Knowledge was indeed power. Did she hope to be knowledgeable about relations between men and women?

Even as the thought rose, he could envision her looking at the illustrations. How far had she read, or had she seen only the first few illustrations and closed the book for good? He shook his head. Not Joanna. She would not allow her own sense of propriety stand in the way of learning something new. But if she didn't plan to marry, what would be the purpose if she couldn't apply that knowledge?

And if she did marry? Would her husband be pleased or displeased that she knew so much? Among the *ton*, it could be either. Irritation flashed through him and he clenched his fists. Only a fool wouldn't appreciate all she brought to a marriage. He stalked to the sideboard and poured himself a scotch. In one gulp, he threw it back. The burning from the drink did little to chase away the irritableness in his gut. It was illogical to be so concerned.

He stilled. Or was he the fool?

CHAPTER SIXTEEN

JOANNA STOOD IN the transformed ballroom of Haven House next to her sister Mariel, Amelia having already found a friend she just had to speak to. Mariel wore a deep blue gown that made her chestnut hair appear lighter than it was. She, herself, had chosen a warm maroon that made her hair appear darker. Lady Astor had outdone herself. She'd created the illusion of a flower garden, complete with fountains, vines, and what appeared to be white doves made of the stone Eleanor Coade had invented. She could just imagine James commissioning a hundred white doves just for his cousin's ball.

The doors to the real garden were closed as the weather was still cool, but she had no doubt once the dancing started, they would be opened. She would wait until then to sneak outside to their coach to retrieve *the book* and return it to the house. She spent the last day reviewing most of it which had given her rather explicit dreams. Because James was in those dreams, she'd blushed while talking to him in the receiving line. Her only hope was to return the book, so he'd think she never had it.

"I believe they are going to start the dancing." Mariel leaned in. "Lady Elsbeth looks absolutely radiant tonight."

She did. The young woman wore the prettiest shade of lavender accented with pale blue and deep purple ribbons on her dress and in her hair. The colors brought out the flecks of violet in her blue eyes. "I hear that she and the duke will open the evening with a waltz."

Mariel's eyebrows raised at that. "It appears you have much influence over the young lady."

"Not yet." She grinned.

The musicians made the last adjustments to their instruments as James and Elsbeth stepped to the middle of the floor. Couples began to join them. She noticed Teddy headed her way. They had agreed to join the first waltz. He bowed graciously. "My lady."

She gave a quick curtsey. "My lord."

He led her out onto the dance floor. This would not be an easy dance with Teddy constantly focused on Elsbeth, but she would do her best to make him appear skilled. She glanced in the direction of the guest of honor and her gaze was intercepted by James. He gave her one of his usual truncated nods in acknowledgement before taking his cousin's hands. She gave him her nod of approval before she and Teddy clasped hands.

The music began and at first, they glided along well. She couldn't help watching James. His steps were sure as he moved through the beginning of the sets. When the turns were about to start, she glanced again at James' form, pleased to see he'd lowered his hand for Elsbeth.

"Joanna." Teddy's whisper startled her. He grabbed her hand forcibly as she'd been too intent on James' form to pay attention to Teddy.

She grimaced. "My apologies. I just wanted to be sure they did everything well."

As he spun her, he frowned. "You should be worrying about me. Have you seen all the men here? Every time she greeted one, my heart stung. I vow, tomorrow I am asking for her hand."

Concerned by the fervor in her cousin's voice, she gave him her full attention. "Do you want her to choose you because you're the only one she knows or because you're the one she feels strongest about?"

His hands squeezed hers hard. "I don't care as long as she's my wife."

"Teddy, take a deep breath. You're losing your step. You want her to think you graceful, right?"

He adjusted their pace to flow better with the other dancers. "I love her with all my heart. I've never wanted anything so much."

As she gazed into his stormy gray eyes, she could see he meant every word. But his passion made her concern for him grow. "I understand. We will just have to be sure she sees how fortunate it would be to have you as a husband."

That seemed to calm him, and as they moved back into the first set of the dance, he even smiled. When it was over, he immediately headed for Lady Elsbeth and Lady Astor, where James had led her.

She returned to Mariel. "I'm concerned about Teddy."

Mariel looked past her. "I see he is smiling. That shouldn't be a reason for concern."

"That isn't, but his emotions are too strong, and he is jealous of every eligible gentleman in here."

"You don't think he'd compromise her, do you?"

At Mariel's question, she widened her eyes. "I wouldn't have thought that, but I do think he would if it appears her attentions are moving elsewhere."

"Oh dear."

Seeing that Mariel watched Teddy, she quickly pulled open her fan. The exuberance of Teddy's partnering had left her feeling a bit warm. Unfortunately, no one else was heated yet, so the garden doors remained closed. She'd feel so much better once she'd moved *the book* into the house. Maybe she could drop it under the settee in the parlor.

As her younger sister, who never lacked for partners, moved into position across from where she stood, she noticed Lady Caroline was partnered by James. That made sense since he was planning to make her his wife. As the two danced, she watched their interactions, trying to see what Amelia saw, but to her they made a beautiful couple. It was rather ironic that the one man she'd truly despised enough to steal a book from would be the one man in four seasons she'd come to respect. No, that she'd come to care about. The thought made her stomach tight, and she sympathized more with Teddy. She hated seeing James dancing with another.

Mariel turned away from the dancing. "I think I would like some punch."

"I'll accompany you." As they made their way, she scanned the room. Four of the mothers of her students were in attendance, not including Lady Astor. That made her a little uncomfortable as she was not likely to dance with anyone else. She just hoped those mothers wouldn't hold it against her. As long as she behaved in an appropriate manner, so they would be pleased to put their daughters into her care, all would go well. Though that did make her consider whether to accept future invitations to balls.

As she and her sister obtained their punch, the dance ended, and another began. She secretly wished she could sneak into the library and read, but she needed to be present when the doors to the garden opened. She would keep an eye on Teddy as well as Lady Caroline. The last thing she wanted was another confrontation, especially at Elsbeth's ball.

"Lady Joanna?"

A shiver ran down her back at the sound of the male voice behind her. She turned to face James. "Your Grace." She dipped a curtsey, wondering where Mariel had wandered off to.

"I thought I might see if your next dance was spoken for?"

Her heart leapt at the idea, and she smiled. "Since I have no dances promised for the rest of this evening, I'd be pleased to dance with you."

He frowned. "No one has requested a dance?"

"I'm rarely asked to dance." She waved her hand, a bit uncomfortable by how forbidding he appeared. "It's of no consequence. Having few to no dances promised leaves me free to mill about as I choose."

His brows raised before he chuckled. "For anyone else, I'd be doubtful, but for you that makes sense, so I approve."

She lifted her glass. "I'm so pleased you do for whatever would I do if you didn't?"

"I'm sure whatever suited you."

She'd just taken a sip and almost spit it out as a laugh attempted to come out. Instead, she coughed. "Excuse me. I'd best set this down."

"Yes, because I believe our waltz is the next dance."

She froze. "A waltz?"

He smiled. "I assure you. I was taught by an expert teacher."

She swallowed hard. Two waltzes with the first part of the evening was unusual. Certainly Lady Astor was aware of that.

"Come, I insisted on one for us." As he led her out to the dance floor, she felt the gazes of all those in the room for the first time. Even if they weren't looking at her with James, she felt them anyway. For him to ask her to dance the second waltz of the evening sent the wrong message. Did he know what he did?

He took her hand in his and smiled, something in his eyes causing her heart to jump. "Enjoy the dance, Jo. Let's give them something to discuss in their morning calls tomorrow."

At the assurance that he did know what he did, her chest filled. He wanted to dance the waltz with *her*. She smiled. "It would be an honor."

His own smile grew and then he winked at her. She was so caught off guard by his action that she stumbled into the first steps with him.

He didn't seem to mind, guiding her in the patterns until she regained her equilibrium. "Your dance with Lady Elsbeth was flawless from what I observed."

"I did as you commanded. I practiced. That is what applied learning is all about, is it not?"

She nodded before facing forward as they danced side by side. As that pattern completed, he turned her toward him and grasped her about the waist. She lifted her arm and swore there was a twinkle in his eye as his hand enclosed hers. Before she could comment, he swept her into the turns.

She couldn't seem to look away, his gaze changing, his blue eyes darkening. Or was it simply the lights in the ballroom? It was as if they floated across the floor, the music entwining around them, through them, tying them together in its notes as if they were one. It was magic, pure and simple, beyond reason, beyond logic, beyond thought. In that moment, she understood being part of another person. Her split-apart.

Neither of them said anything and yet it felt as if they said everything. Dare she hope he felt it too, the feeling that they were supposed to be together?

As the music stopped and the dance ended, his arm left her, as he trailed his hand along her back. He brought their entwined hands down, tucking hers in the crook of his arm. "I think it's time to open the garden doors."

Without asking, he guided her off the dance floor and to the closest set of doors. His footmen immediately opened them, and he led her out onto the terrace she remembered. She should say something about his expert dancing, but the words lodged in her throat. That wasn't what she wanted to say.

He walked her down into the gardens. There were no flowers, but there was much greenery as he led her past the cupid fountain. Once on the other side of it, he stopped and turned her to face him.

She looked up expectantly, her heart pounding, anxious to hear what he would say.

As he cupped her face in his hands, he whispered. "My Jo." His face lowered, and he lifted her chin to brush his lips against hers.

She closed her eyes as tingles spread over her skin. His mouth pressed harder, until his tongue slipped between her lips. She grasped his arms to hold herself up, her body feeling like melting ice cream when his tongue touched hers. Hesitantly, she tasted him, the punch he must have drank mixing with his own flavor. It was intoxicating. Anticipation built like a hot air balloon and as she breathed in his fresh scent, it floated her away.

His arms wrapped around her, pulling her flush against him, exactly where she wanted to be. His mouth on hers became more demanding, and she met his request with demands of her own. Lifting her arms around his neck, she grasped the hair at his nape, the silkiness adding to her senses.

She could feel his heartbeat against her chest and swore they matched. The heat she'd occasionally experienced with him seemed to rise higher and engulf her. This was passion, and she couldn't get enough. She wanted to be closer, to feel more, taste more, touch more. A need started deep in her belly, demanding he satisfy it.

He growled deep in his throat, the vibrations sensitizing her mouth more before he pulled his lips away.

No! Out of breath, her knees weak, and her head light, she tried to calm herself.

He pressed his forehead to hers. "Jo, I didn't mean…I mean, I did…I mean—"

"Shh." She ran her hand along his cheek and through his hair. "I know what you mean." She took in two more breaths before continuing, surprised she could even stand. Though she probably couldn't without his help. "I think this is beyond our control."

His lips quirked. "I think my ego protests your assessment, but I have no better explanation."

She couldn't respond, the view of his lips so close making it impossible to think.

"Joanna." The whispering female voice coming from the terrace, had her snapping her head in that direction, but the fountain hid her from view.

James dropped his hands, but didn't move.

"Joanna, are you still out here?" Mariel's worry came through as she raised her voice a little.

"My sister."

"Yes. She followed us out onto the terrace, which is why I brought you out here. I could not refrain from touching you."

His words sent her heart racing all over again. She gave him a crooked smile. "She's very good at protecting my reputation, when I get carried away."

His brows raised. "Does this happen often?"

"This? No. Never. But I can become distracted from propriety on occasion."

"Joanna, please tell me you're still here."

She grimaced, sorry for the worry she'd caused but not sorry for her actions. Glancing once more to James' lips, she shook her head and took two steps back so she could see her sister. "I'm coming." Turning, she hurried along the path they had taken.

Mariel raised her hand to her chest. "Oh, you gave me such a fright." Her sister peered into the garden. "Is the duke still out here?"

As much as she hated to, she lied. "No, I think he went to the stable." She hooked her arm in Mariel's ready to return to the ballroom. "He said something about a new foal he wanted to check on."

Mariel frowned, clearly not believing her. "After the way you two danced together, I'm surprised if the duke can think of anything but you."

The way they danced? Surely no one else could feel what had seemed to occur between them. "I'm not sure what you mean."

Mariel resisted her tug on her arm. "Joanna, everyone could see it. There's something special with you two. You danced as if you floated. It was as if you were of one mind."

Split-aparts. "It's probably because I taught him how to waltz, so he was used to me as a partner. Can we go inside now? I was warm before, but now I'm chilled."

Her sister finally moved. "If anyone inquires, you and I were talking out here, and the duke went directly to the stables."

She didn't contradict Mariel since they had already entered the room, and more than a few pairs of eyes turned in their direction. That those same people continued to watch the doorway meant speculation was rife among them. Fudge, what had she been thinking? She led her sister straight to Lady Astor who stood with two other ladies of a similar age to forestall any untoward rumors.

The lady welcomed them with a smile. "Are you enjoying the ball?"

Joanna gestured to the vines seemingly growing around the half-column closest to them. "You have transformed this into such a beautiful garden."

"I believe it's a bit warmer in here though than the real one outside. I noticed you went out there with Lord Northwick. Do you know where he is?"

Mariel's hold on her arm tightened.

"Yes. He deposited me with my sister and said something about a new foal?" She cocked her head as if puzzled by that.

Lady Astor's eyes twinkled. "Ah yes. He's had that foal on his mind quite a lot. He even left us at dinner the other evening to check on it."

Obviously, the older woman knew that their tale was nothing more than that, but was happy to keep her secret. Grateful, Joanna steered the conversation to a safer subject. "What of Lady Elsbeth. Is she enjoying her night?"

The older woman looked to her companions before answering with a beaming smile. "She has not had a chance to take a breath. It's better than I had anticipated. So many of these young men are anxious to learn more about her."

Her stomach tightened and she forced herself not to frown or scan the immediate area for Teddy.

Mariel answered. "We are so pleased for her. She's such a lovely woman."

"Thank you." Lady Astor turned her palm upward. "Then again, so are you."

"Me? No, I am a widow. My days for love are long gone."

Seeing Lady Astor about to push the matter, Joanna broke in.

"If you don't mind, I'm quite thirsty. Would you excuse us?"

At the woman's nod, she steered Mariel away.

"Thank you."

"It is the least I can do for my secret-keeper." At Mariel's frown, she chuckled and patted her arm entwined with hers. "You must realize how boring your life would be if I were not about to make it more interesting."

Mariel smiled. "I like boring."

Laughing, they approached the table they'd left earlier and gathered another cup of punch. Dinner would be occurring soon and would no doubt be a fascinating affair. She could find a seat near Teddy since she wouldn't have a partner for the supper dance. Turning from the table, she scanned the ballroom. Lady Elsbeth was once again dancing with another gentleman. Knowing Teddy would be near, she studied the opposite side of the room between dancers. He was there, leaning against a column, his gaze following the young woman's every movement. "I'm concerned about Teddy."

"So am I. Except for you, he hasn't danced with any other ladies. He just stares at Lady Elsbeth. It's not proper."

She understood that, but that wasn't what worried her. "I think he feels too passionately." She turned to look at Mariel. "Is that possible?"

A sadness filled her sister's eyes. "Yes, I believe it is possible. When I received the news that Marcus had been killed, I felt as if my soul had been ripped from my body. I must have loved him too passionately. When George died, I did not feel so."

If she had been Mariel, she would have felt great joy when old George died, but she shouldn't think ill of the dead, especially because his fortune had saved their family.

"Oh, look, here comes Lady Dulac." Mariel gestured with her half-finished cup.

As the older woman approached, Joanna smiled. The older woman was not only a longtime friend of their mother's, but also a mother of one of the young ladies who would be attending her new school. "Lady Dulac." She gave the woman a short curtsey.

The woman acknowledged the courtesy. "Lady Joanna, I wish to speak with you."

"Of course. You don't mind if Mariel is included, do you?"

Lady Dulac appeared startled that Mariel was present and quickly brushed off the concern. "It's of no concern to me. I wanted to tell you that I have changed my mind about Eleanor attending your school."

Had her dance with the duke done so much damage then? Her heart twisted at the idea of losing one of her pupils before she'd even started.

Mariel spoke before she could. "But why? It is such a wonderful opportunity for Eleanor to expand her mind."

"Oh, I agree. But her first duty is to marry well, and I do not want her to ruin her chances." The woman lowered her voice. "She's a wonderful young lady, but even I know she's not the most beautiful flower, nor the most graceful swan, so I need to be sure that nothing else detracts from her person. I hope you understand."

Joanna shook her head. "I do not. How would having more knowledge to bring to her marriage and future family take away from her prospects?" The old frustration at people's inability to open their minds to new ideas boiled hot, and she grasped her skirt with her free hand to try to keep her outward appearance proper.

"My dear, Lady Joanna. I'm afraid the reality is that men of the peerage do not want a woman with a mind." She shook her head. "It is a pity, but a good hostess, a calmness of spirit, and a biddable partner is what they want. I'm sure your school will be no less…interesting without Eleanor there." The woman patted her shoulder like she'd pat a lap dog. "Now, I really must make my salutations to your mother. Enjoy your evening."

Joanna frowned at Lady Dulac's back as she made her way to the other side of the room. Of all the closed-minded, fickle, ignorant, demeaning decisions. No, that was wrong. It had been a closed-minded, demeaning, fickle, and ignorant decision on Lady Dulac's part to remove Eleanor from the school.

"Are you upset?" Mariel's soft words and concerned gaze, had her snapping her head around.

"Yes. I'm insulted and feel angry for Eleanor. She is an incredible, intelligent woman, who is bored with her role in life. She'd been very excited." She put down her half-finished cup of punch, afraid she might spill it in her frustration.

"You cannot blame Lady Dulac. It is what she was taught was the way of life."

"But she'd agreed. It hadn't even been that hard to persuade her. Did I let her think about it too long? Should I have waited until August to find my students?"

"I don't know." Mariel shook her head. "I'm not sure there is an answer to your questions. You are paving a new way, against the norm. I'm sure you knew there would be setbacks."

That was true. It was one of the reasons she wanted to keep it all a secret. The less society in general knew of her enterprise, the less it would try to reject the project before it started. "I didn't expect to lose a student before I'd even started." She tried not to frown as she watched the dance come to an end. James had not returned to the ballroom, but many people were enjoying themselves, nonetheless. Obviously, the host needn't be present.

Amelia came toward them as she exited the dance floor. "I must have a drink and a seat." She scooped up a cup of punch and promptly sat in the closest chair.

Joanna rolled her eyes. "You cannot be complaining that you are so sought after."

"I can." Amelia took a gulp of punch and then followed that with a proper sip. "I may have many partners, but it appears that you have caught the attention of the duke himself."

She schooled her features to show no reaction. "What do you mean?"

"Don't pretend ignorance. You are far too intelligent for that. He danced the second waltz of the evening with you. No, that's not what happened." Amelia took another sip of punch. "He took you out on the floor for a waltz and transported both of you into a world of your own."

She forced a chuckle. "You exaggerate. We did nothing but waltz. We've simply done so before, so we know each other's nuances."

Amelia shook her head. "That's not it, and I'm fairly certain you know that. Everyone is talking about it."

Involuntarily, she scanned the room as if she could hear what every conversation was about. She looked down at her sister. "I highly doubt that."

"And then to take you out in the garden." Amelia took another sip, but she looked up through her lashes with knowing eyes. "That was quite unprecedented."

"Surely after an energetic dance, your partner, if solicitous, walked you outside to cool off."

Amelia lifted her right shoulder and let it drop. "I suppose, but I doubt my dance partners have ever looked so purposeful." She lowered her voice. "Did he kiss you?"

She sucked in her breath. "Is that what everyone thinks?"

"I have no idea what's on the minds of these people. What I can tell you is that you and the duke make an exquisite couple, speaking on an aesthetic level."

Her heart leapt at her sister's evaluation. "As that is just on an appearance level, I will take that as a compliment. However, it hardly means the duke has an interest in me. In fact, he was quick to head to the stables while I spoke with Mariel. Something about a new foal." She waved her hand as if her heart wasn't beating faster than a race horse at Ascot.

Amelia studied her. "The stables? Very well, I will be sure to explain it as such."

"Explain…never mind. It was a dance. That's all." It was far more than a simple dance. It was far more than a simple kiss. An explanation she'd read in *the book* came to mind. It had said there were many types of kisses. She needed to check that again before she slipped it inside and see if she could identify the kiss. Had it simply been passion that brought their lips together or was it something more?

As if he'd heard her thinking about him, he strode into the ballroom from the inside doors. Before she could think to tell him of Mariel's explanation, her older sister was at his side, chatting with him, obviously anxious to protect her reputation.

Amelia rose and stood next to her. "We are very lucky to have a sister like Mariel."

She silently agreed. Too much attention had been stirred by her dance with James. She'd have to wait until dinner to slip out and retrieve the book. If she could find a minute or two to look up the explanation on kisses, she would.

"Come with me. I need to tidy up."

At Amelia's request, she nodded, and followed her sister out of the ballroom and down the corridor where a room had been set up for the ladies. They were about to enter when Lady Preston tapped her on the arm. "Lady Joanna, may I speak with you?"

As this was another mother of one of her soon-to-be students, she was quick to assent. "Yes, of course."

The older lady looked about then motioned toward the parlor, its door open and showing it as empty of guests.

Guessing it must have to do with the school if the woman was so careful as to keep their conversation private, she was happy to repair there. As long as the woman didn't pull her daughter from the school, Joanna would welcome any conversation about it.

Lady Preston stopped in the middle of the room and faced her. "I won't be allowing Dorothea to attend your school."

Not a little shocked by the blunt statement, she forgot to mask her surprise. "Why not? You said it was a wonderous idea."

"I was wrong." The woman worried the sapphire necklace that lay on her chest. "I can't allow it."

"You said it would help Dorothea choose her future husband

wisely. You don't want that anymore?" Frustration was slowly changing to anger at the absurdity of the woman's decision.

"I do, but if she goes to your school, she won't have any choices." The woman glanced worriedly at the open door before continuing. "Men wish their wives to be biddable, calm, and good hostesses. My Dorothea already has too many ideas. Please don't tell anyone I ever considered it."

She pushed her anger aside as she recognized the three qualities from her earlier conversation with Lady Dulac. Something was amiss. "Lady Preston, why do you think those are the qualities that men would prefer in their wives?"

The woman looked away, leaving off fiddling with her necklace to wring her hands, clearly very agitated. "The duke said as much. None of the duke's friends would ever consider a woman as a wife who attended your school, and too many eligible men take their lead from the duke. I'm very sorry." With that, she brushed past her and exited the room as if afraid someone would see the two of them conversing.

The duke? James would counsel young men not to marry her students? She stood in shock, her heart so full a moment before, now frozen and numb. The anger she'd pushed aside for clarity now reared its inflamed head. "Of all the devious, cruel, underhanded, malicious actions to take." Her words came out in a hiss and her hands curled into fists of their own accord. "And I don't give a bloody damn if my words are out of alphabetical order."

He'd done it purposefully. He'd lulled her into believing that he agreed with her, even encouraged her, just to undermine her. Why? Because he disagreed with her? Because he wanted to prove something. "Oh." She sucked in her breath, feeling as if someone had thrown their fist into her belly. He wanted to prove she was like every other woman. No doubt the kiss he stole was to show her she was no different. And she'd thought him enlightened!

Tears stung her eyes as her chest squeezed, barely allowing her to breathe. The treachery was beyond anything she'd ever experienced. Far, far worse than Amelia throwing her favorite book into the fire. She'd respected him. Liked him. Begun to even love him. So foolish!

She'd thought she'd won the debate, but he'd capitulated to win the battle, and he'd struck to wound. His aim had been true. She collapsed into the closest chair, tears running down her cheeks. Why had she let him persuade her so? Was it simply what she wanted to hear? She shook her head. No, it was because the only man who agreed with her was her father, and when she thought she'd convinced James, that logical success connected to her emotions. She'd allowed herself to think kindly of him because he agreed with her and now her heart would pay the penalty. She wrapped her arms about herself, trying to ease the ache in her chest, but it did no good. He'd stolen her feelings and her dreams.

She sat in her misery, vaguely aware of the sounds coming from the other room. The clink of glasses and muted conversation filtered down the corridor into the parlor, everyone enjoying the festivities as if she hadn't just had her life's values dispersed like the ashes that littered the fireplace. Now all she needed was for a maid to come sweep them all up and she'd have nothing. He was no doubt enjoying Lady Caroline's company, confident in the lesson he'd accomplished. A lesson, she had no need of learning.

She swiped at her face, her gloves absorbing her tears. If he thought he'd killed her plans, he was as full of hubris as Achilles. He underestimated her if he thought she'd hand him the victory. Grasping onto the fury within her, she rose and started to pace.

CHAPTER SEVENTEEN

JAMES NOTICED THE moment Joanna left the ballroom. Though she hadn't glanced his way, he understood, thankful to Mariel for protecting her sister's reputation. What had he been thinking to whisk her off the dance floor and straight outside? He smirked. He'd been thinking he needed to hold her close and taste her sweet lips. His body's reaction to her had been fast and intense, the main reason he'd stayed away from the ballroom so long.

"Your Grace, would you agree that Almack's is becoming too selective?"

At Lady Holburn's direct address, he returned his attention to Lady Caroline and her parents. "As I have no plans to enter those hallowed halls, I have not formed an opinion on it."

Lady Caroline, who stood to his left, raised her brows. "Do you not intend for Lady Elsbeth to go to the assembly rooms? You would then know that the men there are of the highest quality."

Her words bothered him, and he could only reason it was because in the course of a few hours, his feelings had moved in another direction. He gestured to the room. "Do you think that my aunt and I have not done well in providing Elsbeth with a selection of possible husbands?"

"Oh, I'm sure you have chosen only the best for your cousin based upon your knowledge of London society. But the ladies at

Almack's are much more aware of all that happens among the *ton*." She preened. "In fact, I have been invited there."

The young woman obviously had not heard the rebuke in his voice.

Lord Holburn cleared his throat. "I think the duke is smart to avoid such censure."

Obviously, the man understood the insult his daughter had cast upon them. "Far too many rules there for men. An atmosphere such as this is much more conducive to true conversation."

As another couple, who had overheard the conversation, engaged the Holburns, Caroline moved to stand before him. She looked lovely in an ivory dress with pure white lace and gold ribbons. An ivory ribbon encircled her throat, and she wore golden dragonflies in her hair. The effects made her shine in a golden light, but he found the rich maroon of Joanna's dress more to his liking. Despite its color, or because of it, she seemed warm and welcoming, while Lady Caroline appeared like a porcelain doll, cold and breakable.

"Your Grace, I would speak to you privately."

He hadn't expected that from a woman who just touted that she was beyond reproach when it came to propriety, and therefore, invited to Almack's. His aunt's words just a few nights ago, whispered through his mind. *She's too perfect, I guess. Almost to the point where she seems not quite human. There is no emotion, and if there is, it is hidden. You deserve a woman who would be honest with you about what she's feeling.*

He motioned toward the corner, not comfortable with being out of sight of his guests once again. One faux pas was plenty for the evening. He wanted people to remember his cousin, not him.

Lady Caroline's lower lip came out and she pouted prettily, but she didn't say a word. Instead, she glided toward the corner empty of people, but still in full view, especially of her parents. When she stopped, she turned to face him. "This ball for Elsbeth is absolutely lovely. I so wish I had met you at my coming out ball."

His curiosity was piqued. "Are you saying your affections are with another? If so, I understand." If that were the way of it, he felt relieved.

She shook her head. "Oh, no. I did not mean to give you that impression. I was just daydreaming how wonderful it would have been to know you all season."

She paused as if purposefully drawing out what she had to say in hopes of keeping him riveted. What he wished to do was turn around and see if Joanna had reentered the ballroom.

"Though it's probably for the best that we have known each other for a short while. Already, I find myself on the end of insulting barbs couched in smiles."

He frowned. "Why would the length of time we have known each other cause such rudeness."

She took out her fan and fluttered it. "I'm afraid that jealousy in women can be quite hateful. There are women in this very room who have made it clear they don't like that I have so much of your attention. You must understand that many of them would prefer you spend time with them instead of me." Her coy smile didn't fit the situation.

Curious about why she brought this to his attention, he decided on a different tactic. "Then it's best that as the host, I dance with more ladies. I do not want any of my guests to feel slighted." He gave her a nod and turned away.

She sidled up to him in a moment. "Of course you have your duties. I really don't mind that they are jealous because I do so enjoy your company."

He continued to walk toward his aunt, curious as to why Joanna's younger sister was in the room but not she.

"Don't forget we have another dance after dinner."

He stopped, having indeed forgotten. "I think, considering the atmosphere you are having to endure on my account, that we forgo that dance. I don't want anyone, you, or my other guests to feel uncomfortable."

"Oh, I'm sure you don't have to go to such extremes."

He looked her in her eyes until she stopped smiling. "Nevertheless, that is what I will do."

Her mouth dropped open in surprise, but he ignored her and strode toward his aunt. Taking out his pocket watch, he was pleased to see that it was almost time for the announcement of supper. He reached his aunt who watched her daughter on the dance floor. The supper dance was finishing up. He glanced among the dancers and not seeing Joanna, leaned in closer to his aunt. "Has Lady Joanna returned yet?"

His aunt's gaze did not leave Elsbeth. "Not since you made such a stir dancing the waltz with her."

"A stir? Because I escorted her outside for cool air before checking in on Venus's foal?"

"Please, James. You don't have to lie to me. I'm well aware of what occurred, though our guests are just speculating." She turned her head, her chocolate gaze critical. "You need to decide what she means to you before you have another word with her." She returned her gaze to Elsbeth.

She hadn't spoken to him like that since he was two score, after he'd been caught in his cups with not one but two naked women in his bed at Oxford. Now, as then, it kindled his arrogance. "I will speak to her when I deem it appropriate. At the moment, she has not returned to the ballroom."

The music ended to laughter and clapping before Harrison announced dinner. The repast was set up along one long wall of their formal dining room with various tables scattered about. It allowed people to congregate as they would for the meal. Despite his aunt's reprimand, he'd planned to escort Joanna in. With that lady suspiciously absent, he did not want Lady Caroline to find him after their last conversation. "May I have the privilege of escorting you into dinner then?"

She didn't say anything at first, noting instead the young man escorting Elsbeth out of the room. Finally, she cocked her head at him. "Wouldn't you prefer to dine with someone closer to your age?"

"I feel as host and hostess that we should go in together."

"Hmmm, very well." Clearly, she knew that was not his reason, but at the moment, he was happy for her cooperation. As they entered the dining room, he scanned the area for Joanna, but she wasn't present. Had she gone to his library to ruminate on their kiss? Even at the thought, his mood improved. He very much wanted to know what she thought.

Two old friends of his aunt invited them to sit just as a footman found him. He didn't need to hear the message to know it had to do with Joanna. Fear skittered up his back. Had she fallen? Did someone else try to kiss her? He motioned to the exit and the footman followed him out. In the relatively quiet corridor, the man gave him a small note.

Some of his anxiousness melted away. Mayhap she wished to meet in private again. Opening it, he read the two words beautifully written across it. Terrace. Now. Not exactly the romantic gesture he'd thought, but nonetheless an invitation to privacy. He nodded to the footman and retraced his steps to the ballroom. All the doors were open now and the night air cooled the suddenly empty room. Striding across the floor he would consider Elsbeth's night a success. He stepped out onto the terrace. Looking both right and left, he saw no one. Then movement by the cupid fountain caught his eye and he grinned. Jogging down the steps, he strode forward, his arms itching to hold her once again.

As he came upon her, he slowed his anticipation, shifting from the physical to the intellectual. She paced briskly back and forth, which could only mean one thing: she had something on her mind. He stopped, ready to give counsel, advice, reassurance, new ideas, whatever she needed. If he could be as excited by her mentally as physically, could that mean he had discovered that illusive emotion called love? He was very fond of her, but love? He would need to ponder that more fully, though just the idea seemed to lift a weight from his shoulders. "Joanna? You sent for me?"

She started, stopping at the sound of his voice, her back to him.

She must have been deep in thought about this issue to have been unaware of his presence.

Turning to face him, her left hand landed on her hip. "I did. I have a question for you."

Her calmness in light of her former pacing must mean it was no large matter. So why not ask him at dinner? "What is your question? I will do my utmost to answer it."

"Why did you suggest I start a school only to then tell everyone that such a school would make my students unmarriageable and to stay clear of them as wives?"

He blinked, trying to comprehend what she'd said, but it made no sense. "I wouldn't."

Her eyes narrowed. "But you did. I spoke to all four mothers who are here, who had originally planned to send their daughters to me, and they all said the same. In fact, they said the same exact thing, that you would not recommend their daughters to your friends if they were to attend my school." She dropped her hand and took two steps toward him, her gaze intense among the garden lanterns.

He shook his head. "That's ludicrous. Why would I do that?" Was she foxed? Nothing she said made sense.

"I can think of only one reason. You wished to prove to me that I was wrong in my views on education for my peers. But you did far more than that."

His patience with her outlandish claims waned. "First, I did not talk to any of the women here who are mothers of your students. Second, I have not spoken to anyone of your school at all. Third, if I wanted to prove you wrong, I could have done so in a much easier way. What is all this foolishness?"

"Foolishness?" Her hands at her sides curled into fists. "Yes, it is foolishness. I was foolish to have believed you, trusted you, agreed with you. I thought you were better than my first impression of you, but I have discovered you are far worse. You are well beyond arrogant. You are devious, calculating, malicious, and cruel. You gave me hope then destroyed it, but even worse, you distracted me with a kiss as if you cared."

A tightness formed in his chest. "Enough. I will not stand here to be spoken to in such a way."

She pointed to the open doors of the ballroom. "Then go. Go back to Lady Caroline. You two will make a perfect couple, crushing people's feelings for your own enjoyment. And I," she pointed to her chest, "I will have my school in the country far from your judgements and opinions."

At the thought of what waited him inside, his stomach tightened. He didn't want Lady Caroline. What he wanted was the Jo he'd come to know, not the harridan that stood before him. That she could think he would do something so vicious, pushed him past confusion and into hurt anger. "*Your* judgment of my character is greatly misconstrued. I see no reason to further take this insult."

He turned on his heel and headed for the house. Inside the doors, the stone doves greeted him. Barely refraining from smashing them to the floor, he stalked through the room, his future seeming to stretch before him as one endless counting of days. Insulted and furious, he stepped into his library and closed the doors, locking them.

The pain in his chest spread with the need to lash out. Stomping to the chair before his desk, he punched it. It toppled to the carpet below but gave him no satisfaction. Spotting the open space on his bookshelf where the missing book, the book *she'd* taken, should have been, he thrust his hand in it and sent the entire shelf of books crashing to the floor. Breathing hard, he cleared another shelf and another. How dare she?

Still not able to find control, he strode to the side board and opened the decanter of scotch. Filling a glass, he then gulped it down, the liquid fire connecting with the pain inside. He recognized the pain. He'd felt it when his father dropped the note that stated his mother and sister's ship had wrecked off Fire Island just before reaching America. He felt it the afternoon his father stared at him, and with tears in his eyes, said he could no longer look upon him because it was like looking upon his mother. It was the pain of being rejected by someone he loved.

Pouring another glass, he threw back half, then strode to the window, his heart starting to race. The darkness outside was complete, no moon to shed light on how she could conclude that he would do something so heartless. Joanna had lured him in and rejected him. His own mind wouldn't work, the emotional pain too much.

His chest tightened, his breaths shortening. The lamp in the room suddenly felt too bright. He moved from one to the other, snuffing them out until only the light from the fire lit the room and still it felt like too much. He strode to the wingback chair before the fireplace, his breaths coming quickly. He dropped into the chair as his chest burned for air. He lowered his head between his knees. He needed to focus on Burhleigh Park, but the image of Joanna in full anger would allow nothing else.

Darkness crept in, beckoning him until he succumbed.

A knock at the door woke him. He was on the rug in front of the fireplace. Sitting up, he stared at the darkness beyond the firelight. As his conscience awoke, so did his mind, and coldness swept through him.

"James, are you in there?"

Aunt Louisa. The ball. Elsbeth. Swallowing hard, he pushed away the encounter with a cruel Joanna and sat in the chair. "Yes, I'm here."

"Our guests have finished dinner. Will you be joining us soon?" The concern in her voice was obvious.

He slowly stood, wobbling a little as he pulled down on his waistcoat. He had duties to perform and people he was responsible for. That hadn't changed.

Walking to the door, he opened it. "Yes, I'm here." Stepping out, he closed the door behind him. Strains of music filtered into the corridor corroborating his aunt's statement that he'd missed dinner and the dancing had begun again. "But we can tell anyone who missed me that I had to oversee the caring of the new foal."

His aunt lowered her brows. "What's wrong?"

"Nothing I wish to discuss. Shall we return to the festivities?" The distraction would help him get through the rest of the evening. He owed it to Elsbeth. This was her night. He offered his aunt his arm.

"Did you find Joanna? She didn't come to dinner, and Harrison said the Mabry carriage is gone."

He forced a smile. "Yes, I did. Now let us make sure Elsbeth continues to have a night to remember."

His aunt's gaze searched his, but he refused to reveal the pain she would recognize.

"Very well. We can talk tomorrow."

As he led his aunt back into the lively ballroom, he perused it, noting where each Mabry was situated and determined to be nowhere near them.

CHAPTER EIGHTEEN

JOANNA SAT AT the desk in the library adding numbers to the family ledgers. Numbers were safe. They weren't good or bad. They didn't make memories nor make her cry. They simply were. Adding her final column, she set the quill aside and blew lightly. The Mabry family was very comfortable; however, the work she'd contracted on Silver Meadows would make a dent in the funds Aunt Mabry left her with the house. She would have to figure out costs for students and teachers and then determine a price. She'd already mapped out a schedule, though she had no students yet. She doubted Elsbeth would be attending, and Lady Astor must know by now that their friendship was at an end thanks to what James had done last week at the ball.

The spike of pain in her heart made her gasp. The Greek poet Menander said time healed all necessary evils, but her heart hurt as if the ball was yesterday. Every task or conversation made her cry or made her angry. Only planning for her school kept her functioning. Amelia avoided her, Mariel offered empathy, and her father bought her books. But her mother had been her silent champion. Confessing all to her family, who agreed they should not tell Teddy, she'd found some comfort from talking with them. She discussed her plans with her father and admittedly cried on her mother's shoulder. Her mother didn't judge her for her own stupidity or lack of foresight. In fact, her mother had purposefully avoided the two events she'd planned to attend, knowing the Huntingtons would be going.

The one secret she kept from her mother had been about *the book*. She glanced at the cabinet. It had come home with her. Almost every day, she took it out once and remembered what it was like to feel such an intimate connection to a man. Her broken heart still not accepting that James could have been so cruel, but her mind, wrathful, determined to prove him wrong. The first night she almost threw the book in the fire, but it was a book, something to be treasured despite its owner. She was its new owner now. There would be no returning the book. But she would never open it again.

She rose from the desk and walked to the window. The gardens outside the library were full of small green leaves, but like most homes, the colorful flowers never appeared in the cold temperatures of their unusual summer. She didn't mind. Her soul didn't want to see bright cheery flowers. As her gaze drifted past the bushes, it landed on the ice house near the kitchens. The sadness of missing Belinda tore at her new heartache, and she spun to face the room again. She needed to do something, anything to engage her mind and let her heart heal.

She started for the door, but it opened before she could reach it. "Teddy." He rarely came into the library when he visited.

"I need to talk to you." His hair was disheveled as if he'd run his hand through it a number of times and his cravat was a mess.

She frowned. "Have you been drinking spirits?"

He strode in, dropping into the wingback chair her father used. Probably because it was the closest seat to him.

He waved off her question. "She has too many suitors. What am I to do?"

She didn't have to ask who he spoke of. Elsbeth was the only thing he'd talked about since he met her. She better understood how he felt about the young woman now. Dragging the chair from the desk over to the area where he sat, she tamped down her irritation at his constant need for support. Maybe it had to do with being an only child. Of course, James was an only child and had lost both his parents as well, and he didn't seem to need support at all. Then again, he had to be at least eight years older and had no heart, while Teddy did.

She took a seat and patted his hand. "Come, tell me everything."

He pulled his hand away. "I did. She has too many suitors. I go to call on her and there are at least five other men there. Five." He held up his five fingers as if she didn't know how many that was.

She let the insult pass. "But you were there too, were you not?"

He threw one leg over the arm of the chair. "It doesn't matter. I'm just one of many. I had to literally trip a bloke in order to reach her first at last night's ball. Even dancing with her has become a major accomplishment."

"You are no longer the only gentleman she knows. You knew this was coming."

His brows lowered into an ugly scowl. "That's not helpful."

She sat back, studying him objectively. Did he really love Elsbeth or was he enamored of her? "What is her favorite book?"

"Huh?" His head jerked back as if she'd tried to hit him.

"I asked what her favorite book is."

"I don't know." His gaze darted toward the bookcase across from him before he looked at her. "We haven't talked about books. But we have talked at length about her. Her favorite color is violet, and she can't wait to marry so she can wear it. I told her I would buy her dozens of violet gowns."

That wasn't much. "And what is her favorite food, fondest memory, greatest interest."

He pulled at his cravat. "Why are you quizzing me? You're supposed to be supporting me. Telling me not to worry."

Irritation burned hot, like everything else about her emotions lately. "How do you expect me to tell you that when I don't have the facts?" She rose and walked to the bookcase to lean against it. "You tell me you love her. So what do you know of her?"

His gaze shifted to someplace far away. "I know she's beautiful and kind and would make a wonderful mother. She's always polite and gracious. As the hostess of a marquess, she would be perfect. She has a gentle smile and a lovely laugh. Her pale blue eyes have a touch of violet in them, and when she smiles, they crinkle at the corners. She listens to everything I say and even asks why I made certain comments." He returned his gaze to her. "You'll also be happy to know that she has a quick wit and an adorable sense of humor."

Everything he listed disappointed her. She'd thought she'd had some influence on him, but he sounded like every other man looking for a wife. Did he not care that Elsbeth wanted to learn and even start a collection. She opened her mouth to comment, but he held up his finger.

"And before you ask, she is well-read and very intelligent. Though I don't know her favorite book, I do know she likes to study rocks and minerals and has much knowledge of astronomy and literature, but doesn't care for philosophy." He lifted his brows as if expecting a compliment.

Relieved at least some of what she'd taught him had taken, she was still not sure he loved Elsbeth, but she would accept that he did for argument's sake. "I'm pleased that you know so much about her. She must know about you if she listens to your every word."

Color rose in his cheeks. "I'm not saying she agrees with me all the time."

"Good. That's the first indication that there is some mutual respect."

He dropped his leg and sat up. "That's not fair. Of course we respect each other."

His attitude was grating on her. "Does she love you?"

Teddy stood. "Of course she does. Why wouldn't she? What are you saying?"

She shrugged. "You can't simply tell by a person's face if they love you. Their actions and their words are more important." And even those could be meant to deceive as she'd discovered.

"Does she make time for you, or does she share her time equally among her suitors to be fair?"

He scowled. "How would I know how she spends her time with other gentlemen? When she's with me, she focuses wholly on me."

"And maybe she does the same with other men. She's just come out and has a number of men who are interested in her. I'm sure, if she is intelligent as you say, she is weighing their characteristics and deciding which would best suit her."

Teddy ran his hand through his hair as he walked away before he turned back, his eyes narrowed. "And what about love? Love is an emotion. It's not a logical weighing of pros and cons. Love is something you feel." He snorted. "But what would you know of that? I should have searched out Mariel. At least she has a heart."

Insulted and hurt, she rounded on him, dropping her arms and pointing a finger at him. "Do you know that Elsbeth loves you? Has she told you so? Has she let you kiss her and whispered in your ear that she loves you and wants to be your wife?"

His face turned red. "I would never kiss her unless she felt that way."

The pain in her heart seemed to burst inside her chest. She lashed out. "And have you kissed her?"

He stared, her implication reaching him.

She nodded curtly. "You'd best figure out what you will do if she doesn't fall in love with you."

"I don't have to stand here and listen to you. You have no idea what it's like to be in love. It's not all logic and knowledge. No wonder no one wants you for a wife."

Her heart stopped beating for a moment, but when it started, anguish filled her.

Teddy stormed out, and she crumpled to the floor. She did know what it was to love and not be loved in return, and despite all her efforts, it was killing her. Tears flowed as silent sobs wracked her. If only she could go back to being ignorant about love. The knowledge was far too painful.

CHAPTER NINETEEN

"J AMES, YOU NEED to talk to Lady Joanna."

At his aunt's unannounced entrance, he stiffened. He sat back in his chair, the book he was reading, or trying to read, still open on his desk. "Actually, I don't."

She strode forward, uninvited and stood across from him. "Yes, you do. I don't know what caused this rift between the two of you, but you need to be the gentleman and repair it."

"Me? I'll have you know I did nothing. She came at me accusing me of despicable acts and then left. It's clear the woman doesn't know who I am."

Unfortunately, his aunt decided to sit in one of the two stuffed chairs before his desk. "What did she say?"

He crossed his ankle over his knee. "The words were too unladylike for me to repeat."

"Oh please." She waved him off. "I'm a grown woman. Tell me."

He sighed. He'd known this would happen eventually. It had been a week, and she had held her tongue, but even she noticed there were no Mabrys beside Lord Mabry at any event they attended. It was as if they'd vanished. Mayhap they had returned to their country estate. He'd tried to carry on as if nothing was amiss, but his aunt was far too intelligent, and she'd obviously deduced that him being in his library the night of Elsbeth's ball had something to do with Joanna.

She patted the arm of the chair. "Come, James. You know I only want the best for you. I've helped you many times before. Don't you think talking about it might help you with a plan of action?"

Oh, she was good, appealing to his intellect. It was also an exact quote from himself, and she knew it. "Fine. Lady Joanna accused me of telling her students' mothers that I would not recommend their daughters to my peers if they attended her school."

Her eyes widened and her hand found her chest. "James, you didn't."

He scowled. "Of course I didn't. I told you, the woman doesn't know me."

"What else did she say?"

He blinked in surprise. "Isn't that enough?"

"No. What else? Tell me everything."

He thought back to that night, as he had every day for a week, though he didn't want to. For the first time, he'd not simply known what he wanted in his life, but he had craved it. Her accusations had been crushing. "She said when I kissed her, I pretended to care."

"You kissed her?"

He dropped his foot to the ground and stood. "You know I did. After our waltz, in the garden. She was wrong. I did care. But she thinks I encouraged her only to undermine everything she planned. It was ludicrous."

His aunt pondered that then shook her head. "We are missing something. What made her think you had told the students' mothers that you wouldn't recommend their daughters for marriage?"

He shrugged. "I don't know. No, I do. She said they told her I said that. But I didn't talk to anyone about the blasted school." He strode around the desk and leaned his hips against it. I'm telling you, the woman must believe anything she hears, even gossip against me. Perhaps her unusual intelligence has a downside."

"That doesn't sound like Lady Joanna."

"No, it doesn't. But it is. The whole episode is a moot point. I'm calling on Lady Caroline's father today to ask for her hand in marriage. I believe he will accept, don't you agree?"

His aunt looked like he felt, crestfallen. "There's no rush. The season doesn't end for another four weeks. I want to investigate this." She rose.

He pushed away from the desk. "You may do what you like, but my mind is made up. I will visit the Holburns today.

"No." Elsbeth's voice came from the doorway.

He and his aunt looked at her as she walked in as if walking toward a corpse. Her hands were clasped, and her shoulders slumped forward. He was in no mood for emotional theatrics. He knew how much she liked Joanna, but he would not delay or change his plans because his cousin, who could well be married and living in her own home soon, didn't like his decision.

His aunt held out her hands to Elsbeth. "Why do you look so dispirited? Is it because you don't like your cousin's choice of bride?" She threw him a warning look not to say anything.

He kept silent as his cousin took her mother's hands.

"What did you want to tell us, dear?"

Elsbeth looked at her mother, then dropped her mother's hands, straightened her shoulders and faced him. "I was the one who revealed the secret school. I was just so excited. I was chatting with Lady Caroline as I assumed you had told her. At least, she didn't seem surprised by the school, but she asked me a lot of questions. I'm sorry. I shouldn't have told her. I wonder if someone overheard us and told all the mothers."

He glanced at his aunt who looked at him. He doubted very much that anyone overheard them. Lady Caroline had purposefully caused the rift between him and Joanna. It made so much sense, it angered him he hadn't figured it out.

"Elsbeth." His aunt put a hand on her daughter's shoulder. "I understand, and I'm sure your cousin does, too. I just have one question. Did you know who the other students were and relate that to Lady Caroline?"

She nodded at her mother, then turned to him. "Do you forgive me?"

"I do." At least now he knew why Joanna was so upset. It still stung that she hadn't believed him. Worse, that she could think he had planned to crush her dreams for over a month.

Lady Elsbeth started out the library door, but stopped when her mother spoke.

"Do close the door, please. I would like a private word with James."

Elsbeth's gaze moved to him before she gave an abbreviated nod and pulled the door closed.

He took the initiative. "Did you have something else that is pressing? I do want to visit the booksellers today. Avery put aside a volume for me that he thinks I will be particularly interested in."

"I'm sure I misheard you. I believe you meant to say you'd be calling on the Mabrys, correct?"

He frowned. "Why would I want to call on the Mabrys? It's obvious that Lady Joanna's opinion of me is hardly complementary."

"But that's because she doesn't know the truth." His aunt studied him. "Surely you aren't going to still request Lady Caroline's hand, are you? What she did was purposeful with the intent to do harm. Heaven forbid she were to take a dislike toward me or Elsbeth. What if she turned on her own husband? He could well meet with a questionable accident and then—"

"Enough." He raised his hand. "No need for melodrama. I am not so enamored of Lady Caroline that I cannot see what type of person she is based on her recent actions. You can rest assured I will not be calling on her again."

She raised her chin a fraction. "I never doubted that. I simply looked for confirmation. Now as to Lady Joanna."

"There is no Lady Joanna. If you still wish to teach at her

school, and Elsbeth still wishes to attend it, I will not hinder you from doing so. I do not see a need to be in her presence again." As he said the words, his chest tightened, but he knew them to be the best course of action to take.

"What?" His aunt gestured toward the library door. "You heard Elsbeth. Lady Caroline caused this misunderstanding between you two. You need to tell Joanna the truth."

"I did, and she didn't believe me." He pushed away from the desk and walked back to his chair. "She chose instead to believe that I lied and schemed. She believes I am a monster. I see no reason to further our acquaintance." He sat and turned the page in his book. In time, his feelings for the unusual Joanna would fade. Perhaps if Elsbeth had an offer before the end of the season, they could all repair to Burhleigh Park. He'd just have to come back another season to find a bride.

"Further your acquaintance?" His aunt stood and stepped to the front of his desk. "You two went far beyond acquaintances. You were even more than friends. You kissed her because your heart told you to." She slammed her hands, palms down on the desk in front of him. "Your pride may be hurting, but it's nothing compared to how you will feel if you let that remarkable woman slip through your fingers."

She pushed away from the desk and crossed her arms over her chest. "Use that intellect of yours. Have you ever thought what it must have been like for Joanna to have her dreams crushed? Whether it was by you or anyone, but for it to be laid at your feet, the man she respects, admires, and who she has come to care deeply for, had to have hurt her far worse than any wounded pride you may be suffering. Remember, James." She dropped her arms and pierced him with her dark gaze. "Lady Joanna has never had a suitor. Not one. Not one man willing to get to know her and who she is. She has no experience with what was happening between you two. You are the first man not to reject her out of hand because she can think!"

Her chest rose and fell rapidly as she spun away from him and stalked toward the library doors. When she reached them, she turned back and pointed at him. "You think long and hard about this, and make the right decision based on the facts, not on your wounded pride." With that, she strode out, slamming the door behind her.

He stared at the dark panels, in shock at his aunt's outburst. She always controlled her emotions. He'd only seen her like that once before. It had been the day she'd arrived at Burhleigh Park and found out his father had left to live apart from him *and* the memories he stirred because he looked so much like his mother. Their butler took the brunt of her tirade that day, but to his credit remained, in full agreement.

Both his parents had abandoned him. His mother first, risking her life to voyage back to America to see her family, only to drown, taking his sister with her. Then his father, who couldn't stand to live with him and passed three years later. They said he'd died of a broken heart. It was that notion that had him looking for a wife who would fulfill the duties of a duchess and be a pleasant companion, nothing more.

Joanna had abandoned him, too. But she was still alive and her reason for doing so made sense now. But what he felt for her, if he were honest, was far more than simply pleasant. Unexpectedly, his feelings for her had grown deep, deeper than he ever wanted to feel, stronger than anything he'd felt before. That scared him.

He leaned back in his chair, crossing his ankle over his knee and grasping it. Was this how his father had felt for his mother? That unnerved him. He searched his mind for memories of his parents together before his mother left on her fateful voyage. It seemed as if his memories started that day. The day she took his sister but wouldn't take him.

Dropping his foot to the floor, he stood. His instinct told him he needed to remember. He needed to know if he were to make the right decision now. Strolling across the room, he stopped in front of the bay windows. The cold morning with the sun peaking in and out of the clouds gave the limited greenery a cold shimmer. It reminded him of his first snowfall. There had only been a light dusting, but he found the sight wonderous and insisted on going outside.

His heart filled with aching warmth as the memory of his mother buttoning his coat filled his head. He closed his eyes and breathed in, almost smelling her light vanilla scent. She'd smiled at him, her blue eyes twinkling with excitement. When she finished, she kissed him on the nose, and rose to don her coat as well. She couldn't button it because her stomach had grown so large. She was expecting.

She took his hand and they stopped at his father's study where she opened the door and told his father they were going to play in the snow. His father had frowned, warning her to take care. She'd laughed.

He opened his eyes as her laughter filled his head. He'd forgotten her laughter. It always made him happy. They'd gone outside and within minutes his father had joined them. He had been smiling as he approached them while they tried to catch the snowflakes on their tongues.

Sinking into the closest chair, he concentrated, holding the memory close. He'd forgotten the man could smile. His father watched them for a moment before a low growl came from low in his throat and he wrapped his arms around his wife and kissed her.

Stunned at the images floating through his mind, he tried to analyze them, but the memories started to assail him. His mother looking up from a book she read to him as his father walked into the parlor. His father's gaze filled with love, not shuttering the emotion when his mother looked up at his entrance. His parents walking hand in hand in the gardens at Burhleigh Park as he investigated a frog ahead of them, his sister skipping far ahead. The four of them sitting at the table having dinner together, his mother insisting her children be with them, her American ways, foreign but accepted by his father.

His heart pounded as buried feelings of childhood happiness filled him. He gripped the arms of the wingback chair as those memories dissipated under the onslaught of the usual ones. The next three babies had not made it and he felt his mother's tiredness, though he didn't understand it. His mother leaving to visit her family, taking his sister with her. She had struggled to live up to English standards. As a child, he didn't understand why it mattered that their neighbors had thought her manners were poor and she had odd ways with him and his older sister. He also didn't understand what she'd meant by the pressure to give his father another child. All he knew is she'd left him to visit her family in America and died in the crossing.

He never wanted to love like his father had. It was far too risky. But Joanna was not American. Nor did she care what others thought of her except to the extent it would affect her family. In fact, she had planned to purposefully challenge society in order to move it forward. She was far different from his mother.

As his logical side kicked in, he stood. All this time, he'd been following society's dictates. He'd looked for, found, and courted a woman who would fit the role of duchess perfectly and not expect any deep emotion from him in return. While he'd been convinced of Joanna's argument, he'd still continued on his course to marry Lady Caroline. He was a hypocrite!

He strode back to his desk. In his estimation, there was nothing worse for a well-read man to be than a hypocrite. He wanted to rail at himself, but that was a waste of time and emotion. Joanna's unwillingness to believe him made far more sense now. She saw that he continued on his old path while professing to believe in women being equally educated. He'd not even considered her, who was the epitome of such a woman, as a wife. He'd been so blind to his own hypocrisy that he'd fallen in love with her despite it.

He stood before his desk, staring at his bookshelf. He'd returned all his books to their proper place, not allowing the staff in until he'd done so, and had closed in the space where the book she'd taken had been. It was as if he could close off his feelings for her, but he couldn't. He loved her. He knew it now with far greater assuredness than he had denied it.

Walking around his desk, he pulled out a plain piece of paper. He needed to explain what happened, but first he needed to make things right. He dipped the quill in the ink and wrote:

Call on parents of students
Call on Lady Caroline and family
Go to booksellers for a special book as a gift
Call on Lady Joanna.

He set the quill back in the inkstand then reread his list. It made sense. The only task on it that made him uncomfortable being the last. Strengthening his resolve, he stood. His aunt was correct. No matter what he had to go through to have Joanna in his life again, he had to do it because he couldn't imagine life now without her. Striding to the door, he opened it and bellowed. "Harrison, have my coach brought around."

CHAPTER TWENTY

JAMES STOOD AT the window in the parlor. His aunt and cousin alighted from the coach and slowly made their way to the door. He turned expectantly, forcing himself to remain where he was and not rush out into the entry way. He stared at the closed doors of the room, willing them to open.

After fulfilling his list of tasks to win Joanna back, he'd visited Craymore Hall four times in the last week. Each time he'd been told she was not at home. It was obvious she didn't want to see him, but how was he supposed to explain, if she wouldn't see him? Finally, he enlisted the aid of his aunt and cousin, who were delighted to be of service.

The parlor doors opened, and his aunt stepped in.

"Well?" He couldn't keep from taking a step forward. "Did she see you?"

His aunt gave a brief nod. "She did, but only if we promised not to talk about you."

He turned away, not willing to let his aunt see how much that news hurt. He spoke over his shoulder. "But you were gone half the afternoon."

His aunt's chuckle had him turning back.

"It was only an hour. Really James, we did have more to talk about besides you."

"I don't appreciate your levity."

"No, I don't suppose you do. I apologize." She settled onto the settee.

"How did she look?" He steeled himself to hear that she was as vibrant as ever.

His aunt shook her head. "When we arrived, she was quite stiff and unhappy. As Elsbeth said, she looked like a ghost."

At the mention of his cousin, he glanced toward the open doorway. "Will Elsbeth be joining us? I'd like her insight as well."

"No, she has a ball to attend tonight, so she has gone to rest, which we both should do as well."

Of course. He'd forgotten about the ball, his mind focused only on seeing Joanna. He hated the feeling that the longer it took, the less likely she would be willing to listen. It had already been over a fortnight. "Were you able to mention anything to help my cause?"

His aunt grinned. "Oh, yes. My daughter is quite ingenious. I like to think that she is much like me. She talked about how excited she was that Eleanor's and Dorothea's mothers had changed their minds and were allowing them to attend Lady Joanna's school. She innocently asked if she might know anyone else who would be attending."

Despite his mood, he gave her a crooked grin. "I think I have been underestimating my cousin."

"I know you have." The pride on his aunt's face reminded him of his mother's when he'd recited his alphabet to her. Ever since the afternoon in his library when he'd forced himself to remember events from when they were a happy family, snippets of memories would surface at the oddest times.

"And did Lady Joanna mention the other two women?"

"She did. Of course, then we began to talk about the school. She has such wonderful plans. She already has construction started on Silver Meadows. I admit we talked at length about the school. She asked us about coming up with some possible names."

As pleased as he was that she continued to move forward

with her plans, he wanted some hint that she'd be open to talking to him. "Did you mention Lady Caroline?"

"I did. I asked her if she had heard Lady Caroline was betrothed to the Earl of Montrose. She hadn't and was quite surprised. From what I gathered, she hasn't been attending any social events." His aunt paused as if choosing her words carefully. "She made it sound as if she has been so busy with her plans for the school that she hasn't had time for society, but I think she's hiding."

That got his attention. "Hiding? Hiding from what?"

"You, maybe? There was a brittleness about her that concerned me. The only time it left was when we discussed her plans. My opinion is that her heart is broken, and she's trying to heal."

His stomach tightened at the thought of Joanna in such a condition.

"Elsbeth saw it too and feels responsible. Poor dear was almost in tears on the way home."

He shook his head. "It is not Elsbeth's fault. It's mine. I'm the one whose actions belied my words." Now, if he could just get her to see him.

"That may be true, but it won't assuage Elsbeth's guilt. I think that's only part of it."

"What do you mean?" He studied his aunt as she sighed. Something obviously troubled her.

"For all Elsbeth's intelligence, I fear that her coming out has not done her well. She is too easily flattered by all the attention and now she is questioning her feelings for Lord Mabry."

Surprised, he moved closer, taking the chair opposite her. "I thought you preferred that she not settle on Lord Mabry."

"That's correct, but only if it's because she truly does not have feelings for him. Now, with all the young men paying attention to her, I don't think she knows what she feels. She may no longer be interested in Lord Mabry simply because she's known him the longest and the others are like...they're like a shop full of new hats."

He understood what she meant, having seen the effects of Elsbeth's entrance into society. She'd not only charmed half the eligible bachelors, but the matriarchs of the *ton* as well. "Then we must do our best to guide her." Though he felt ill equipped to guide his young cousin after the failed results of his own pursuit.

"Yes, well, perhaps I'll tackle that on my own as you have your own tangle to unravel. What do you plan to do? Accepting every invitation as you have been, won't put you in her company if she isn't going out. And if she refuses to see you at home, I'm not sure what your options are."

He didn't either, but he'd think of something. Now at least, she knew she had her students back and that he had no interest in Lady Caroline. He could write her a letter, but that was a last resort. If she was still hurt and angry at him, she might not read it, and he'd never know. He wasn't quite desperate enough to hire a Bow Street runner to follow her so he could arrive wherever she went, especially if she wasn't leaving her house. "Perhaps if I call on her daily, she'll finally see me."

Her eyes widened. "You wouldn't."

"No, at least not yet. Maybe I could give a lecture at the Royal Institution."

"Can you do that on short notice? What would you lecture on? And more to the issue at hand, if she knows you're the lecturer, wouldn't she avoid it?"

"Valid point." There had to be some way to draw her out. The Paris panorama was due to remain for the entire month. He didn't want to wait another fortnight to see her. Though she might visit another museum, there was no way of knowing which one. "I could ask Lord Mabry about their next outing."

She perked up at that idea, then her shoulders slumped. "No, that won't be of use. He's the only one attending events. From what Lady Joanna said, her younger sister is preparing for an exhibit and her older sister is visiting a friend in Bedford. Lord Mabry is attending every event Elsbeth attends, so that won't help you."

He rose again and moved toward the window. "There must be something I can do to see her." The first time he had arranged to see her, he'd gone to Vauxhall because Lord Mabry had mentioned they would be there, but even Joanna said she only ventured into the Pleasure Gardens when Monsieur Armand served his mascarpone ice cream. He stilled. "That's it!"

"What's it?"

He scanned the parlor, looking for his papers. His aunt and cousin often skimmed them when he'd finished with them. "Is today's *Chronicle* in here?"

She shook her head. "No. I didn't see anything of interest and had Harrison take it below stairs. Why?"

"I need it and any other we may still have."

"But James, there will be a new paper tomorrow. Whatever would you want with old news?"

"You're right. Why wait for a paper? I can go straight to the source." He strode to the door.

"Wait, where are you going?"

"I need to go to a confectioner."

CHAPTER TWENTY-ONE

"Joanna, he's not here."

At her mother's voice, she returned her attention to her parents. They had just settled in at a table at Vauxhall. "I'm sorry."

Her mother patted her hand. "It's fine. With how much you feel for him, I can understand not wanting to see him."

When her mother phrased it in such a way, it made her sound foolish. "I'm just confused. Why would he tell my students' mothers that he wouldn't recommend them for marriage if they went to my school, and then call on all of them to endorse it?"

"I don't know dear."

"I do."

At her father's words, she looked to him. "Please, enlighten me. I find the male mind unfathomable."

He laughed. "That is what we men think of you women. But I can shed a little light on this particular puzzle. The duke is an idiot who played with your feelings."

Her father's words were like a warm hug. "Thank you."

"Maybe that was all he wanted was something for his own entertainment. You didn't deserve to be treated so." Her mother's gaze remained sympathetic.

He might have convinced her students' mothers to let their daughters attend her school again, but he could never undo the damage he'd done to her heart. She'd realized she loved him, and that he was not worthy of love, all in one night. It had been too much. Her appetite was gone, and she could no longer sleep through the night.

"Ah, Lord and Lady Wakefield, and the lovely Lady Joanna, I am so pleased you have come." Monsieur Armand smiled at her. "I can depend on you to see my advertisement, can I not?"

She welcomed the distraction, happy to drop the subject of James. "You can." She made herself smile.

"Tsk, tsk, what is this? You are not your usual happy self."

"Monsieur Armand, you are very observant." Her mother silently squeezed her hand. "Our daughter has been unwell, but she would not miss your exquisite ice cream."

"You flatter me, my lady." Monsieur Armand studied her. "Oui, I see sadness in your eyes. Let me bring you happiness." He clapped his hands and a waiter appeared. "We must bring mademoiselle Joanna a dish of mascarpone ice cream *toute suite*."

As her parents ordered their own desserts, she took the opportunity to scan the crowd again. She hadn't seen Teddy since their argument, so she couldn't ask him where he would be dancing attendance on Elsbeth. James would be there. So seeing Teddy would give her fair warning. It didn't take long to check everyone as the crowd was sparse. The cool weather had turned even colder at sundown, and only those dressed warmly had braved the chill.

Her lips quirked upward. And here she was about to eat ice cream outside. Then again, she'd rarely followed the norm, and as long as James was not about, she could relax and enjoy her outing. The band still played despite the cold, and a number of people danced about below them. Since her school would be open in the coldest times of the year, she would have to devise some outdoor activities to engage her ladies in relevant exercise.

She turned toward her mother to ask her opinion on the subject and froze. Monsieur Armand walked toward them with James. She had an immediate urge to run but where could she go?

Turning her head, she found her father's brows lowered as he looked at her. He was clearly not happy with the appearance of James and for that she was grateful.

Monsieur stepped up to their table. "*Mes amies*, I have brought a lone monsieur who needs company, might he join you?"

Her mother spoke. "That will be up to my daughter."

She swallowed hard, not even daring to look at James. If she did, she was sure she'd start crying again and probably rail at him like an unbalanced person.

"Lady Joanna, would you walk with me?"

The deep tones of his voice made her shiver with both dread and remembered passion. She shook her head, unable to speak.

"If you prefer, I could join you for ice cream instead."

She didn't want that either. She didn't want to have anything to do with him. Why did he keep trying to talk to her?

Her mother's hand grasped hers behind the table. "Perhaps it is best to hear what he has to say so that you can stop avoiding him."

The logical side of her brain agreed, but her heart didn't want to hear it. She raised her gaze to her mother's. There was sympathy, but also pride. Finally, she forced herself to look at James. He was as handsome and commanding as the last time she'd seen him. His blue wool greatcoat made his eyes seem lighter in the lantern's light and her chest tightened. She'd been strong enough to confront him, she could stand to hear what other torture he had in mind for her. At that thought, she straightened her spine. "We can walk."

"Are you sure?" Her mother's hand squeezed hers again.

"I'm sure." Rising from her seat at the table, she stepped down from the dais and moved toward him.

He held out his arm, but she refused to take it. Finally, he dropped it and motioned toward the main walkway, where but few people meandered. "It is good to see you."

His voice flowed over her, but she kept her eyes on the lit

path. She despised the fact that she felt the same about seeing him. She wanted to hate him. He deserved that. "Why did you come here?"

"I have been trying to talk to you because I've discovered what happened at Elsbeth's ball."

She snapped her head around to stare incredulously at him. "Discovered? Was not being there and manipulating your plan not clear enough for you?"

He winced at her attack, but instead of making her feel good, it just made her feel worse and even more angry. "What could there possibly be to discover?"

He didn't answer immediately. Finally, he gave his usually truncated nod as if bracing himself. "Like you, I accepted what occurred that night. I had not spoken to anyone about your school, so when you accused me, I was angry that you could think I would do something so cruel."

She opened her mouth, but he held up his hand. "Please, allow me to explain."

Snapping her mouth shut, she crossed her arms over her chest, hoping it would help her hold her tongue.

"As you are aware, I did not call on you immediately afterward because I was angry that you, whom I respected, would lay such insulting allegations at my feet."

She squeezed her arms tight to keep her mouth closed, but her body now burned with a need to yell at him.

"It wasn't until a fortnight past that I discovered the source of the problem. It was Lady Caroline."

She couldn't keep quiet any longer. Stopping she faced him. "Lady Caroline? How you can blame Lady Caroline, the perfect lady. She didn't even know about my school."

"Until that night." He stared at her as if trying to figure out what she thought, but there were few lanterns where they were, and for that she was thankful.

He sighed. "You are correct. Lady Caroline did not know at the start of the ball, but Elsbeth assumed the lady knew because she was aware that I planned to ask her to be my duchess."

Hearing the words aloud had her stomach rolling over in pain. Why should she care?

"Lady Caroline did not disabuse Elsbeth of that and proceeded to ask questions. Elsbeth told her of all the young women who would be attending with her. She had no idea that Lady Caroline had become jealous of you and wanted to undermine your plans, so as to make you less appealing to me."

She took a step back. "Lady Caroline was jealous of me? I find that difficult to believe."

For the first time since she met him, he wouldn't meet her gaze. His right hand fingered one of his coat buttons and in that brief moment, she could imagine him as a little boy, abandoned by his parents and unsure of how to proceed in the world. The image was revealing, cutting through some of her own pain.

Though he continued to look down, he finally answered her. "That was my fault. I realized after I had kissed you that I had been walking one path but believing in another. I had been raised like any other young man, to look for certain qualities in a woman and so upon meeting Lady Caroline, I had pursued her as she met every one of my standards."

Even though she was well aware of it, hearing him say it had her swallowing hard, determined to argue the point further. "Exactly, so why should she be jealous of me, of all people?"

He finally met her gaze. "Because my standards changed when I came to know you. Everything about you is the opposite of what I was taught, yet it was you I wanted to spend time with. It was you I talked about with her because it was you I wished to converse with. It was you I wanted to hold in my arms and kiss until you couldn't stand on your own feet any longer."

She sucked in her breath as his words sent a thrill ricocheting throughout her body.

"I finally recognized that I didn't want a woman like Lady Caroline and without saying so, I pulled away from whatever our relationship might have been construed as. She felt it at the ball, and I believe that is what motivated her."

He dropped his hand from his coat and straightened. "Though Elsbeth revealed your school and Lady Caroline went about undermining it, I was the root cause. Despite changing how I felt about what I wanted in the woman for me, I continued in my old behaviors. The reason I have been trying to talk to you is to ask your forgiveness."

Her mind was awhirl with all the information, but her heart beat so hard, she couldn't think.

He stepped toward her. "I haven't begged anyone to take me since my mother left Haven House to sail for America. Not even after her ship sank in a wreck off Fire Island taking her and my older sister to a watery grave, did I beg my father to take me." He reached for her hands and grasped them in his. "But Joanna, I'm begging you to take me. Forgive my mistakes. I am not infallible as much as I try to be. You have opened my eyes to what a life between equals could be like, and it is wonderous."

She sniffed, her eyes filling with tears. Never in her wildest imaginings did she envision a humble James baring his soul to her. Her heart squeezed as his gaze searched hers, hope in his eyes. Swallowing down the lump in her throat, she licked her lips. "Yes, I can forgive you."

His eyes widened before his lips moved upward into a brilliant smile. He dropped her hands and cupped her face. "I love you, Joanna Mabry."

Before she could say a word, his lips descended and she was wrapped in the scent of bergamot, her body seeming to float as happiness filled her from the very core of her heart. She kissed him back, every second washing away the pain of the last month, the hurt dissolving in the honesty and warmth of the man before her.

A man cleared his throat nearby, and she stiffened.

James immediately broke their kiss, brushing a tear from her cheek.

The man grinned and winked before attending to the conversation of the lady on his arm.

"I suppose this is not the proper place to be kissing you, but I can't say I'm sorry." He grinned like a young boy caught with his hand in the Christmas pudding.

She still reeled from his confession, too delighted to dredge up any concern about impropriety, but she did feel her own sense of guilt. "I should not have accepted what I heard. I know the kind person you are. I should have listened to you. Maybe we could have figured this out together that very night."

He tucked her arm under his. "All I care about is that we now know what occurred and you are back in my arms. I don't believe I have ever been this happy before. I wonder what the great philosophers would say about that."

She could feel it too. "Robert Herrick said 'it takes great wit and interest and energy to be happy. The pursuit of happiness is a great activity. One must be open and alive. It is the greatest feat man has to accomplish.' Of course, he was a poet, so his wisdom is circumspect."

"True, but I do think there is a kernel of truth in that last sentiment. Happiness does feel as if it is a great accomplishment. I believe many people simply exist in a comfortable place, but is it a happy one?"

She tried to keep her mind on their conversation, but it was difficult. As much as she enjoyed their talks, she felt more like jumping, or running, or spinning, though she'd learned that was not the best idea. She was just too filled with joy. "My thought is that there are multiple levels of happiness, everything from contentment to blissful joy."

He halted them at her comment. "I want you to know blissful joy."

"I think I already do." She smiled at him, her own feelings for him filling her soul.

He shook his head far longer than usual. "No, not yet. But I promise you, you will."

Something in his gaze, now lit by the myriad lanterns near

the pavilion, promised her something beyond the realm of her experience and her breath caught as tingles of pleasure skittered along her skin.

"I'd best you get you back to your parents before they grow concerned."

She waved off his comment. "They know I'm fine."

He gave her a lopsided grin. "No, I meant they might be concerned about me being in your presence so long. It was obvious you told them what happened, and they are not happy with me."

"True." She chuckled. "Will you join us for ice cream?"

He shivered. "No, I need to make an appearance at a recital and let Elsbeth know if you are talking to me again. She was worried you'd blame her. She felt very guilty."

They walked by the other diners, but she was quick to assure him. "Of course I don't blame her. That she was so excited to attend my school, does make up for it."

"And the blame is on my shoulders." He stopped them in front of her parents as he said it.

She nodded. "And partly on mine. In fact, I will call on her tomorrow to reassure her."

"Thank you." He disengaged his arm from hers and turned to her parents. "I hope to see you again soon."

She couldn't help watching as he strode back toward the entrance of Vauxhall. The Duke of Northwick loved her. And she loved him.

"Joanna, is everything all right?"

She turned toward her mother and smiled. "Everything is wonderful." She stepped up onto the dais and took her seat. At least, she hoped it was. Then she proceeded to explain what James had discovered.

CHAPTER TWENTY-TWO

"**I**'M SO PLEASED that you found the Dresden's dinner enjoyable. I have heard their daughter perform before and I was quite impressed."

As Mariel continued to talk about social events with Lady Elsbeth, Joanna searched for some reason to ask after James. Not wanting any secrets between them, she'd wrapped up *the book* and brought it with her on their call to Haven House. It was sitting on the table for calling cards in the entry, and she was anxious to confess her theft. Or would it be unknown borrowing?

"Lady Joanna?"

At Lady Astor's question, she returned her attention back to her hostess. "Yes?"

"I asked if you would like more tea."

Lady Elsbeth grinned. "What she would like is more of my cousin."

"Elsbeth!"

It was the opening she'd hoped for. "No, it's fine. Do not be cross with her." She smiled warmly at the younger woman who had gained so much confidence since her ball. "Actually, I do need to speak with His Grace. Is he home?"

Lady Astor gestured toward the door. "Yes. He was wrestling with his ledger." She cocked her head. "Perhaps you can help him? I can have Harrison show you to the library if you like."

Surprised that Lady Astor was inviting her to be alone with James, she looked to Mariel. "Will that be acceptable to you?"

Her sister and chaperone for this visit knew exactly why she needed to see James alone. When Mariel had understood she was returning the book, she'd been relieved.

Mariel waved her hand. "Go, but don't be too long or I'll come looking for you."

Grateful to both her sister and Lady Astor, she ignored the knowing look the older woman threw her way and made haste to exit the room. Finding no one about, she quickly grabbed up *the book* wrapped in brown paper and headed for the library. She paused just outside the doors. Had he not known they'd arrived and so had not joined them, or had he known and not wanted to.

Either way, it didn't matter. It was time to confess. Straightening her shoulders, she knocked on the door.

A growl came from within. "I told you, I do not want to be disturbed until I can get these devil-made columns to add up."

She smirked. Well, that explained why he hadn't joined them. She opened the door and stepped inside. "Perhaps I can help."

James, whose head had been bowed over his desk, looked up. He was in his shirtsleeves, and his hair was a mess as if he'd run his hand through it multiple times, a habit of Teddy's that she hadn't seen James ever perform. He stood, a slow smile forming on his face. "Joanna. I didn't know you had arrived."

She sauntered forward. "Or you would have hauled me in here sooner to help your columns balance?"

He grimaced. "Heard that, did you? I apologize. But now that you're here?"

She stopped in front of his desk and set the package down on it before dipping a quick curtsey, keeping her gaze away from the open neck of his shirt. "I've brought your book back."

His brows raised, but before he could say anything, she continued. "I know you deduced that I borrowed it. I need you to know that I had no idea what was inside."

"You are correct, I did know you took it." He walked around

his desk like a tiger hunting its prey, his movements calculated and his gaze never leaving her.

A small thrill went up her spine. "I want to return it. I know how much you value your collection."

He stopped right next to her and leaned his hip against the desk. "I do. I appreciate that you brought it back." He cocked his head. "But I am curious as to why you absconded with it in the first place."

Heat filled her cheeks at having to admit her incorrect first impression of him, but if he could confess, then she could too. "I originally took it for a number of reasons but the foremost was that I thought your views on women archaic and that all this," she gestured to the whole room, "was simply for show. I can't stand the thought of books being used as decoration or to impress but never to be read."

He crossed his arms. "So you thought to steal one of my books and that I wouldn't notice." His blue gaze grew intense. "But I did, especially after I realized which one you took."

She took a deep breath. This was harder than she'd thought it would be. "Yes, well, as I said, I didn't know what was inside. It appeared to be an antiquated philosophy on what women should know."

A slow grin formed on his face. "But it's actually a modern, forward-thinking book on what men should know, don't you agree?"

If she agreed or disagreed, she'd have to admit to reading the book. She just couldn't do it. "Then it's not meant for women after all? So why the title?"

His grin widened, a knowing glint present in his eyes. "No, it's for young men. But it is a false cover book. This is done on purpose to hide the real book inside."

"This is done? What do you mean? That this is a common practice so men can—oh." The false cover was purposeful so the lady or ladies of the house wouldn't suspect what the man of the house was reading. She frowned. "This is common practice?"

He pushed away from the desk to fill the space between them. "No, but enough that I wanted an example in my collection."

She was forced to raise her head to meet his gaze. His eyes had darkened, and her skin felt particularly sensitive as his scent filled her nose. "So you just wanted it as part of your collection, not to read it?"

He lifted his hand and played with the curl she always left to fall over her collarbone, the backs of his fingers, lightly brushing her skin just like in one of the first illustrations. "I read everything in my collection."

Her breaths turned shallow, and her red dress felt unusually warm. "Everything?" Her words barely made it past her lips and came out in a whisper.

His gaze moved to her mouth. "Everything." As he said the word slowly, his head descended, his face drawing closer.

She licked her lips, anxious to feel his again.

He stopped, just a hairsbreadth away. "Did you read it?"

The words, so softly spoken, the air from his mouth teasing her own, didn't penetrate her brain at first. When they did, her whole body seemed to light like a lantern wick. She should step away. It wasn't proper to want a man to kiss her, despite his professed feelings for her. But she could no more step away than she could force words past her lips. She met his gaze and with the smallest of movement, she nodded.

His nostrils flared as air whooshed through his lips to brush her own. That was her only warning, before his mouth met hers and he crushed her to him, wrapping her in his arms.

She opened her mind, body, and heart. His tongue sweeping inside her mouth made her feel desirable, while his hold had her feeling loved and treasured. She wrapped her arms around his neck, her tongue tangling with his as she pressed herself closer. Every part of her felt alive and excited. He broke their kiss and pulled his head back. "Jo, I want you more than I want to breathe."

His words made her toes curl inside her boots. Thanks to his book, she knew exactly what that meant. "I want you, too."

His whole body stiffened, then with no warning, his arm moved from behind her back to her knees as he bent and swept her into his arms. Not expecting it, she tightened her hold on his neck.

He carried her across the room past the stairs to a secluded spot where a wide armchair sat next to a small window and a bookcase. He set her on her feet and immediately cupped her face. "I need to know while I still have control of my actions, do you understand what it means when you say you want me?"

She gave him a sly smile. "I know more than I ever expected to know. Your book was quite enlightening."

He lowered his forehead to hers. "It shows you what can happen between a man and a woman, but it does not do justice to the feeling involved." He lifted his head and gazed into her eyes, his own dark and riveting. "I want to make you feel the wonders of the flesh. I want to bury myself inside you and make you mine."

Her heart jumped with awareness. Tingles spread from her chest throughout her body, making her knees weak. She licked her lips. "I want that too. I want to know."

"This is more than knowledge." He let go of her face, but one hand moved to her neck to caress the soft skin at her nape. "This will change you forever." He looked away. "It will change me forever."

If he felt half of what she felt, she could understand his hesitancy. She laid her hand on his bare flesh where his shirt opened, wanting to do so since she'd walked in. His skin was warm and his heartbeat strong beneath her palm. "I think we have already changed. Show me what is left to know. I want to feel everything with you."

His gaze returned to her, and his brows rose. "Everything?"

At the devilish look in his eyes she swallowed hard. If he'd thought to scare her away, he was mistaken because now her pulse raced with anticipation. "Yes, everything."

His hand on her neck pulled her forward. "Only because I love you." His lips met hers for a thorough kiss that made it hard to stay upright. As if he sensed when her knees began to fail her, he stopped, sat down in the chair, and pulled her onto his lap.

"Oh." She hadn't expected that, but as she now found herself eye level with him for a change, she took advantage of it and released a few buttons on his shirt.

He held completely still so she released a few more, marveling at the hard planes of his chest and stomach as she spread the material wide. It made her want to touch more of him. Knowing what a man looked like beneath his clothes and what he *felt* like were two entirely different experiences. She ran her hand over his shoulder, pushing the white fabric aside as she stroked the corded muscle beneath. She hadn't expected to want to touch him or that he would feel so good. Not happy that the shirt wouldn't move farther, she started to tug it from his pantaloons.

"Wait." His fingers wrapped around her wrist.

She snapped her gaze back to his. "Why? I want to touch you."

"I know." He paused as if searching for words. "I need you to be patient and allow me to touch you first."

Though disappointed, the heat that rose deep in her center distracted her. Images of the scenes from *the book* flashed in her mind. "I think I would like that."

His lips quirked up on one side. "You will definitely like it."

She was about to protest his arrogance when his finger trailed along the neckline of her dress leaving tendrils of sensitive skin behind. Maybe she should wait to argue and see what he would do first. Again, images from the book crowded her mind so that when the back of her dress loosened, she shivered.

James lowered his head and kissed her shoulder before moving to her neck. She let her head fall back, allowing him access, fascinated by the desire beginning to fill her. Not only did her limbs feel weak, but her body flushed.

She held onto his bare shoulder with one hand as he dipped her lower, his lips following the descent of her dress. Even as he found the top of her breast just above her stays, she wished to be out of them. She should be shocked at such a feeling, but she knew what he sought, and she wanted to feel his lips there.

Though she hadn't felt him loosen her dress and petticoat, she noticed the second her stays were released. Instinctually, she arched upward, wanting to be free of the layers of cloth covering her. James pulled her stays down, effectively revealing her to his gaze.

She sucked in a breath as her hot flesh felt the cool air of the room.

"You are so beautiful." His words came out of him on a breath, barely audible before he kissed her breast.

She'd thought having his touch there would satisfy the need to be naked, but it seemed to fuel her desire. When his tongue darted out and licked her, she gasped.

He pulled away, and she grabbed his head, grasping the hair at the back of his neck. "Don't stop. Please."

He chuckled. "As you wish."

For the next minutes, she wasn't sure where she was, all she knew was James' mouth and the titillating movements he made as he paid homage to her breasts. Strong, sharp pangs of need started deep inside her. The juncture of her thighs felt like the entrance to Dante's inferno, blazing, craving what *the book* had alluded to, but never described. This was beyond her, taking her to something else. "James." She panted, barely able to fill her lungs enough to speak. "I want so desperately."

He lifted his head from her and gazed into her eyes, his so dark they appeared black. "What do you want? Tell me."

She searched her mind for the words, not sure what it was. "I don't know." Frustrated by her inability to think, she welled up.

He stroked her cheek gently. "You don't have to know. This is when you need to let yourself experience the wonder and stop thinking."

She frowned, not sure that was possible, but trusting him, she gave a hesitant nod. How could anyone stop thinking?

"My intelligent Jo. Let me take you beyond thought."

For some odd reason, his words made more sense when phrased that way. "Yes."

His gaze filled with love as he gave her a soft smile. "For you."

She wasn't sure what he meant by that, but when his mouth returned to her breast, her focus shifted. The spikes of wanting returned immediately and then he sucked. She moved one leg off his lap and pushed her hips upward, craving even more.

As he moved to her other breast, his hand began to move up the leg still on his lap beneath her dress, petticoat, and shift. An image from *the book* took away any question as to what he was about. Now she understood why a woman would want a man to touch her there. But she was far beyond simply wanting. When his hand passed her stocking and found her warm flesh, he hesitated.

No! She tried to speak, but her throat was tight. Instead, she moved her free leg further away, inviting him in. When his hand continued upward, her anxiousness abated but her need increased, everything inside her growing tight.

He released her breast, and she almost cried out, but he lifted her head to his lips at the same time his fingers found the juncture of her thighs. *Yes! Yes!* She wanted to yell, but his tongue dominated her mouth, demanding she surrender.

Then his fingers found her intimate folds and the spot she'd only seen drawings of. Her hands turned to claws as she held onto him while he pillaged her mouth and played lightly with her sex. Her body seemed to spin in a spiral, higher and higher, the feelings escalating beyond comprehension until suddenly, without warning, a wave of ecstasy engulfed her, pulling her along exquisiteness so joyful as to be beyond human existence.

As the wave released her slowly, pure satisfaction enveloped her, floating her safely back into James' arms. She found her head resting against his bare chest. At some point, she must have broken from his kiss. To not know one's own actions was disconcerting, yet she understood why now.

His heartbeat continued to race, while hers had slowed. She lifted her head to view him as the feel of a large lump beneath her made her seat uncomfortable. Recognition dawned. "You didn't have any satisfaction."

He gave her a strained grin. "Not yet. I wanted you to know what it was to experience the thrill of lovemaking."

She frowned. "But it's not the same. I know how this works. You need to be inside me." The hard staff beneath her moved.

"Believe me, I want to be there more than you can know, but our first time together must be broached slowly."

"Oh." She'd forgotten the chapter titled simply "The Virgin." But if the book had done such a poor job of describing the actual feelings of fulfillment, then it may have done little justice to the feelings upon consummation. "Tell me what to expect. Will it hurt?"

His cheek twitched. "I hope not."

She understood the mechanics and after what she just experienced, she was nervous, but she trusted James, and he had no satisfaction. She could feel how much he needed it. She wanted to give it to him. She wanted to feel everything with him, as she'd said. "Please James, take me now."

✦

CHAPTER TWENTY-THREE

J AMES CHOKED BACK a pained groan at Joanna's statement. Her words made him even harder, and it was already unbearable. He wanted her to feel as much with him as she'd just experienced already. Though wishing more than anything that they were in his bedroom after their marriage, he still couldn't bear to wait another moment to make her his. His body was in full agreement.

Gently, he lifted her, leaned over, and laid her on the rug covering the small corner. Following her down to the floor, he lay down next to her on his side. They were both half-undressed, and as wrong as it was for him to take her this way, he could no longer wait.

She lay on her back staring at him, curiosity clear in her hazel eyes. "Take your shirt off."

Sitting up, he did as she asked.

She angled herself upward, causing her breasts to become exposed again, and she reached out with one hand to stroke down his chest to the edge of his pantaloons. "The illustrations do not portray how hard men are."

At her choice of words, his erection pushed to be released. If she only knew how incredibly desirable she looked at the moment. Her innocent touch threatened to make him forget how new she was to this experience. He grasped her hand and gently laid her back, his mouth finding hers in a kiss. The feel of her full breasts pressed to him made it even more difficult to stay in control. Quickly, he moved his lips down her throat and back to her exposed flesh. Covering one hardened peak with his mouth, he gently sucked.

Her gasp sent a thrill down his spine even as her hands in his hair encouraged him to enjoy her. Again he wished they had more time to explore each other, but he was not unaware that the door to the library remained unlocked and the only thing keeping servants out was his earlier foul temper. While leveraging himself with one arm, he reached down with his free hand and bared one of her legs and the juncture of her thighs.

She moaned, moving her limb further to the side, inviting him to take what he would. He forced himself to breathe deeply and blow across the tight peak before him, straining for control, forcing his body to wait. She felt so good against him, like she'd been created just for him. As he ran his hand up the softness of her skin, her hands gripped his hair. She knew what to expect this time and wanted it.

He wanted it too. He loved everything about her from her sharp mind to her playfulness to that single lock of hair that had mesmerized him from the first. He moved his mouth to her other breast, giving it the same attention even as his fingers found her slick opening and her pleasure point. This time he spent more time where he would enter her, playing with her and getting her used to the feeling. Holding himself back when he wanted nothing more than to make her his was going to be the death of him.

"Please. James. Take me." Her panted words were impossible to ignore as he responded with impatience.

Pulling his hand from her silkiness, he unbuttoned his placket, the temporary relief allowing him to think more clearly. He moved over her, not wanting her to see him and tense. He kept his weight from her chest, to allow her to breathe.

She opened her eyes, now glossy with passion. "I love you, James. I can't wait any longer."

Unable to delay another moment, he kissed her, even as he positioned himself to enter her. The heat of her called to him like the sun called to the wildflower. Slowly, he nudged her legs apart, letting her know now was the time.

Instead of stiffening, she widened her legs, bending them, and before he knew what she was about, she thrust her hips upward.

His body instinctively pushed downward, and he stilled, pulling his head back to see her, fear that he'd hurt her filling his chest.

She also lay immobile, her eyes closed and her brows lowered.

"Jo. I didn't expect you to—"

Her eyes snapped open. "You were taking too long."

Nervous humor started up his throat, and he swallowed it. "I was trying to be gentle."

She cocked her head slightly to study him. "Now you can be gentle."

He didn't know what to say to that, admiration for her filling him, along with the knowledge that she was his forever now. "Look at me."

Slowly, he pulled his hips up and then gently sunk down, her warmth surrounding him feeling so right. Her brows were still lowered, but her lips parted. He repeated the action and this time her brows rose, her body beneath him relaxing.

"It's not as bad as I expected." Though she gazed at him, she wasn't seeing him.

He had the distinct impression she focused on the feelings from where they were joined. He couldn't help a smile. Her and her curiosity. It made him feel alive. He carefully increased the rhythm, enjoying every glide into her, noticing little nuances as she tightened around him or let out her breath.

Soon though, when she wrapped her arms around him and brought her lips to his, he lost his focus. He was far too intoxicated by her mouth, the feel of being inside her, her scent surrounding him as they climbed closer to the peak of fulfillment.

He held himself back, wanting her with him this first time.

She broke their kiss, small moans coming from deep in her throat. He tilted his hips, giving her the stimulation she craved, until he felt her release start. Finally, he let himself go, biting down hard to keep his own shout from revealing their joy. As he spent himself inside her, an instinct buried deep in his psyche reared up with ferocity. Triumph and possessiveness filled him, blocking out any logical thought, and he grasped her to him.

She was *his*.

"James?" Her whisper wound around his heart.

He loosened his hold and leveraged himself higher so he could look at her. Her face was flushed and her lips reddened from their kisses. She was breathtaking. "Yes?"

"I liked it. Do you know why this position is called the missionary position?"

He barely held back his laugh. "Actually, I don't. We'll have to find a book about that."

Her gaze wandered. "That's the basic one, right? When does a couple try more complicated ones?"

This time his body reacted at the thought of her on top of him or splayed out on his desk.

She sighed. "I wish we had time to try another."

At her mention of time, the precariousness of their situation cooled his blood instantly. Not wanting to scare her, he slowly pulled away. "Stay right there and don't move."

He strode desktop the door and quietly turned the lock. Tucking his shirt back in, he buttoned himself up all the way to his neck.

Returning to Jo, he was surprised that she had done as he requested, until he noticed her eyes were closed and her breathing was even. For the rest of his life, he'd remember the image of her half-unclothed, thoroughly loved and satisfied. A wave of possessiveness swept through him again, and he tamped it down. It felt as if a beast was taking over, and he'd have no part of that. "Jo, we need to get you dressed."

"Uh-huh."

As much as he wanted to let her sleep, he could not. Sitting her up, he knelt behind her and tied her stays before tucking the petticoat back under her dress, buttoning the back, and tying the neckline.

She remained quiet, until he helped her to stand. "Am I supposed to pretend that nothing happened here?"

"Yes, to everyone but me. I will keep our secret."

She touched his face. "I think Aristotle was wrong. You are more handsome with your hair tousled and your whiskers showing." Her hand drifted along his jaw before it came down on his chest. "I'm so glad you have a heart as well as intelligence."

He grinned, but removed her hand, her touch far too enticing. "I have to admit I am pleased as well that you have both. Now, turn around so I can see what damage we have done to your dress."

As if the mention of her dress had somehow penetrated the fog in her brain, she stepped back and smoothed down the new wrinkles in the front. "Is that better?"

"Yes." It was, but it didn't change the wrinkles from being there. "Let me see your back."

She turned around, and looked over her shoulder, her dark lock falling down her back. "Maybe I could don my wool coat and tell Mariel I'm ready to leave?"

"That's a good plan." Especially because the back of her gown was far worse. What had he been thinking to put her in such a position? She was to be his duchess.

She faced him again and smiled slyly. "As far as applying knowledge, that was very educational."

He swallowed a laugh. Life with her would never be dull. "That may be, but we need to get you back to your sister. I don't want anyone thinking ill of my future wife."

Her eyes rounded. "Wife?"

"Of course." He tucked her arm in his and walked her back toward the desk to retrieve his waistcoat. She was obviously still basking in the glow of their lovemaking. She'd had no idea how it could affect her thought process. She simply wasn't thinking of the consequences of their actions. "If you like, I could request a special license, so we need not wait long."

She coughed, but didn't respond.

After donning his waistcoat, he took both her hands in his. "I will call on your father tomorrow and request your hand in marriage."

She pulled away and paced the length of the bookcase. "That might be too much of a surprise for him." She turned and walked back toward him. "I think you should ask to court me first. My family, except Mariel, of course, is unaware of our feelings for each other."

He opened his mouth to object, but she raised her hand. "I know that feelings don't matter in most families, but in ours they do…very much."

He didn't want to wait. He wanted her in his home, here in his library, in his bed.

"Please." Her gaze met his, and he could see exactly how much it meant to her.

Was it her family she was most concerned about, or did she want his attention in public? He dismissed the second thought. Jo wasn't like Lady Caroline. Her feelings for her family were strong and her interest in society was weak, only remaining proper for her family's sake. "Very well. I will call tomorrow to discuss courting you with your father."

"Thank you." She stood on her toes and pulled his head down with one hand to give him a satisfying kiss.

He liked that she learned so quickly. "But it won't be a long courtship and I will request a special license."

"I understand."

Unable to resist her, he pulled her close for another kiss. When his body started to react all over again, he forced himself to step away. "Let me call Harrison for your coat."

She nodded, a soft smile on her face.

Gently, he pulled her single curl back over her shoulder then made himself stop touching her. Turning, he strode toward the door. Just as he reached for it, a knock sounded. Damn.

He opened the door to find Mariel and Aunt Louisa. Both ladies looked beyond him. He raised his brows. "Can I assist you with something?"

His aunt addressed Mariel. "I told you she was probably helping him with his ledger."

At that, he looked over his shoulder at Jo. Her finger was gliding along his columns when suddenly it stopped, and she looked up. "I found it. You have an error in your computation on line twenty-one." She smiled, obviously feeling quite triumphant.

"Thank you." He turned back to the women. "I believe Lady Joanna wishes to go home now." He looked pointedly at his aunt. "Please have Harrison retrieve their coats."

Though his aunt left to do as he bid, Mariel stepped past him and into the room.

"So, this is the infamous library my father and sister talk about so much." She meandered over to the two wingback chairs by the fireplace as if looking for something in particular.

He took the moment to comb his hair with his fingers then strode to where she stood, not wanting her to look too carefully at her sister. "This," he lifted one of the two books on the table between the two chairs, "is Coleridge's most recent poetry. Do you enjoy poetry?"

Her sharp green gaze studied him, suspicion clear in her eyes. "No. I find it to be melancholy. I much prefer a Shakespearean comedy so as to lift one's spirits."

It was an odd remark, but considering the woman was a widow and had sacrificed much for her family, he could understand her feelings. In his peripheral vision, he noticed Jo slipping out of the room. "I understand one is to be performed next week."

"Really, which one?" Her gaze did not move from him as if she suspected him of something.

"*As You Like It* will open at Drury Lane." He leaned in as if they could be overheard. "Do you think your sister would enjoy it?"

She shrugged. "I have no idea. She has very particular tastes."

He gave a short nod. "I understand that well. In fact, I will be calling on your father tomorrow to request permission to court her."

At his announcement, Mariel's eyes rounded, and in that moment, he recognized a true resemblance between the sisters. Her stiffness left, and she smiled warmly. "I am pleased." She glanced toward his desk then scanned the room. "Has my sister departed?"

He looked behind him and noticed the wrapped book. "I believe she has, but she forgot something." Striding to his desk, he tucked the wrapped book under his arm. If he wanted to shorten their courtship, he had a feeling his book could help. One thing he was absolutely sure of was that he could depend upon Jo's curiosity. Now that she knew how it felt, he had no doubt she'd want to review what she'd seen and read. He grinned as he walked toward Lady Mariel. "Let us find her."

※

CHAPTER TWENTY-FOUR

JOANNA STARED OUT the carriage window, excited, confused, happy, and concerned. Or would that be confused, concerned, excited, and happy? Either order, it was how she felt. She didn't regret their intimacy at all. But she didn't know what was to come of it. James would only be so patient. She wasn't sure how she knew that, but she did. He was anxious now to ask her father for her hand and that was the crux of her quandary.

She'd *never* planned to marry. She liked making her own decisions about her day, her finances, her life. Now she had a school to start. If she married James, he'd be in control of everything unless she legally protected it. Would he accept that?

A husband. She wished she could continue to spend time with him and still have her independence, but that wasn't done among women of her class unless she wanted to be shunned by society. Then she'd have no students.

On the other hand, she loved him. She wanted to wake up next to him, debate the latest news over breakfast, balance his ledgers, enjoy his family, and read every book in his collection, even the ones like the one she'd already read. She glanced at the seat next to her, the book still wrapped in brown paper, his gift to her. The cool coach suddenly felt warm at that idea. She wanted to try every position and—

"You're very quiet, Joanna. What is it?"

She started, completely forgetting about Mariel. If there was anyone she could talk to, it would be her. "I'm torn."

"Tell me. Mayhap I can help."

"I'm in love with James, the duke."

Her sister smiled warmly. "I know."

"You do?" She threw her hand up. "And here I thought I hid it so well."

They both chuckled. It felt good, but it didn't take away her problem. "But I never plan to marry. Am I to give up my independence for something I never wanted?"

Mariel's hand flew to her chest. "Did he propose?"

"He made his intentions clear, but I distracted him. All my reasons for not marrying remain. All that has changed is I've fallen in love. I want James *and* my independence. How can I do that?"

"I don't think I understood exactly how important it was to you to remain independent until this moment. To love someone and not want to marry him is beyond my understanding."

She sighed, her hope for help melting away. "It's not that I don't want to be with him. I do. But I can't change who I am. I can't suddenly enjoy hosting dinner parties and embroidering. I still want to run my school at Silver Meadows, attend lectures, discover new books. But I want to be with him too." She let her head fall back against the seat. Did she want too much from life?

"Joanna, I wouldn't usually suggest this, but if Lord Northwick knows you as well as I do, and loves you, then I would tell him how you feel just as you told me."

"Tell him? He's a duke."

Mariel smiled. "Yes, but he's a duke who loves you. Trust me on this. If you love each other, you can figure it out, especially with all that knowledge the two of you have in your heads." She shook her head. "Sometimes I think it just makes things more complicated."

"Now that I can agree with." She gave her sister a smile, but wasn't sure. How would she feel if James wanted her in his life, but didn't want to marry her so he could pursue his interest in something else and have his independence. And worse, what if she told him how she felt, and he decided he'd be better off with a more traditional woman? Her heart lurched.

Bloody hell.

JAMES COULDN'T BELIEVE how much more he enjoyed the social events of London now that he officially courted Joanna. To dance with her, talk with her, enjoy her conversation and especially her observations made every new outing an adventure. For a city he despised for taking his mother, he now found a place for it in his life because of Joanna. He ached to have her alone again, but her parents had suddenly become quite vigilant about her reputation, which he was both pleased and frustrated by.

Joanna's hesitancy to discuss marriage was also frustrating. If their conversation moved in that direction, she quickly distracted him with another topic. Tonight, he was determined to ask her directly if she wanted him as a husband. The idea that she would reject him had his panophobia hysterica returning, but his confidence in her love kept it at bay. He'd get a special license immediately if she would agree, but something held her back and he had to discover what.

He scowled as two gentlemen approached her and his aunt. Joanna's emerald-green gown brought out that color in her eyes, making her look particularly vibrant. Introductions were being made, not that he was surprised. What gentleman wouldn't want to meet her? But she was his. Moving through the crowd as quickly as he could with two cups of punch, he almost bumped into her father. "Excuse me, Lord Wakefield."

"Your Grace, I was hoping to discuss this latest invention by Robert Stirling. Do you have a moment?"

The two men before Joanna laughed at something she said. Swallowing a growl, he gave a quick nod. "I would enjoy that very much. I will be sure to call on the morrow so we may do so." Before her father could respond, he was stepping past and around the dancers at the end of the line. He was just feet away when the two men moved on.

"There you are." Aunt Louisa smiled as she held her hand out. "We had become quite parched."

He forced himself to stop scowling as he handed them the drinks. "Who were those men?"

Joanna studied him. "They were Teddy's friends back from the continent. I only met one of them before, so he introduced us." She cocked her head. "Why?"

He shrugged, relieved that the men were too young for her, at least in his estimation. "Curiosity. I hadn't seen them before."

"Are you jealous, James?" His aunt's question made him more than a little uncomfortable.

He raised his brows. "Not that I am aware."

She looked at him askance, clearly having made up her own mind.

Joanna's hand on his arm relieved him of further discussing it. "Have you seen Teddy?"

He thought for a moment. "Not since the second dance when he partnered Elsbeth." He scanned the room. "Where is my popular cousin?"

"Third couple in the second set." His aunt answered without hesitation."

He grinned. "I see you do not take your duties as mother and chaperone lightly."

"I do not. Nor do Joanna's parents." She nodded toward Lord and Lady Wakefield who spoke to friends but were faced their way.

"Yes, and I appreciate it. I would not want Joanna's reputation to be harmed in any way by my attentions."

She laughed. "Your attentions toward me are making me far more popular than I ever was. In fact, I have gained two more students. You didn't have anything to do with that, did you?"

"I may have. Are they the daughters of Lady Dowling and Lady Egerton?"

She nodded.

"Then, yes." At her surprised expression, he expanded on his answer. "I want to see this application of theory succeed. Every man deserves a wife as intelligent as mine."

She froze. It may not have been obvious to the casual observer, but he knew her well.

What the devil was wrong with being his wife? They needed to discuss this. "I think it would be good to take some air, don't you?" He dared her with his gaze. "It's grown quite warm in here. Shall we?" He offered her his arm.

Her smile did not reach her eyes. "Yes, a brief walk in the cooler air would be welcome."

He led her along the side of the ballroom, the two doors to a small courtyard had been thrown open earlier to allow the cold air to freshen the room full of bodies. Lord and Lady Stockton had invited a few too many guests for their home.

Once outside, Joanna removed her arm and sat stiffly on the stone bench within the light of the ballroom. Where was the woman who had visited him in his library unaccompanied?

He stood before her, every muscle tensed for rejection. "Do you love me?"

Her eyes rounded at his question, then her whole body relaxed as a soft smile appeared. She lifted her gloved hand and took his. "I do. Very much."

His tension eased, and he sat next to her, not releasing her hand. "Then why do you avoid the topic of marrying me?"

She would have pulled her hand from his, but he refused to let her go. "Tell me. There should be no secrets between us. We are of like mind and like heart, but there is something."

Shaking her head, she gave him a weak smile. "Your keen observation is one of the reasons I have fallen in love with you. You need to know that my hesitancy is not about you." She pressed her other hand to her chest, opened her mouth and closed it.

While she relieved some of his concern, that she couldn't quite explain to him hurt. It would seem that loving someone made his heart very sensitive, something he would have scoffed at earlier in the season. "If you are not hesitant about me, is it marriage that you fear?"

He'd swear there was confirmation in her gaze, but she turned her head at that moment to look toward the ballroom.

"Oh, good. I'm so glad I found you." His cousin almost ran to them, his aunt following behind.

He stood. "Elsbeth, what is it."

"It's Teddy." She turned to Joanna, who had also risen at her approach. "He's gone."

Foreboding had him taking his cousin's hand. Teddy never left an event until Elsbeth had. "Did something happen between you?"

She looked down before finally meeting his gaze. "I told him that I cared for him like a brother, but I didn't see him as a husband."

"Why would you have broached this with him now?" Joanna was clearly angry.

Elsbeth wouldn't look at her. "He asked me to marry him after our dance. I had been dreading telling him, knowing how much he cared for me." She finally turned back to Joanna. "I had hoped he would come tell you."

"He did not."

Though it was a crushing blow to the young man, James didn't see the reason for alarm. "He probably went home to mourn your loss in privacy."

Elsbeth shook her head. "That's why I came as soon as I heard. One of his friends said he planned to get fuddled at the Devil's Own pub and didn't care what happened after that."

"The Devil's Own pub?" Joanna looked at him. "I've never heard of that, and I know almost every establishment in the area."

Elsbeth squeezed his hand, her eyes clearly watering now.

"It's down by the docks."

"Bloody hell." Joanna's swear caught them all by surprise. "It's been hours since that dance. Why didn't you tell us sooner?"

He patted his cousin's hand in his. "That's a fair question."

"I didn't know he left until I danced with his friend. When I discovered he was at this pub, I searched you out immediately." Two tears had now started down her cheeks.

He gave her hand one last squeeze. "It's not your fault. "You were right to tell us."

"We have to find him." Joanna picked up her skirts to walk back in.

He let go of Elsbeth and caught Joanna by the hand. "Wait. You aren't going anywhere."

She spun to face him. "You can't stop me."

"Joanna, let me do this. It's not safe down there."

Her eyes narrowed and she pulled her hand from his. "Either I go with you, or I take our coach, but one way or another I'm finding my cousin and bringing him home."

There was no way he was letting her go without him. She was right. He couldn't stop her as he wasn't her husband, but he doubted even that would make a difference. Was that why she feared getting married? As if the sun had finally shown itself from behind the clouds, he knew he was right. Relief and determination swept through him like a winter storm. "We will take my coach."

"James."

At his aunt's voice, he paused. "Yes."

"Be careful and take a chaperone."

He understood the look she threw him. While Teddy's disappearance was paramount, keeping his future duchess's reputation was equally so. "We only have two footmen with us."

"We have two as well. Let me get my cloak." With that, Joanna strode back into the ballroom.

His aunt held Elsbeth, who now cried in earnest. She spoke over her daughter's shoulder. "I suggest Lady Mariel. She is discreet and will do as you ask."

Because Joanna wouldn't. He understood the message. Giving her a quick nod, he went in search of Lady Mariel and her sister, and to let their parents know he would retrieve Lord Mabry.

He found Joanna outside with the Mabry footmen. She'd called for his coach and paced as she waited. He moved toward her to halt her frantic movement, but Lady Mariel tapped his arm. "Let her be. She needs to expend her worry this way."

He remained where he was, wishing he could help alleviate that concern immediately, but it was out of his hands at the moment. Finally, his coach pulled up and they piled in. Luckily, his driver knew where the Devil's Own pub was. Asking for directions along the docks in the middle of the night, was not something he had wanted to engage in.

The streets were empty, everyone home or wherever they planned to be for the night. The Stocktons' ball wouldn't end until early morning and it was still just after midnight. There were far fewer streetlamps as they drew closer to a side of Town he'd spent very little time in. They drove by two urchins stealing a drunk man's coin as he wobbled down an alley, and his protective instincts rose. Though they were there to find Teddy, Joanna would be his priority.

They had ridden in silence, but Mariel broke it. "Joanna, I'm concerned you made the wrong decision."

Joanna had been observing everything outside the window, or what could be seen when they drove by a lantern. She didn't take her gaze from the streets. "Wrong decision about what?"

Mariel took a deep breath as if finding her patience. "With coming down to the docks ourselves. I'm sure His Grace could handle this without us."

"Of course he can. And when Teddy refuses to come with him because he's in his cups, a fight will ensue in which either Teddy or Lord Northwick will be injured."

"And you think we can keep that from happening?"

Joanna finally turned away from the window, but she didn't turn to her sister beside her. Instead, she met his gaze. "I've seen Teddy in his cups before. He won't come with you. He'll only cooperate if I cajole him."

If she thought he'd let her walk into a pub with the dubious name of Devil's Own located on the docks, where every cutthroat and thief resided, she wasn't using her brain. "You will stay in the coach. I will retrieve Lord Mabry."

Her brows lowered. "You cannot force me to stay here."

"Actually, I can. You are in my coach and therefore under my protection."

Her eyes narrowed once again as she murmured something under her breath.

"Joanna!" Mariel's exclamation told him it couldn't have been very complimentary.

He didn't care. What he cared about was keeping her safe. If he thought for one moment he could do that by leaving her at the ball, he would have, but even with her parents watching her, he had no doubt she would have commandeered their coach and gone after Teddy by herself.

The coach came to a stop, but there was no pub anywhere in sight. Wishing he had his flintlock with him, he held up his hand to forestall any questions. One of his men would inform him of why they were stopped if it would be longer than a few moments. Conversation came from above and since there had been no shout of alarm, he could only surmise they were not being robbed.

The door opened and one of his footmen appeared. "Your Grace. There seems to have been a bit of a brawl and the road is blocked. However, the driver said that you could take this alley to the next street and the pub is across the street on the left."

He peered down the alley behind his footman. It was filled with trash and only the breadth of three men standing side by side. As much as he didn't care for walking through it, it would keep the women safely away from any immediate scuffle. "I will take you and my other man. Tell the Mabry footmen to stand guard around this coach. Understand?"

"Yes, sir." The footman closed the door.

He rose to exit, but Joanna grabbed his arm. "You can't. It's not safe."

The worry in her face sent away all his doubts about her feelings for him. "I'll be fine as long as I'm not worried about you."

She stared into his eyes and reluctantly nodded.

He stepped out to find the Mabry footmen stationed on either side of the coach and his footmen waiting for him. After briefly explaining what they needed to do, he led the way down the alley. The limited light shining into the area made it difficult to see what he was stepping on, but that could be for the best. As they traversed the tight space, the stench grew stronger then seemed to dissipate. He wouldn't be surprised if there was a dead body among all the filth. Emerging onto the next street, he found a myriad of people wandering about. Most appeared drunk, though many of the women were working and finding a willing man to pay them for their services. Just as his coachman said, The Devil's Own was to the left. He led his men to the pub. As he reached for the door, it opened, and a woman and man staggered out.

"Oooh, it be a gentleman and all." The woman winked at him and licked her lips, but her partner pulled her away, swearing about too many gents in one night.

He hoped that meant that Lord Mabry was still inside. "Stay behind me." At his men's nods, he opened the door to loud music, boisterous voices, and the smell of sweat. Resisting the urge to cover his nose, he stepped inside and quickly scanned the patrons. He almost missed Lord Mabry simply because he was one of only three people who weren't moving. Hoping the man was just drunk and not dead, he made his way between the tables and bodies. The chaotic crowd and loud noises threatened his control. He didn't want to take deep breaths, so he kept them shallow and focused on the man sitting in a chair slumped against the wall. Just as he reached him, a dark-haired serving woman with pretty eyes stepped in front of him.

She hooked a finger over her shoulder. "You come for him?"

He gave her a nod.

She held out her hand. "He owes me two shillings."

He raised his eyebrows and stared down his nose at her. "Are you telling me he doesn't have two shillings?"

She lost her bluster. "He may have, but they're thieving all over and he hasn't paid me yet. If I don't have at least two shillings from him, Morty will beat me."

Hell and damnation. He reached into his waistcoat. Not planning on needing money, he only had a crown and three shillings. He handed it all to her. "Give Morty the shillings and keep the rest and find yourself another occupation."

The woman stared at the coins in her hand before closing her fist tight and throwing herself at him, hugging him hard. "Thank you, sir."

Luckily, as quickly as she'd grasped him, she let go and was heading for the bald man behind the bar.

Anxious to get out of the place, he motioned his men forward. "There. Let's get him out of here." As the footmen pulled Lord Mabry from his chair, his head lolled, but he still breathed.

He led his men out, focused on the door. Only four steps from it, a burly man with scraggly hair and a short beard stepped in front of him. "Where ya goin' with me pal?"

He pulled himself to his full height and looked down his nose. "That man is my wife's brother, and if I do not get him home posthaste, I'll be sleeping in my cold coach tonight."

The man stared at him as if he had seven heads, then let out a loud guffaw. "Dancing to yer woman's tune? Poor bastard." He moved aside and slapped him on the back.

Not wanting to show any weakness, he forced himself to keep his feet planted like he'd learned in school. He jerked his head toward the door. "Even now may be too late." Then he moved forward again, opening the tavern door while his footmen passed. As they crossed the street with Lord Mabry, he couldn't help feeling that they had barely made it out alive, and Joanna had expected to waltz into a place like that and coax her cousin out?

"Is he still breathing?" He looked over his shoulder as he and his men headed into the dark alley.

"Yeah, but he reeks of beer."

Beer? He needed to teach the man that Scotch was a better option if he didn't want to suffer for his excesses the next day. Then again, Lord Mabry probably didn't want to remember this evening come the morrow.

Seeing the footmen standing before the coach at the end of the alley, he wished to quicken his pace. He wouldn't be content until he had Joanna out of there. But he had to think of the men behind him. Tripping over what may have been a broken chair, he caught his balance by grabbing the wall, not wanting to fall into the filth at his feet. Looking at the exit so close, he stopped. The footmen had disappeared.

Fear for Joanna ran up his spine, and he ran toward the coach. As he exited the alley, a fist caught him in the stomach. He folded over but came up swinging, catching his assailant in the jaw. He swung around to search for Joanna and Mariel and found them standing next to the horses, two footmen on the ground at their feet and his coachman fighting another thug. Hearing movement to his left, he spun, ducking just in time to avoid a fist in his face.

His footmen were fighting two others, but no one attacked the women. "Get in the coach!" He didn't have time to see if they did, since his attacker jumped on his back. James backed into the wall of the building hard, causing the breath to leave his enemy, which loosened his grip. Pulling away, he spun to confront him.

The man smiled as he whipped out what looked like a large fishhook. "Come on, gent. Let's put you down so we can enjoy the pretties."

Backing out of reach of the weapon by inches, he wished he'd thought to bring his cane. As they circled each other, he had to do something, so he faked a fall, grabbed the dirt from the road and threw it in his attacker's face. As the man stumbled back, trying to see, James swung with all his might. The man spun around and fell to the ground, the weapon skittering from his hand.

Snapping his head around to check the coach, he was in time to see one of his footmen on the ground and a man trying to get in the coach. He ran forward and pulled the blackguard around, slamming his now sore fist into the man's stomach. Unfortunately, that did little to stop him. The big man roared with indignation and shoved James against the coach. Hands found his throat and started to cut off his breathing.

He grabbed onto the meaty fists, determined to pry the fingers from his neck, but his vision started to blur. Suddenly, he was released, and the man stumbled back. He gulped in air and grabbed the door frame of the coach, only to find Joanna standing there, the handle of a broken chamber pot in her hand. He would have shaken his head at her if he had time, but he was just able to avoid the big man's clutches.

Joanna's strategy made sense. Scanning the entrance to the alley, he grabbed what looked like the handle of a broken axe. Now he had what he needed. Blocking the miscreant's attempts to reach him with the wooden handle, he finally connected with the man's head and he went down.

Breathing hard, he surveyed the scene. The coachman had a bloody lip, but his assailant ran down the street. The Mabry footmen were just sitting up, and one of his men felled the last attacker. With all their assailants down or gone, he checked on the women by sticking his head in the doorway.

He was grasped so hard, he would have thought he was being attacked again, but the scent of spicy sweetness and the softness of the skin against his face told him otherwise.

"I thought they were going to kill you." Joanna's voice cracked as she held onto his neck, which was quite sore, but he didn't mind. He wrapped his arms around her and held her, looking over her shoulder to see Mariel fanning herself. Satisfied they were all in good health, he extracted himself from her arms. "I need to get your cousin so we can leave here." His voice was barely a whisper.

She cupped his face, tears running down her cheeks. "Hurry."

It took them less than a few minutes to get Lord Mabry and the unconscious footman into the coach, before the coachman set them moving and turned down the first street to get away from the docks.

He and Joanna sat on one side with the footman propped in the corner, while Mariel tended to Lord Mabry on the other. Joanna held his hand tightly, refusing to let go. He brought her bare hand to his lips and kissed it, glad that she had thrown her gloves away before they left. "Jo, I'm fine," he rasped.

She rounded on him. "You are not fine. You can barely speak. You almost died. You can't die on me. I won't have it."

"What would you like me to do then?" He thought to chuckle but ended up coughing.

"Don't you say another word. Just listen."

He reached his arm around her and pulled her closer, not caring that Mariel was with them. Joanna would be his wife sooner rather than later. Now that he hadn't been strangled to death. "The chamber pot was an appropriate weapon. Where did you get it?"

She frowned at him. "It was on the side of the street as I made my way back into the coach. I think I'm going to add classes in protecting oneself to the school curriculum. Now, I told you to listen, not talk."

He gave her a short nod.

She set her hand against his face. "Since I tended Belinda while she was sick, I wanted to avoid marriage. Then after Aunt Mabry died, I realized I could. From then on, I was set on never marrying."

He couldn't help tightening his grip as she paused. It was his fervent wish to make her his wife. She was his life now.

"But then you came along and made me fall in love with you."

He grinned. "Didn't make you."

"Shh, yes, you did. You treated me as an equal, something I never expected any man to do. Loving you and remaining independent are impossible. For weeks I have tried to figure out a way that I could have both, but…"

"But that's impossible." His stomach twisted as she nodded.

"I've been so torn, but when I thought I would lose you, I realized that all my independence and my school wasn't worth living for if you weren't by my side. I love you, James Huntington, Duke of Northwick, and I would be honored to marry you."

His chest filled with joy as he pulled her head to him and kissed her with all the love he felt for her.

Her response was equal, as she was in everything. She'd stolen his heart like she'd stolen his book, but he hadn't even known it until it was too late.

Mariel cleared her throat. "It would be remiss of me as your chaperone not to remind you that I am here with you."

He smiled and Joanna laughed, effectively ending their kiss.

She brushed back his hair. "Of course, there will be conditions."

He would have groaned if he had any voice, then he grinned. "The first is that I be allowed to teach at your school."

She pulled back and stared at him. "You mean you want to…don't mind…oh, James." Throwing her arms around him she kissed him again.

Loving the feel of her in his arms, he welcomed her with his whole heart. Now and forever. Breaking the kiss, he looked into her eyes. "I cannot wait to share the rest of my life with you."

As the coach moved through the better parts of Town, the light grew inside the interior and he could see her glowing face and the twinkle in her eye. "I guess Lady Caroline was correct after all. She said I was stealing the duke."

He pulled the long lock that had fallen over her shoulder to the front. "You can never steal something that is freely given. My heart is yours."

"And mine yours." She sat back against him, holding his hand and sighed. "Now what shall we name *our* school?"

An uncharacteristic wetness formed in his eyes at her use of the word *our*. "What do you think?"

"I think we should discuss it when you have your voice back. It would be far too easy to get my way now."

He smiled. As long as he had her for the rest of his life, he was content to let her have her way…half the time.

EPILOGUE

Haven House library
June 1816

J OANNA HUNTINGTON, DUCHESS of Northwick added the final number and set the quill back in the ink stand. Blowing on the paper, she set it aside. The tuition would cover everything but the changes she'd made to Silver Meadows. The estate would be ready for them to open the Belinda School for Curious Ladies come September. She rose and stretched, before walking to the bay window where her husband sat reading the newest collection to their library.

She flopped down into the chair next to him.

He immediately set down the book. "Are you finished?"

She nodded. "I believe so. I can't imagine there could be anything else. Of course, once we get through the mandatory sampling of courses with the three of us, we will need to hire additional teachers, dependent on the subjects requested."

James' gaze turned wicked. "And what if one of our students requests to be instructed in the pleasures of seduction?"

Her body reacted to his question far faster than her mind. In the month they had been married, they had already enjoyed the majority of positions illustrated in *the book*. She rose and lifted the new book from his lap and set it on the small table, then she took the place of the book and wrapped her arms around his neck. "I think if we wished to teach such a subject, we would have to open a school for married women and mistresses, don't you?"

His gaze moved to the neckline of her turquoise day gown. "The only woman I'm interested in teaching is right here." He lifted the fine material from her chest and blew air down her cleavage.

She placed her finger under his chin and nudged his head up. "Are you sure there is anything left to impart?"

His head dipped and he caught her finger in his mouth. As he held it lightly with his teeth, he sucked.

Her body flushed with remembered pleasure from the night before.

Letting her finger go, he grinned. "There is far more to learn than what is in a single tome." His hand came up to cup her breast, his finger grazing over her now-taut peak through the cloth. "Remember I have other volumes, one which you already began to read. I believe it started with something about how a woman must be available for a man to take her whenever, wherever, and however he wished."

The promise of pleasures she'd had yet to experience glowed in his predatory gaze and her core tightened with need. "I don't remember it saying *however*. Maybe I should write a book about how a man should be available to his wife whenever, wherever, and however she pleases."

He grasped her breast and squeezed. "You haven't done enough research yet."

Oh, but she wanted to. An idea sparked. "Then I must go find that pamphlet again at once, so I can learn all about this." Fully intending to do just that and read more of it aloud, she pulled away from his touch and tried to stand, but he grabbed her about the waist.

"No need to do research. What you need to do is apply your knowledge." His grip was strong but gentle.

His response had her insides quivering, and the imp in her

demanded she push it. "No, I still need to amass more information on the subject. I really must go up there and find that pamphlet." She attempted to wriggle from his lap.

He growled.

In the next instant he had thrown her over his shoulder and stalked toward the door.

"James, put me down." She was caught between excitement and laughter. "James Garrison Huntington, you put me down this instant."

"I'll put you down when I—"

A knock sounded at the door, and he halted. Slowly, he set her feet to the floor. "What is it?"

Harrison opened the door. "Her Grace's sister, Your Grace."

"My sister?" Immediately, her good mood evaporated. "Which one?"

"Lady Amelia."

She glanced at the clock on the fireplace mantel. It wasn't even after noon. No one called before noon. "Something's wrong."

James nodded. "Let us see what it is."

His words kept her from panicking. She was still getting used to having him support her. He opened his arm to allow her to precede him. As they strode down the corridor to the parlor, his hand remained on the small of her back, his signal that they would face this together.

When they entered the parlor, Amelia turned from the window and ran to her. "Oh, I'm so glad you're awake. I knew you would be, I just knew."

She embraced her sister then sat her back. "Now tell me what brings you here so early. Is it Father? Mother? Mariel?"

Amelia waved her hand. "No, no, they are all fine."

Her heart lurched. "Teddy didn't make it to France."

Amelia frowned and shook her head. "Of course, he did. The ship has already returned to London." She spun away, her hands in the air as she walked toward the settee. "By now he's enjoying his grand tour. I have no doubt within the month he'll forget all about his heartache."

At the feel of James' hands on her shoulders, she looked at him in question. What could it be?

He shrugged before looking at Amelia. "Could you tell us what brought you here so early?"

"I'm just so furious." Amelia sunk down on the settee then arranged her skirts, careful to be sure they didn't wrinkle.

Completely confused now, Joanna walked across the room and sat next to her. "What is it?"

"It's my exhibit."

That made no sense. Amelia's exhibit had opened with many compliments in the papers. Even a distinguished artist had been quoted as saying she had great talent. Had something happened to it? "What about your exhibit?"

Amelia rose again and walked to the window. "It's embarrassing."

James moved to the door. "I'll get Harrison to order some tea." In an instant he had left the room.

Her husband was not only intelligent but understanding. "Amelia, tell me what happened. I can't help if I don't know."

Her sister didn't turn from the window. "They said I obviously knew nothing about the male anatomy."

Oh, that would greatly hurt her sister's pride. "Who did?"

Amelia faced her. "Two men, who didn't know I was the artist *and* that I was standing next to another one of my pieces talking with Lady Spencer. How can that be? I based the painting on the book you lent me. I was so sure I had it correctly that I made the three men in the foreground quite large."

She swallowed down a chuckle. This was a significant event in her sister's life. "Are they the only two who had a critique?"

"I don't know." Her hand went up again as she spun back toward the window. "But if they noticed, others did. My reputation as a painter could be ruined now. I need to fix this. I pulled the painting from the exhibit and replaced it with my painting of the Seine."

Amelia didn't like that particular painting, which just proved how upset she was. "How many more days is your exhibit?"

"Two. There's nothing I can do now." She turned and returned to the settee and sat, a little calmer. "But I must figure out what is wrong with my male figures. How come I can recognize a forgery so easily, but I can't determine what's wrong with my own figures? These were much better than the ones I based off the ancient statues. I must have missed something in that book. Can I borrow it again? I need to compare."

The door opened and the footman brought tea.

Joanna waited, as Amelia poured, not sure how to respond. As a married woman, she now knew the significance of the illustrations.

Amelia took a sip of tea and looked at her expectantly.

"Are you sure? If you already used it, why do you think it can help now?"

"I'm sure I must have missed something. I only drew a few sketches from it, as I was in a hurry to start painting."

Perhaps the book could help Amelia. But what if she actually looked at the content and read the information instead of just figuring out the art of it?

Since Amelia did plan to marry well one day, Joanna couldn't see how knowing what to expect could be a detriment. With her decision made, she left her cup where it was, and stood. "Let me see if I can find it."

Her sister rose and gave her a hug. "Oh, thank you."

She hugged her back then quickly exited the room. Her sister obviously viewed the illustrations in *the book* as artistic sketches. Since she had no great eye for art, she'd have to accept that her sister knew what she was about. She entered the library and as she suspected, James was back to reading.

He looked up at her entrance. "Did you discover why she's so concerned?"

"Yes. It was a critique of the males on one of her paintings.

She's asked to borrow *Educating the Feminine Species*."

He raised his brows. "Does she know it is the *Illustrated Pleasures of Seduction?*"

She strode to the shelf where they kept their favorite books. "She does. I let her borrow it once before, but I'm not sure she viewed the intimate pages. She's intent on getting the male form correct in her paintings."

"Ah, of course. She wouldn't know much about that."

She lifted the book from the shelf. "I told her I'd have to look for it. I didn't want her to know we kept it nearby. That would surely ruin your reputation."

He wiggled his brows. "I wasn't aware I had one."

She waved him off. "Oh yes. It's quite sterling, especially after marrying me."

At his incredulous look, she laughed and slipped out the door. If she had known how fun marriage could be, she would have been eager to try it. Then again, not every man was a Duke of Northwick with a handsome face, intelligent mind, and passion to make her toes curl. She was quite sure that stealing his book was the best decision she'd ever made.

By the time she entered the parlor, Amelia had finished her tea. "Did you find it?"

She held it out. "I did."

Amelia reached for it, but Joanna pulled it back. "You must not let anyone at home see this book."

Amelia's brows lowered in confusion then she smiled. "Oh, because it's about reproduction? Of course, I won't."

Still stymied by her sister's comfort with the illustrations in the book, she handed it to her. "I hope it can help you."

"I dearly hope so, too. I don't see how I could get a live male model without risking my reputation."

"Amelia, you wouldn't!"

Her sister shook her head. "I can't. Though it would be so much easier, it's just not done. I will be sure to return this when I've discovered what I'm missing."

Relieved, she walked with Amelia to the entry where her sister donned her cloak. "Tell Mother I will call on Wednesday as usual."

Amelia nodded and left a much happier artist.

Joanna returned to the library, still confused but pleased she could help. With the book gone for reference, maybe it was time to explore others of its ilk.

As she walked in, James set his book aside and rose. "Does Amelia feel better now?"

"Yes, though I'm not sure how much I helped." She walked toward him. "I've never been able to fully understand Amelia's creative impulses. She is the creative one, while I'm more comfortable with math and science, but she's my sister and I adore her."

James took her hand. "And I adore you."

"How perfect." She cocked her head. "Because I adore you as well."

"Good." He grinned. "Now where were we? Oh, yes."

She let out a squeal as he threw her over his shoulder. "What are you doing?"

He laughed. "Whatever, however, wherever I want with you."

Lightning shot through her limbs at his statement even as he climbed the stairs to the second level. When he reached their favorite spot, the two armchairs across from the large window, he moved the small table away with his foot and set her feet down, her back to the wall. Then before she could move, he pinned her there.

Her pulse started to race, but she looked up into his eyes, playing the innocent. "It might be a bit difficult for me to retrieve that particular pamphlet unless you move."

He shook his head, a devilish grin forming on his lips. "You already know all you need to know from it." Capturing her hands, he lifted them over her head and held them with one hand.

Her breaths came fast now, the image of The Prisoner clear in her mind. He planned to bring her to ecstasy, and she couldn't be happier. "I know that I love you. Was there anything else?"

He tilted her head back further. "Yes. You need to know that I love you and will forever." His head lowered and his mouth found hers.

Her last logical thought, as his tongue breached her lips, was that she would enjoy forever very much.

The End

About the Author

Lexi Post is a New York Times and USA Today best-selling author of romance inspired by the classics. She spent years in higher education taking and teaching courses about the classical literature she loved. From Edgar Allan Poe's short story "The Masque of the Red Death" to Tolstoy's *War and Peace*, she's read, studied, and taught wonderful classics.

But Lexi's first love is romance novels so she married her two first loves, romance and the classics. Whether it's dashing dukes, hot immortals, sizzling cowboys, or hunks from out of this world, Lexi provides a sensuous experience with a "whole lotta story."

Lexi is living her own happily ever after with her husband and her two cats in Florida. She makes her own ice cream every weekend, loves bright colors, and you'll never see her without a hat.

Website: lexipostbooks.com
Lexi Post Updates: app.mailerlite.com/webforms/landing/c1w1g3
Facebook: facebook.com/lexipostbooks
Twitter: @LexiPost
Instagram: instagram.com/lexipostbooks
Amazon Author Page: http://amzn.to/1IEL2cc
BookBub: bookbub.com/authors/lexi-post
D2D: books2read.com/author/lexi-post/subscribe/1/16171
Goodreads: goodreads.com/goodreadscomLexiPost
Instagram: instagram.com/lexipostbooks
Blog: happilyeverafterthoughts.com
Pinterest: pinterest.com/lexipost77
Email: lexi@lexipostbooks.com

www.ingramcontent.com/pod-product-compliance
Lightning Source LLC
Chambersburg PA
CBHW071220210726
48293CB00002B/504